His blue eyes locked with hers. "Miss Carpenter, we have a situation."

Charlotte's chest tightened. What in the world did he mean? "I have arrived on the day we arranged. I am ready to leave on the trip you mentioned in your advertisement. I cannot understand why we have an issue."

Perhaps he no longer needed her services but didn't know how to tell her? Maybe she should decline as Emily's caretaker? Although, she had no idea what she'd do for money or where she'd live until the teaching job started at the Long Valley School.

"Mr. Harrison, if you no longer need a caretaker for your daughter, I release you from any obligation. When I start my new position in September, I will repay the cost of the train and stagecoach tickets."

"Ma'am, I do need a caretaker f̶̶ ̶ ̶ had a chaperone—she ̶ ̶ ̶ ̶ ̶ ̶ ̶ trip— but she left ̶ ̶ ̶ ̶ ̶ ̶ ̶ ̶ . You can't travel ̶ ̶ ̶ ̶ ̶ ̶ ̶ …we'll have to get ̶ ̶

D0834478

Kate Barker loves life. She's fed cattle in deep snow, doctored cows, horses, chickens, pigs, goats and sheep, driven a team of horses, made soap, spun wool, opened a tearoom, had tea in a *ger* in Mongolia, viewed the Three Gorges Dam in China and waved to the Queen of England. Today, Kate lives in Northern California and writes sweet forever romance stories. She loves connecting with readers. Find her at www.tea4kate.com and www.Facebook.com/writerkatebarker.

Books by Kate Barker

Love Inspired Historical

The Wrangler's Wedding Pact

Visit the Author Profile page at LoveInspired.com.

The Wrangler's Wedding Pact

KATE BARKER

LOVE INSPIRED
INSPIRATIONAL ROMANCE

LOVE INSPIRED®
INSPIRATIONAL ROMANCE

ISBN-13: 978-1-335-63096-4

The Wrangler's Wedding Pact

Copyright © 2022 by Kathryn Barker

Love Inspired
22 Adelaide St. West, 41st Floor
Toronto, Ontario M5H 4E3, Canada
www.LoveInspired.com

Printed in U.S.A.

Trust in the Lord with all thine heart;
and lean not unto thine own understanding.
—*Proverbs* 3:5

To my sweet husband in heaven,
thank you for believing in me and pushing me to
follow my dream of writing. Here we go!

To my beloved children and grandchildren,
never give up on your dreams! You can do it!

To my precious mother, you always told me
I could be a writer. You're my inspiration!

To my editor, Emily Rodmell,
I treasure your availability, your patience
and your persistence in helping me in every way.
Thank you for taking a chance on me.

To my cherished writing group, Quills of Faith,
thank you for continuing to fuel my dream.

To my dearest writing friend, Cathy Elliott,
thank you for celebrating every little step with me!

Chapter One

Late July, 1895

"Whoa! Whoa, now!"

The driver yanked the reins, and the stage rocked back. Six lathered horses skidded to a halt.

Puffs of dirt drifted under the leather window curtains. Two days ago they'd left Reno, Nevada. Were they out of that sage-infested desert yet?

Charlotte lifted the curtain and looked around. Was this Cedar Grove, California?

She stared at the wrinkled advertisement spread out in her lap. "URGENT: Caretaker needed for a thirty-day journey to help with five-year-old daughter. Chaperone provided. All expenses paid."

Mr. Paul Harrison's advertisement had intrigued her. Why did he need help for only thirty days? Was his wife sick or an invalid? Was he a widower? Why a chaperone? She'd pondered those questions from Boston to Reno during the strenuous seven-day train ride.

From Reno to Cedar Grove she'd prayed Mr. Harrison would not be disappointed with her. Charlotte had spent most of her life seeking to please her guardian, Aunt Arilla, who found reason upon reason to criticize her. The more Charlotte strove to win her aunt's approval, the greater her aunt's irritation.

No more would Charlotte grapple with her aunt's dissatisfaction. It was Mr. Harrison's good opinion that counted now. Charlotte believed her flight from Boston meant she'd rescued her confidence and gained her freedom. Most important, though, she'd thwarted the arranged marriage her aunt had negotiated with that rich, grizzly old captain. Charlotte grinned. She'd accomplished this clever escape without confrontation. Altercations twisted Charlotte's thoughts and made her perspire. She avoided conflict like she sidestepped spiders and bugs of any sort.

The stage door opened. The driver waited. Charlotte's hands trembled as she held tightly to the drawing tablet and pencils she'd brought as a gift for Paul's young daughter.

Charlotte grasped the hand of the tall, rugged cowboy standing beside the coach. In his arms he held a rosy-cheeked girl with golden-red curls. Her yellow dress highlighted her deep blue eyes.

There wasn't a scuff mark anywhere on her shiny black boots. Did he carry her everywhere? Charlotte clamped her lips together, concealing her response to such a fantastical notion.

Her eyes met his.

He was young. He was handsome. He was staring at her.

His eyebrows arched. "Ma'am, are you Miss Charlotte Carpenter?"

Charlotte stepped down and took a deep breath. "Are you Mr. Paul Harrison?"

He let go of her hand. "Yes, ma'am."

"I am Charlotte Carpenter. I'm pleased to meet you and your daughter." She smiled at the little girl. "I brought a drawing tablet and some pencils for you." Charlotte handed the package to the child, who looked down without a word.

Paul gazed at Charlotte, took the tablet and pencils and pointed to a white-washed, two-story building. Black letters above the door said Cedar Grove Hotel. Small shops lined the wooden walkway. This town was simple and full of charm, she thought. Not like the stately stone structures huddled side by side in downtown Boston. In this wide openness Charlotte could breathe.

"Um, we…we need to talk," he said.

The driver handed Charlotte her valise. Mr. Harrison snatched it and bounded up the steps, then strode in the direction of the hotel. Charlotte trotted after him, alarmed at his hastiness. Like he needed to escape.

It wasn't his speed or the July heat that caused her breath to come in spurts. She relished exercise, especially fencing.

It was Charlotte's nerves. The cowboy she tagged along after took her breath away. Mr. Harrison was not what she'd expected. Not at all. Younger than she'd imagined. By far the most handsome, athletic-looking man she'd ever met.

A nail in the wooden sidewalk snagged her shoe. "Owww…" she squealed and fell to her knees.

He stopped and set down the suitcase and his daughter. He touched the little girl's cheek. "Emma, wait here."

Paul walked back to Charlotte, reached down, pulled her to her feet and stared into her eyes. "Are you okay?"

She nodded. He dropped her hands, turned and proceeded toward the hotel.

A tingling sensation swept up Charlotte's neck and cheeks. Her mouth was dry. Her throat ached. She swallowed and wiped a gloved hand across her forehead.

Something must be wrong.

Was he upset? Was he on the verge of a frenzied tirade like her aunt? With his child present, wouldn't he maintain a sense of decorum? She was proud she'd not mentioned her trip to Aunt Arilla and avoided a showdown.

Paul held the hotel door open for her. Charlotte scooted inside. Mr. Harrison swept passed her and marched into the dining room, plopped her travel bag next to a round table and settled his daughter in a chair.

The air inside the hotel smelled clean. The primitive beams and hardwood floor looked sturdy enough to withstand a hurricane. Starched white curtains flanked the windows.

Mr. Harrison took off his cowboy hat, pulled out a chair and nodded. "Miss Carpenter."

She slid onto the chair. Her hands shook as she adjusted her blue traveling jacket and brushed at the wrinkles in her skirt. He seemed distressed. She couldn't imagine why. Had she troubled him already? She'd just gotten off the stage.

Mr. Harrison flipped a chair around, straddled it and sat down. His brow furrowed; he cocked his head. His blue eyes locked with hers. "Miss Carpenter, we have a situation."

Charlotte's chest tightened. What in the world did he mean? She drew a deep breath. "Mr. Harrison, are you upset?" She swallowed. "I have arrived on the day we arranged. I am ready to leave on the trip you mentioned in your advertisement. I cannot understand why we have an issue."

His eyes met hers again. His eyebrows rose. His lips pursed. He flipped his hat onto the floor and rubbed his forehead with his fingers.

Charlotte stared at him, clasping her hands together.

With a deep sigh, he said, "Miss Carpenter, I'm sorry. I have forgotten my manners. I am sure you are tired and parched after the coach ride from Reno. Would you care for a cup of coffee? Something to eat?"

"Coffee sounds good."

He turned to his daughter, who clutched a small rag doll with yellow hair. "Emma, how about a piece of apple pie and milk?"

Emma looked up at him and nodded. He patted her hand and smiled.

"Hey, Bob," Paul called on his way to the counter.

"Mr. Harrison, how are you today? Would you like coffee for you and the lady?"

"Yeah, two coffees. A glass of milk for Emma. And a slice of apple pie for each of us, please."

"Sure thing." Off to the kitchen, Bob looked back and whistled. "She's a beauty, Mr. Harrison."

Charlotte felt heat flood her cheeks.

The waitress grinned at all of them when she served the coffee and pie. "Nice day, ain't it, Mr. Harrison?"

He nodded with a smile. "Yes. Thank you, Sally."

Charlotte removed her gloves and set them next to her reticule. The aroma of strong coffee filled the air. Strong, like the man sitting across from her. His chiseled jaw and rugged features couldn't hide his dimpled grin when he smiled at his little girl.

Perhaps he no longer needed her services but didn't know how to tell her? Maybe she should decline as Emma's caretaker? Although she had no idea what she'd do for money or where she'd live until the teaching job started at the Long Valley School. She'd counted on Mr. Harrison's position for food and lodging for the month in exchange for taking care of his daughter. Her employment by Mr. Harrison and the school district meant she'd have her own income. Her decisions would be her own. A liberty she had never known thus far.

She put down her fork and looked at Paul.

"Mr. Harrison, if you no longer need a caretaker for your daughter, I release you from any obligation. When I start my new position in September, I will repay the cost of the train and stagecoach tickets."

Paul's head pounded. Like someone had whacked his skull with a chunk of firewood. He was stunned. Dumbfounded. The moment she stepped out of the coach, the air had been sucked right out of him. A mistake. He'd made a horrendous blunder. She was too beautiful. Too well-to-do. Too out of place. Every time he peeked at her his breath caught. Forbidden feelings rattled around inside his head and heart. He'd never wanted to feel this way again. Beautiful women were treacherous. He knew it for a fact. Every time he thought about his deceased wife, his stomach soured.

Emma. He had to think about Emma. And his ranch. His daughter was what mattered. Emma's well-being counted. Not his feelings.

Charlotte's application said she was a teacher. He'd pictured his third-grade teacher from the orphanage school. Older. Plump. With her dark hair pulled straight back into a tight bun. Not at all like the stunning female who sat across from him. Why hadn't he asked for a photograph?

Thoughts roared through his mind like a freight train. His insides rocked like a boat in a storm. He raked his fingers through his hair. Their eyes met. He took a deep breath. Might as well get to it. No use beating around the bush.

"Ma'am, I did not have you come out here under false pretenses. I do need a caretaker for Emma. I had a chaperone—she was also my cook for the trip—but she left town unexpectedly this morning. You can't travel with me without a chaperone…so…we'll have to get married. Then I can make this trip, sell my horses, save my ranch and make sure Emma is well cared for."

Whew. He'd done it. Said what needed to be said. Laid out the whole truth of the situation. He had not kept anything from her.

He looked at Charlotte. Her cheeks changed from rosy pink to pale gray in seconds. Her eyes narrowed.

She scooted backward. The legs of her chair scraped on the wooden floor. She rose slowly. He watched her hands tremble when she grabbed the edge of the table.

Charlotte swallowed several times, took a deep breath and fastened her eyes on him. "I… I will not… marry. I do not wish to be married. I abhor the institution of marriage." She continued, "I will not be shackled."

She swiped her forehead. "I wish to teach school, to make a difference in the world. I agreed to come here as a caretaker, not a wife." She tilted her head. Her green eyes flashed with fear, like a deer caught unaware.

Paul stared at this small woman. Fiery little thing, he thought. And spooked.

He'd promised himself the day Emma was born that she would not have a childhood like his. She'd have a home and security. No lovely, rich, educated woman would deter him from honoring his pledge to his beloved daughter. Emma had gone mute the day her mother left. Paul hadn't yet told Emma her mother had died weeks later. She was too fragile. Emma had to have a caretaker for the trip so he could sell the horses.

Charlotte lifted her head and straightened her shoulders. The plume on her tiny black hat sashayed with every move. Captivated by her defiant emerald eyes, he lingered to see if she had more to say, then drew in a deep breath, got up and sauntered to the window without a word.

"Lord, help," Paul whispered, gazing out the window. "I have a dilemma."

Tall cottonwood trees lined the dirt road that led out of town toward his ranch. The sun hung in the sky like an orange ball suspended in the middle of two mountain peaks. Pain gripped his heart when he glanced at his precious daughter. He prayed one day she'd talk and giggle and dance around again. He'd worked hard to give Emma the security he'd never had. A place to belong. To be loved. Would all his plans crumble now like a winter rockslide?

"Lord, I need wisdom. You know the situation. Help me, please."

When he returned to the table, he smiled at Emma and sat down beside her. "Please sit, Miss Carpenter. I have a—"

"Mr. Harrison," she interrupted. "I repeat, I do not want to get married. Not to you. Not to anyone. Ever," she snapped. "I'd suffocate. I'd strangle. I'd wither... I'd be a prisoner. Marriage is like being locked in a dungeon...forever."

Paul closed his eyes and held up his hand. Boy, she was as opinionated and talkative as she was pretty.

"Don't say one thing more. Please. Hear me out." He had an alternative plan. One she might agree to.

She stared at him. "Go ahead. Say what you have to say."

Paul took another deep breath. "I must sell my horses to pay off the loan on my ranch. The buyer is about two hundred miles away, so I have to make this journey. It will take at least a month. I cannot leave Emma. She's delicate and must come with me. I need someone to care for her on the trip while I tend the horses. I have no mother, sisters or cousins to help me. Widow Miller, who was my cook and would have been our chaperone, was called away to care for her sick daughter and left on this morning's stage. I had no way to get word to you. I cannot ask you to travel alone with me for such a length of time unless we are married. Your reputation would be spoiled. Your upcoming teaching opportunity might be revoked. Also, if you do not go with me, you will have nowhere to stay and no job."

He paused to let to let this information take hold in her mind, and then he continued.

"This would be a marriage on paper. Nothing more. I don't need, nor do I want, a wife." He stared into her eyes.

Her face turned cherry-blossom pink. She plopped onto her chair.

Paul knew it was strange, but he figured it was the best way to manage both situations. "If you accompany me, as Emma's caretaker for a month, I promise, when we return, I will have the marriage annulled."

Emma needed to be with him. He needed Charlotte. Not forever, but for thirty days. The sale of his horses was how he'd provide Emma a home and security. He would do what he had to do. He refused to tarnish Charlotte's reputation or to leave her stranded when he'd brought her so far from her home.

"After the trip, you'll be free to continue with your plans to teach."

Charlotte's hand moved to her throat. "One month?" Squinting at him, she leaned closer. "That's all you'll ask? No strings attached? You pledge it's only for thirty days and my duties are only to take care of Emma?"

He nodded. She scanned her pie. "I don't know how to cook."

"I'll hire a cook."

Charlotte bowed her head, closed her eyes and remained silent for several minutes. Then, her fingers curled around her coffee cup, she lifted her head and said, "I must be assured you will keep your word."

He nodded.

Her eyebrows raised and their eyes met. "I'll write down what you have proposed, and if you'll sign it, I will go with you as your wife."

Paul sighed. Signing a document he couldn't read was what had gotten him into this predicament with the bank. He didn't want this college-educated woman to know he was untaught. He'd learned to write his name at the orphanage school but couldn't focus long enough to understand the rest of the alphabet. No one except Widow Miller and Frank Kenny, the banker, knew he couldn't read.

Without a word, Paul stood up and strode to the counter. "Bob, I need a pen, ink and some paper." Bob tore a blank sheet from the register. He retrieved the fountain pen and ink bottle from under the counter.

"Here ya go."

Paul deposited all of it in front of Charlotte. He kissed the top of Emma's head. He would do anything for his sweet daughter. For Emma's sake, he'd even marry and release a beautiful woman he didn't know to save his ranch.

Charlotte penned the words he dictated as he paced round and round the table. She dated the document and they both signed it. When it was dry, she folded and stashed the paper in her pocketbook for safekeeping.

Paul picked up Emma and Charlotte's valise. "Now, Miss Carpenter, let's find the minister."

Chapter Two

The farm wagon rolled along the dusty road. The picturesque town of Cedar Grove intrigued Charlotte. What a delightful contrast to Boston's crowded streets, where three-story structures and noisy, smelly electric trolleys dominated the scene.

She sighed when they drove past the little white church where they'd become husband and wife. She was a wife. An absurd thought. Not for long, though. Charlotte's suffragist friends had schooled her in the downsides of marriage, and she'd vowed to resist the trap. She glanced at Paul. Her stomach churned. *Lord, what have I done?*

"Mr. Harrison, where are we going?"

His jaw clenched. "Don't call me Mr. Harrison. Call me Paul."

She wrinkled her nose. "Very well. Paul. Where are we going?"

"To the ranch."

"I know that's where we're headed now, but on this journey you need me for, where are we bound for? Is it a big town? Will there be stores there? Do you think they might sell books in one of the shops?"

"Do you always ask so many questions?"

"Of course." Charlotte tilted her head. "My college professors encouraged us to ask questions. That's how one learns."

"Well, I'm not a professor and this isn't school. Lyonsville is the town."

Her chest tightened. Was this his nature, or were the circumstances causing him to be so irritable? Good thing her focus would be Emma. Not him.

The wagon bounced along the rutted road. Charlotte gazed at the wide-open spaces and the expansive blue sky. Junipers and cottonwood trees dotted the rippling sea of silver-tipped sagebrush. A sweet, earthy aroma filled the air. Charlotte smelled freedom. She choked upon remembering that she'd abandoned hers. For only one month. Thirty days. Not forever.

Up ahead, a fast-flowing stream lapped at its flattened banks where the road took a dip. Rocks jutted out of the water. Charlotte searched for another way across.

"Where's the bridge?"

"Don't need one."

Charlotte rubbed her temples. Why was he so prickly?

"Look, Paul, our situation is a bit uncommon, but that doesn't mean we have to antagonize one another. Can't we be friends and get along on this trip?"

Emma dropped her doll and latched on to her daddy's arm.

Paul's eyes focused ahead, and he clicked to the horses. The team picked up speed and raced straight into the water. When the wheels hit a rock, the wagon tipped.

"No!" Charlotte screeched. She clung to the back of the seat. Water rocketed into the air. Droplets peppered them from head to feet. Emma beamed up at her daddy. He grinned. His blue eyes twinkled like shimmering silk.

Paul stopped in front of a small house, hopped down and reached for Emma. She tumbled into his sturdy arms, and he spun around before setting her down. "Hey, my little gingersnap, did you like your shower? Don't forget your dolly."

Paul handed her the rag doll. "Emma, go inside and please show Charlotte which bed is hers. And show her the kindling box. I'll unhitch the team and be there in a minute."

Paul hurried to Charlotte's side, placed his hands on her waist and lifted her down. She stumbled. His strong arms steadied her. She vowed to master getting in and out of the wagon without his assistance. She didn't like what happened to her insides when he touched her. Her stomach felt twisted, like she'd eaten something bad.

"After you put your things away, please start a fire and make some coffee. The boys and I'll have a cup before supper." He leaped back into the wagon and drove off toward the barn.

Charlotte sighed and followed Emma onto the porch. The house reminded her of the rustic cabins used by the caretakers at Lake Oralee, where she and Aunt Arilla had spent many weekends out of the city. Emma opened the door. A fuzzy brown puppy charged into

Emma's arms. She stroked his head, and slobbery kisses were her reward.

The house was simple, neat and clean. Wooden benches hunkered beneath a long rectangular table near the cookstove. Paper-covered shelves held cooking supplies, white enamel dishes, coffee mugs and glasses. Two adult rockers and a small child's rocker faced the fireplace. No curtains hung in the windows.

Charlotte looked at the two inside doors. "Emma, where's your room?" Emma walked to one and pushed it open. She pointed to the bed with a blue-and-white quilt. The small dog jumped up on the other bed and curled into a ball. A bureau separated the two beds. A small mirror hung above the wash basin on the dresser.

"What a lovely room, Emma." Charlotte smiled at her. Emma bowed her head. Paul said she was delicate. Charlotte wondered if she was mute or just shy. Laying her gloves on the quilt, she removed her hat, unbuttoned her jacket and hung them on the hooks next to the bed.

She turned to the little girl. "Let's get a fire started."

The dog followed Emma and Charlotte back into the main room. Emma stepped close to a box full of spindly wood pieces and twigs. Charlotte tried to remember how they started the bonfires at Lake Oralee.

She gathered sticks and twigs, retrieved a match from the tin box and knelt in front of the fireplace to give it a go. The match flame lit the twigs right away. But it faltered and then—poof—nothing.

"Oh, dear." Charlotte fetched more twigs and another match. Once again, she piled the kindling underneath the stick. "Now I remember. We blow on it to get the flames to ignite." She pushed wisps of stray hair back into place, got on her knees again and lit the wood. Drawing a deep breath, she started to exhale but gagged and coughed.

Too much air. The spark extinguished. Ashes burst upward and floated down like soft snowfall, landing in Charlotte's hair, on her face and her skirt. She blinked and brushed residue from her eyes. Emma's eyebrows curved up, her eyes round as a full moon.

"What's going on here?"

Still on her knees, Charlotte watched Paul come through the door, followed by two men. The younger man was lanky, with dark hair hanging to the tips of his ears, and the other fellow had soft brown puppy eyes and wore a droopy hat.

Charlotte stood. Hands on her hips, she took a long breath, arched her brows and said, "I'm getting the fire started—what does it look like?"

Paul swallowed and stared down at his boots.

Paul took off his hat and rubbed the back of his neck. What a sight. Gray ash was streaked across Charlotte's cheeks. Cinder snowflakes dotted her golden hair, undone wisps clinging to her sweaty face. Her bun slid sideways and settled like a bird's nest about to topple out of a tree.

This woman is trouble. She talks too much. She asks too many questions. She doesn't know how to start a fire. She can't cook. She wants to be friends. She makes me laugh.

Paul couldn't remember the last time he'd laughed. It was a long, long time ago. Probably even before Emma's momma ran off with that traveling salesman. Had he been reckless, insisting Charlotte marry him? Maybe.

He'd done what he had to do. Except she quickened his pulse, and he didn't like that.

Paul picked up twigs and sticks of kindling, shoved them into the stove's firebox and lit a match. "I meant start a fire in the woodstove." The tinder burst into flames.

He smiled at Charlotte and then at the men standing in the doorway. "Boys…this is my…wife, Charlotte Harrison. Charlotte, this here is Bernie Wilson, my oldest friend. And the new hired man, Zeke Smith." The men bowed their heads when Paul spoke their names.

"Nice to meet ya, ma'am." Bernie nodded and grinned. His brown puppy-dog eyes lit up.

Zeke took a step toward her. "Pleasure to meet you."

Charlotte extended her hand, saw it was covered in soot and swung both arms behind her back. She curtsied slightly instead. "It's very nice to meet you both. Sorry there's such a mess. Excuse me while I clean it up." Charlotte searched the room for something to sweep up the ashes.

Paul held out the broom and dustpan with a smile. "Here, let me help."

"Sit down, boys. Supper will be ready soon."

Bernie and Zeke pulled out a bench and settled themselves like they'd been doing since Paul's first wife left. Rachel had refused to eat with the hired help. After she deserted him, Paul had invited the men to share meals with him and Emma.

Paul swept the ashes into the metal dustpan Charlotte held, and then she carried it outside.

After he set the Dutch oven on the burner and dumped grounds into the coffeepot, he called to his daughter, "Be back in a minute, Emma."

Paul scanned the yard for Charlotte. She was leaning against the side of the house. Her cheeks were stained with tears and she muttered, "I can't do this. I'm such a failure."

Paul stared at her. His heart leaped. He took out his handkerchief and walked over to her. "Are you okay?"

With her head still bowed, she said, "Yes. But maybe I'm not suited to this life? I don't know how to do things. I botched the first thing I tried." She looked up at him.

He took a deep breath. With the handkerchief, he wiped the ash streaks from her cheeks.

"This is your first day. You had a long journey on a bumpy stagecoach. You're tired. Everything will be okay."

"Are you sure?"

He took her hand. "Yes. You can clean up inside."

With each word, he exhorted himself to ignore the powerful urge to pull her close and comfort her. She had tried to start that fire and had clearly struggled—she looked miserable. But she was trouble, and he needed to stay clear of that temptation.

Paul grinned at Emma. "Thanks for setting the table, honey." She returned his smile. She grouped the three of them together, like a family, across from Bernie and Zeke. He'd have to talk with Emma about the length of Charlotte's stay. He didn't want her shaken by another woman's surprise disappearance.

Paul smiled. He'd been so proud the day Emma was born. Rachel had taken care of the child but hadn't been affectionate with her. In fact, she'd been downright in-different toward her. Paul didn't understand Rachel's response to Emma. He cherished his daughter. Every-one in town marveled at his devotion to Emma.

Charlotte hurried to Paul's side.

"Can I help?"

A rose scent spun around her. She'd repinned her hair bun. He shuddered and moved away to get the dip-per for the stew.

"Fill these bowls." He pointed at five enamel bowls and handed her the ladle.

Paul poured coffee in the mugs for the adults and set them on the table. Emma's glass of milk sat between two of them.

Charlotte placed the full bowls in front of each per-son and then sat down herself. She dipped her spoon into the stew.

Paul nodded. "Let's say our blessing." He reached toward Bernie and Emma. Emma touched Charlotte's hand, and Zeke laid his on top of Charlotte's. Paul bowed his head.

"Thank you, God, for the safe arrival of this woman. Thank You for my sweet daughter. Thank You for our friends, Bernie and Zeke. We thank You, God, for this food and we ask You to bless it with the proper nour-ishment of our bodies. We also pray for a safe journey to sell the horses. Amen."

Though Paul was grateful Charlotte had agreed to be his wife to make this trip, he silently pleaded for God's help to reinforce the collapsing fence around his heart.

"Do either of you know a chuck wagon cook I can hire for this trip to Lyonsville?"

Bernie halted his spoon midway to his mouth. "What about old Charlie over at the Lazy S? Last week he told me he's real tired of that bunch and needs a change of scenery."

"I'll ride over in the morning and talk to him. You boys get the bows on the wagon. When I get back, we'll set the chuck box. After the bows dry out, we'll put the bonnet on and start packing the wagon. We'll leave day after tomorrow."

"Sounds good, Boss." Zeke smiled and Bernie nodded as they pushed their empty bowls to the center of the table.

"You want more stew?" Paul asked.

"Nah. We gotta be turnin' in," Bernie said as he got up from the table. He knocked Zeke's shoulder and winked at him.

"Yeah. Mornin' comes early." Zeke chuckled and tipped his hat to Charlotte.

Bernie and Zeke thanked Paul for supper.

"'Night, ma'am." Bernie nodded to Charlotte.

Paul touched Emma's shoulder. "Time for bed, honey. Wash up and I'll come say prayers and tuck you in." Emma hopped down from the bench and skipped into the bedroom. The little dog trotted behind her.

Paul gathered the bowls and utensils from the table and carried them to a washbasin. He lifted the kettle of hot water, poured it into the basin and added shaved soap flakes. He handed Charlotte a dishrag and another large white enamel bowl.

He stared at her hands. Small and soft, they looked like she'd never washed a dish in her life.

"Wash in this one." He pointed to the basin with floating soap flakes.

"Rinse in this one." He added hot water to that bowl.

"Dry and put away." He pointed to the shelf for dishes. "I'll tuck Emma in and be back to help."

"Okay," Charlotte said. "By the way, what's the dog's name?"

"Prince."

In Emma's room, Paul sat down on her bed. She hopped onto his lap. He took the black brush and pulled it through her hair, chanting, "One hundred strokes every night makes your hair shiny and bright." He'd remembered the rhyme the girls at the orphanage had recited when they brushed each other's hair at bedtime.

He set the utensil on the dresser and turned her face to his. "Emma, sweetheart, Charlotte is only staying a little while with us. When we get back from this long trip, she'll move to another home. She'll be a teacher at the Long Valley School. Charlotte will always be our friend. We will visit her when we go to Long Valley."

Emma's eyes searched his face. Paul ached for his daughter. He didn't want her to grow attached to this woman who would leave them.

Paul tucked the quilt around Emma. They held hands while he prayed. He kissed her forehead, gave Prince a pat on the head and closed the door behind him.

For a moment Paul leaned against the frame and watched Charlotte systematically wash each plate, mug and spoon. Why had he let this beautiful creature into his life? She struggled to lift the pot off the stove. He saw her arms trembling with the weight of the kettle. Paul hurried to take hold of the handle and help her add more hot water to the basin. His hand brushed against hers.

He backed away, shivering like a quaking aspen in a spring breeze. This woman exposed uncomfortable, inconvenient feelings he'd thought he'd buried. Deep.

"You dry, I'll put away," he said. "I know where they go."

Charlotte retired when the last dish was dried and put on the shelf. Paul lit a fire and sat in his rocker near the fireplace. Thoughts about his new wife swirled in his mind. Her clothes, her hands and her lack of practical skills indicated she'd lived a life of leisure back East. Why did she come out West, with all its hardships, to teach school? Was she running from someone or something? Educated and beautiful, her opportunities must have been limitless. Why had she agreed to become Emma's caretaker for a month? Why hadn't she waited until the school sent for her?

This was day one. Her impact on his thinking troubled him. Once this marriage was annulled, he'd find a plain, middle-aged woman to care for Emma and their home.

Right now his mind and heart required boldness and courage where Charlotte was concerned.

He was up for the challenge.

Friends only, he vowed.

Chapter Three

Charlotte stared at the ceiling. Her arms were sore, like after her first day of rowing with the college team. Her leg muscles throbbed too.

She rolled over. Why was there another bed in her room?

Oh, yes. She was in California. "I'm Emma's caretaker. And wife to Mr. Harrison." She grinned. "But that sorry circumstance will be undone in thirty days. Marriage is not for me."

She jumped up.

Where was Emma? Her blue-and-yellow quilt was neatly pulled over the pillow, and Prince was gone.

Charlotte splashed water from the basin on her face and looked into the mirror.

"Oh, dear, my hair." She quickly brushed it and tied it back with a ribbon. She smoothed the wrinkles from her dress and retied her shoes.

No one was in the house. On the table, a mug of coffee sat beside a plate heaped with eggs and bacon.

Where was Emma? She was supposed to take care

of her. Charlotte hurried outside. Down by the barn, Bernie carried a load of long, thin planks. Zeke was in the bed of the wagon, shoving one end of a skinny board through a small metal slat on one side of the wagon. Near the barn door, Emma sat in the dirt with Prince in her lap.

With a sigh of relief, Charlotte hustled to the barn. "Good morning."

"Mornin', ma'am," Bernie said. Zeke nodded.

Bernie pushed the poles into the wagon bed and then turned to Charlotte.

"Ma'am, Paul said to tell ya to eat your breakfast. He should be back within the hour. He'll tell you what to pack in the wagon."

"Where did he go?"

"Over to the Lazy S to talk to Charlie. About cookin' for us on the drive," Zeke answered. "I hope old Charlie comes. I sure do like his apple pie." Zeke grinned as he shoved the other end of the slat into a strap on the opposite side. The pole now formed an upside-down U hoop above the wagon.

Charlotte started for the house, then remembered her charge.

"Would you and Prince like to come inside and keep me company while I eat my breakfast? You can use your tablet and pencils." Charlotte smiled at her. Emma gazed up but offered no smile. She stood, dusted off her dress and walked beside Charlotte. Prince trotted behind them.

Emma fetched her supplies and joined Charlotte at the table. The dog curled up under Emma's feet as he had the night before. Charlotte chatted about when she was a young girl and loved to write her name and draw with her pencils and pens.

"Can you write your name, Emma?"

Emma didn't respond.

"Can I see what you've drawn?"

The little girl slowly turned the tablet so Charlotte could see. The page was filled with butterflies, primitive trees and flowers.

"You draw very well. Your butterflies are beautiful. And your flowers have wonderful details. Your trees are so tall. What an artist you are." Charlotte smiled at her. She thought she glimpsed an upward movement in Emma's lips, as if she were about to smile but changed her mind.

"Emma, I'll teach you the letters of the alphabet so you can write your name." Charlotte pushed back from the table and carried her plate and cup to the basin. "You'll be my first official scholar. You can learn some easy words and I'll create sentences. You'll be reading in no time." She grinned at Emma, who watched her wash the dishes.

"Then when I begin teaching, I can say I've had experience." Charlotte dried the plate and set it on top of the others in the cabinet.

Hoofbeats sounded in the distance.

"I think your papa's on his way, Emma. Let's you and I and Prince go see what he wants us to do now."

Although once in a while, Paul was difficult with her, Charlotte felt a peace in his presence. Like no matter what happened, he'd handle the situation. He inspired confidence. She felt safe with him. He expressed a belief in her that she didn't feel. He commended her attempts to learn even simple tasks, like starting a fire and washing and drying dishes, always assuring her she'd soon master the skill.

She smiled and stretched out her hand to Emma. The girl bowed her head and looked at the ground.

"That's okay, Emma. We can walk together without holding hands."

Emma put away her pencils and tablet and caught up with Charlotte. Prince barked and twirled all the way out the door. Paul dismounted and strode toward them. Emma rushed to her daddy, and he picked her up and swung her around.

"How's my darling gingersnap?" He kissed her cheek and set her on the ground.

Charlotte gazed at him. How she envied Emma—to be loved like that. What would it have been like to have someone cherish her? Could a man ever love a woman that way? Or was that absolute delight reserved for children, and she'd missed her opportunity? Charlotte knew nothing about love between men and women. She remembered her parents being affectionate with her and with each other in a stiff, formal way. She never saw joy in their eyes like Paul expressed when he looked at Emma. Charlotte knew her aunt disliked her and had agreed to be her guardian only because of the extra income. No, Aunt Arilla had never shown any tenderness toward her.

When her girlfriends got married, they'd never spoken of love. They'd boasted about their future husband's potential, his inheritance or his position, but never anything about love. How would it feel to be adored like Paul did Emma? The thought bewildered yet charmed her. Was this a skill one learned? How did one go about loving someone? How did one retrieve another's affection?

She looked at Paul and squished down all those thoughts. "Sorry I overslept and missed breakfast. Thanks for leaving me a plate."

He nodded. "You were tired."

Paul walked toward the barn, Emma skipping alongside him. His stride was long, and Charlotte trotted to keep pace with him.

"Will Charlie be your cook?" she asked.

"Yeah. He'll be here later. He'll help load the chuck box."

"Chuck box?" Charlotte asked.

Before Paul could answer, Zeke shouted, "Hey, Boss! Is Charlie comin'?"

"Sure is."

Paul looked at the bows on the wagon.

"Good work. I'll be back to help with the bonnet."

Paul unsaddled Buck and turned him out in the corral. He headed back to the house with Charlotte, Emma and Prince trailing behind him.

When his feet hit the porch, he pivoted and faced Charlotte. "You'll need to wash and dry all Emma's things for the trip and then pack them. I'll get her travel bag. When Charlie gets here, you can help him pack up the chuck box. The boys will want dinner in a few hours. Can you make coffee?"

Charlotte took a deep breath, straining to make sense of everything. Coffee. Dinners. Packing. Washing. She had no idea how to wash clothes. Back in Boston her maid had gathered her soiled attire and taken it downstairs, and a day or two later, her dresses appeared again in her closet and her other garments were folded and put away in her bureau. She knew how to pour coffee but not how to make it.

She straightened her shoulders. "I've never made coffee, but if you show me, I can learn."

"Okay." Paul walked into the house.

"Add more wood to the fire…" He shoved several sticks of kindling into the firebox. With teasing blue eyes, he grinned at her. "…in the woodstove. Fill the coffeepot with water." He pointed to the large galvanized container on a back burner.

Charlotte poured water into the pot.

"Grind the beans." To the coffee grinder, he added a handful. He demonstrated how to twist the top handle round and round. The aroma filled the room. It reminded Charlotte of pouring coffee from her aunt's shining silver service.

"Smells delicious," she mumbled.

"When the water boils, toss in the coffee." Paul pulled out the drawer from the grinder and tossed the pulverized beans into the pot.

"Give it about five minutes. Then pour in a cup of cold water." He picked up a mug and showed it to her. "That's all."

"I can do that." She smiled at him. She wanted to be helpful—she didn't want to be a burden or a disappointment to him.

He strode into Emma's bedroom and came out with an armload of clothes.

"Here's what Emma needs washed." With a vacant look, Charlotte took the clothes from him.

"The washtub and scrub board are on the south side of the house by the clothesline." Paul disappeared out the door. Why was he always in a hurry? Did he want to get away from her? She suspected he was upset about marrying her to save his ranch. Now he had to show her how to do everything. Maybe he was frustrated. She'd work hard to be an adept pupil, and a fast learner too.

"Emma, want to come with me to wash clothes?" She winked at the girl and walked outside. Emma dashed ahead of her, with Prince bouncing behind her.

Charlotte spotted the washtub and scrub board.

"Well, Emma, I assume cleaning clothes and dishes must be similar." She smiled at the child and traipsed back into the house to find the soap tin. The water bucket was empty. On her way to the pump, she stopped to gaze at Paul helping Zeke and Bernie spread the canvas over the hoops on the wagon.

He was sweet with Emma, handsome and strong. No wonder she felt at peace. Yet every nerve in her body felt like it was on fire when he came near her. Her muscles ached as she pumped water, but it reminded her she needed to build up her strength. In thirty days she'd be on her own, with no man to help her with anything.

Water sloshed from the heavy bucket. Charlotte set it down on the porch to rest for a moment. Loud sizzling sounds came from inside. She dashed into the house, where a stream of brown-speckled water flowed from the top of the coffeepot, danced on the burner and spit onto the floor.

"Oh, no." Charlotte grabbed the coffeepot, but yanked her hand away, screaming, "Ouch!"

Emma rushed to her side. She reached to touch Charlotte's arm and then bolted out the door with Prince racing behind her.

Paul looked up to see Emma sprint toward him. Her eyes round, her hand motioned for him to come to her. He leaped from the wagon and raced to meet her. With tears in her eyes, she grabbed his hand and dragged him toward the house.

"Emma, what's wrong? Emma?" She didn't answer. What had upset her? She continued to tug him toward the house. Prince trotted inside, and Emma pulled Paul through the open doorway. His heart plummeted. Charlotte sat bent over at the table, her head on her arms.

Had she changed her mind about going with them? Had he expected too much from her too soon? Was she leaving like Rachel had left them?

Paul hustled to her side. "Are you okay? What's wrong?"

Charlotte raised her head and coughed. She stammered, "I had to get…water…to heat for the wash. The coffee…boiled over. I grabbed the handle. I—I burned my hand." She held up her red-streaked palm, and a tear slid down her cheek.

He sighed. What a relief. A little burn he could deal with. If she'd changed her mind about the trip, he doubted that was fixable. Was marrying him too much for her? Was she strong enough for this kind of a life? For thirty days?

He snatched a clean dishcloth, dipped his fingers in butter and held out his hand to her. He breathed deep.

Charlotte laid her open palm in his hand and looked up at him with trust in her eyes.

"This should help." Tenderly he rubbed the butter over the burn. He wrapped the cloth around and secured it. "It's not too bad. Should be better real soon."

He prayed her hand would heal quickly. He needed her to take care of Emma. Maybe once they got on the trail, things wouldn't be so hard. Whatever it took, though, he had to save his ranch from foreclosure. For Emma's sake.

Paul went to the stove and cleaned up the coffee grounds, then filled the pot with water for the washtub, set it on the stove and added more kindling.

"While the water heats, warm up something for dinner. The boys need to eat in a while."

"The stew from last night?"

"Sure. Or there's a kettle of beans in the icebox also."

Paul heard Charlotte push back the bench seat as he hurried out the door. He was surprised Emma and Prince didn't follow him. Usually Emma clung to him, afraid he would disappear and never return like her mother.

Moving a herd of horses over two hundred miles required him being away from Emma for hours at a time. With Charlotte to comfort Emma in his absence, he hoped the child's apprehension might be alleviated a little bit. Maybe she'd talk again. It looked like Charlotte had gained Emma's approval already. Paul remained hopeful for his daughter's complete recovery.

Charlie Whittaker was a man people noticed. As his horse trotted up the long lane to the ranch, he sat tall in the saddle, easy to recognize. When he reached the barn, he stepped down and tied his mount to the rail.

"Hiya, boys." Charlie's thick black mustache turned up with his big smile. His dark sideburns were streaked with silver and his big floppy hat looked like someone had sat on it.

"Hey, Charlie," Bernie greeted him.

"You gonna make us apple pie?" Zeke jumped from the bed of the wagon to shake Charlie's hand.

"I will if the boss gets us some apples." Charlie grinned.

Paul shook Charlie's hand. "Just in time to pack the chuck box. I got dried apples at Beiber's store and some fresh ones too. Come on, Charlie, I'll introduce you to Emma and Charlotte." Paul started for the house. A scorched aroma filled their nostrils as they stepped through the door.

"I think something's burning." Paul raced inside, Charlie on his heels. Smoke rose from the pot on the stove. Paul grabbed a dishcloth, wrapped it around the handle and pulled the pot of beans to the side.

"There goes dinner," Paul mumbled, shaking his head.

"Looks like my timin' is good." Charlie chuckled. "I can fix somethin'. What have ya got on hand?"

"Leftover stew. Can you make biscuits to go with it? The boys would sure like that. Haven't had any in quite a while." Paul pointed to the shelf where the flour was stored. "Buttermilk's in the icebox."

Charlie looked over the shelves. "Looks like everything's right here. I'll call ya when it's time to eat. Are ya sure the missus won't mind me bein' in her kitchen?

I know some women are mighty territorial about their cookin' area." Charlie arched his dark, bushy eyebrows.

"Nah. She won't mind." Paul smiled. "I'll introduce you later," he said, as if that would explain it. Paul hurried out the door, grateful Charlie had volunteered to cook dinner. He couldn't imagine how to teach Charlotte to make biscuits if she couldn't even keep from burning a pot of beans.

Paul came around the side of the house and stopped. He stepped back. Astonished. Transfixed.

Charlotte leaned over the washtub. With one hand she pulled Emma's dress out of the water and swirled it in the air. Round and round it whirled as she sang some kind of song about a washtub. Smiling and swaying, she dipped it in the water again and continued to sing to Emma. The scrub board leaned against the side of the tub while the soap bar floated in the water. Emma stood to the side, her eyebrows raised and lips parted, like she might be about to smile. Her little foot tapped in time with Charlotte's song.

Paul was astonished. Emma had not shown any kind of emotion in a long time, except to smile at him. He watched a bit longer, delighted in his daughter's hint of liveliness. The once playful, happy child had been silent since the day her mother drove out of sight and left Emma standing alone on the porch, sobbing.

Paul walked closer. "What are you doing?"

Charlotte frowned at him. She held up the dripping outfit and said, "Washing Emma's dress."

He didn't know whether to burst out laughing or pull his hair out. She didn't know how to wash clothes? Good grief. What had he gotten himself into? Should he show her the right way? If he didn't do it now, he wouldn't have time once they started on the drive.

She troubled him. She intrigued him. He smiled when he remembered her persistence last night washing and drying the dishes. He knew she was very tired, but she wouldn't quit until they were all done and put away. Rachel had always grumbled about the work, complained that he expected too much of her. She'd constantly berated him because they had no extra money to hire help.

Determined to make the best of this situation, Paul stepped forward and rolled up his sleeves. "Look, nothing is going to come clean if all you do is dunk and swirl."

He grabbed the bar of soap and plopped the scrub board into the tub. He held out his palm toward Charlotte. She snorted, rolled her eyes, puckered her lips and plopped the soggy dress into his hand.

"Now watch." Paul held the dress against the scrub board, ran the soap up and down it a few times, then rubbed the frock against the corrugated surface. He plunged the garment into the water several times, held it up to examine it and then repeated the soap and scrub.

"You try," he grunted.

Charlotte scooted next to him, slid one hand in the soapy water and fished around in the tub until she found another little dress. She scooped up the soap, swished it over the fabric and then pulled it over the washboard.

"No, like this." Paul stepped behind her. That rose scent perplexed him. He took hold of her hands and held them a moment too long. At last he pushed the dress firmly against the board over and over. "You have to apply pressure. Scrubbing is what gets the clothes clean."

"Ow." Charlotte pulled her wrapped hand away.

Paul swallowed. "Sorry. I forgot about your hand." His heart thumped in his chest.

"Well, do the best you can. When you finish, pour out the soapy water. Rinse the clothes in clean, then wring them like this." He demonstrated how to twist and squeeze.

"Clothespins are in that feed bag there." He backed away, pointing to a tea-colored sack hanging on the side of the house, and jogged back to the barn.

Once there he ripped off his hat, slapped his thigh and ran his hand through his hair. He willed his heart to stop pounding and his mind to quit racing. This woman was not working out the way he'd planned. This city gal—who was now his wife—kept him out of balance. Her lack of domestic skills was frustrating, but her willingness to fling herself wholeheartedly into learning tugged at his heart.

He found her attempts to master a task a source of delight—and that threw his mind into a turmoil.

From now on, he'd assign one of his crew to help Charlotte.

Chapter Four

A hint of light sneaked through the windowpane. Sunrise. The aroma of fresh-brewed coffee and bacon filled the room. Charlotte rolled over and saw Emma's sweet face lying on her pillow, her curls forming a crimson halo. Charlotte smiled and her heart warmed. Her young charge. For thirty days. "I'll do everything I can to help you, little one," she whispered.

There was a light tap on the door. Charlotte got up and opened it a crack. "Yes?"

It was Paul, hands in his pockets, "We'll have breakfast and be ready to leave in an hour. Can you get Emma dressed?"

"Sure." Charlotte closed the door and leaned back against it. That cowboy smelled of leather and coffee. He was strong. Rugged and capable. She shook herself loose from her thoughts and pulled on her chocolate-brown skirt and the tan-striped blouse she'd laid out last night. She'd not had time to put her clothes in the bureau. Well, in thirty days, she'd have her own place and she'd unpack then.

In her travel bag she found the slim vial of rose perfume. She dabbed a bit on her wrist and her neck and inhaled the fresh scent of her favorite flower. Charlotte was happy to leave a good many things behind for her trip West, but not her rose cologne.

Prince jumped down from Emma's bed, shook himself and came to Charlotte for a few pats. Charlotte touched Emma's arm. "Good morning, little beauty. Time to get up. Today we start on our big adventure." Emma looked startled for a moment. She blinked and then sat up and reached for the outfit she'd chosen the night before. All of Emma's clothes and shoes fit in one small suitcase.

Charlotte marveled at that. She'd had too many clothes when she was young. Aunt Arilla insisted she dress appropriately for each occasion. A dress for play couldn't be worn to dinner. There were clothes for the beach and fancy frocks for tea parties and, oh, how she'd loved her riding habit. Maybe she could find more outfits for Emma on this trip. A bonnet was a must.

Emma slipped on her navy blue dress. Charlotte buttoned and tied its bow and helped her with her shoes. After Emma folded her nightgown and put it in the suitcase, Charlotte brushed her red curls and found one of her own white ribbons to tie around Emma's head. She looked like she was leaving for church. Charlotte smiled and patted her shoulder.

"Let's have breakfast," she said, opening the door.

Seated at the table, the men forked bites of eggs and bacon and slurped their coffee. Fluffy biscuits slathered with butter and plum jam perched on their tin plates. They looked up at her and Emma. "Good morning, ma'am."

"Good morning to you all. It's a beautiful day to start a journey."

"Yes, ma'am." Bernie smiled at her. The others nodded in between bites.

"Eat up boys. Might be the last of the eggs for a while." Charlie grinned and turned to Charlotte.

"Thank ya, missus, for lettin' me use your kitchen this mornin'. I figured since you had the little one to get ready, I could make us breakfast."

Her cheeks warmed. He knew she couldn't cook. Why, she'd burned the beans yesterday and he'd had to fix their supper. Of course, last night he'd mentioned he knew she was washing all the clothes for the trip and wouldn't have time to make dinner. She wondered how many excuses he could make up before this game of pretending got old. Maybe he could give her some lessons. In a month she'd have to do her own cooking anyway.

Charlotte smiled at him. "Thank you for your consideration and for this delicious meal." She strolled over, got a cup of coffee and filled Emma's glass with milk. Paul filled plates for Emma and Charlotte and sat down by his daughter.

"Charlie, you and Charlotte and Emma will go ahead of us in the wagon. We'll have the herd follow the chuck wagon for the first day or so. Get them used to moving altogether in a bunch."

"Sure, Boss." Charlie popped the last bite of biscuit in his mouth. "How's your lead mare?"

"She's a good one. Saddle broke too," Paul answered.

Bernie got up and placed his plate, cup and fork in the dishpan. "Ole Sassy's a mighty fine boss mare. She's been keepin' track of this herd for a while." He headed out the door, and Zeke followed.

Charlie picked up his plate and then hollered, "Hey, boys, make sure your gear is loaded in the wagon! We'll be rollin' outta here real soon!"

Paul stared at Charlotte. Her heart thumped when she met his gaze. He still made her jittery, and his blue eyes and dimpled smile unnerved her. She got up and carried her plate to the dishpan.

"When the dishes are done, take them out to Charlie. He'll pack them in the chuck box. Then load the suitcases in the wagon. Did you pack Emma's cape?"

Charlotte straightened her shoulders and drew in a long breath. He sure liked to give orders. In fact, he treated her like one of his hired hands. *It's only for a month*, she reminded herself. "Yes, sir, Boss," she said, wrinkling her nose.

Paul raised his eyebrows and then hurried out the door. She washed the dishes and carried them out to Charlie. When she came back in the house, she noticed Emma's tablet had not been packed, nor her pencils. She gathered them up, wondering about the best way to keep the tablet from getting torn.

Paul stood in the doorway. "We'll not be taking those. Get the suitcases."

Charlotte whirled and stood for a moment before she spoke.

"I am not your hired hand. Stop shouting orders at me. Emma loves to draw and she's very good at it. I want to teach her the alphabet. When you care for someone, it isn't just about washing clothes and cooking meals. It's about other things too. We will take the tablet and pencils."

She stomped into the bedroom, slammed the door and plopped on the bed. Her whole body trembled. Never in her life had she allowed her temper to dictate her response. Not to her aunt or her friends, not to anyone. What was wrong with her? Who was she? What had she done?

Paul stared at the bedroom door. "That's the most confounded, opinionated, outspoken woman I've ever met," he mumbled. Feisty too—and pretty cute when she got all riled up. He smiled. He'd wanted to hug her when she said she'd teach Emma her letters. He was grateful. Paul wanted his daughter to learn to read. He hadn't thought about the usefulness of the tablet or pencils. Maybe having Charlotte come along wasn't a mistake after all. An apology might be in order. But later—they needed to get on the road.

He untied Buck and rode out to see if Zeke and Bernie were ready to move the horses from the south field. The herd paced about but stayed bunched. On his way back to the house, he watched Charlotte carry the two suitcases out and hand them to Charlie, who tossed the baggage in the wagon and then climbed in and took the reins.

Charlotte lifted Emma and Prince into the wagon. When she stepped onto the spoke, he saw her slap Bernie's hands away. *That was meant for me*, he thought. Poor Bernie. He rode up in time to hear Bernie's apology.

"Sorry, ma'am. Didn't mean to be forward. Tryin' to be helpful."

Charlotte turned. Bernie's sad eyes drooped even more.

"Bernie, excuse me. I'm so sorry. Thank you. Yes, I would like help." She extended her hand and Bernie took it and gave her a little boost.

Paul looked at Charlie. "Ready?"

"Let's roll!" Charlie hollered and clicked to the team. "Hup, Jack. Come on, Belle. Hup, hup." The two sorrel horses leaned forward and stepped together. As the wagon lumbered ahead, Charlotte smiled and patted Emma's hand. "Here we go." She twisted to look behind the wagon. She took a long breath. "Oh, those prancing horses are magnificent, aren't they?"

"Yes, ma'am. Ain't nothin' quite as beautiful as a horse in motion. Mr. Paul's got a mighty fine herd."

"Thanks, Charlie." Paul winked, spurred his gelding and rode back to help Zeke and Bernie keep the herd together. Charlotte's smile and dancing eyes were electrifying. Her outspokenness troubled him, though. He didn't mind her opinions. Sometimes she had good ideas. But he didn't know why she seemed upset with him. Rachel had moaned and complained, but she'd never argued with him. She'd also never had an original thought. He was the one who wanted to teach Emma to do new things. Rachel had fed her and kept her clothes clean, but hadn't really interacted with her own child. Not even as much as Charlotte had in the last few days. Charlotte was a puzzle for sure.

The horses started to scatter. Some dropped behind and some took off in different directions. Bernie stayed with the ones who lagged while Paul and Zeke worked to get the others back to the bunch. After regrouping the stragglers, Paul trotted up to the wagon with a frown on his face. "Pull up, Charlie."

Charlie eased the reins back. "Whoa, Jack. Whoa, Belle."

When the wagon stopped, he asked, "What's up, Boss?"

Paul pointed inside the wagon. "I need Sassy's bell. The herd's all over the place."

Charlie looped the reins over the brake handle. He leaned into the wagon and rummaged through the pile of bedrolls. "Not in here. Did ya ask the boys where they mighta throwed it?"

"Let me get in there, Charlie."

Paul dismounted, and Charlie stepped down out of the wagon. Paul hopped up and bumped into Charlotte, who shuddered, her cheeks turning pink.

Paul looked at her. "Are you cold? I can get a blanket."

"I'm fine. Thanks." She looked away.

He kissed the top of Emma's head. "Hey, gingersnap. How are ya doing?" Emma smiled. Paul climbed inside the wagon. He pawed through the gear for a few minutes and said, "Guess it didn't get packed."

He jumped down and frowned. "Too far to go back."

"Yeah, we'd probably end up in a fuss. Better to keep movin'." Charlie shook his head.

"When we stop for dinner, I'll take another look. Find us a good spot, Charlie." With that, Paul mounted and rode off, glancing back at the wagon where Charlotte was smiling down at Emma.

His heart filled with gratitude. He tipped his Stetson as a gesture of thanks and watched Charlotte's eyes widen and a flush sneak across her cheeks before she bowed her head and turned back to Emma.

"Why does he need a bell?" Charlotte asked as Charlie clicked to the team.

"There's always a boss mare in a herd. They go where she goes. When they hear her bell, they follow and stay closer. Right now, sounds like those horses are kinda scattery 'cause we're outta their territory. Mr. Harrison must be havin' trouble keepin' them together. We'll be stoppin' soon, though."

Emma yawned and leaned her head on Charlotte's arm. Specks of gold flickered in her long red curls.

"Emma reminds me of a doll I used to have. One with big blue eyes and a little round face. None of my dolls had such beautiful ginger-colored hair, though." Charlotte stroked Emma's hair.

"There's a stoppin' place." Charlie pointed in the direction of a meadow. A ring of pine trees bordered lush green grass where scattered wildflowers grew in clusters. A small creek zigzagged through the middle of the meadow. He guided Belle and Jack onto a flat area close to the trees and halted the team.

"What should I do about Emma?" Charlotte inclined her head toward the sleeping child.

"I'll get a bedroll and we'll let her rest under the wagon." Charlie reached back and grabbed one of the canvas tarpaulins, then hopped down.

Paul rode up. "Good stopping place, Charlie." He pointed at the bedroll. "Are ya planning to take a nap?"

"Ha." Charlie smiled. "Emma's asleep. Thought we'd let 'er rest under the wagon. Okay with you?"

"Sure." Paul tied his horse to a tree branch and came over to Charlotte's side of the wagon with his arms outstretched. She lifted Emma to him, then gathered her skirt and proceeded to back slowly down the side of the wagon wheel. Her foot slid on the spoke, but Paul's strong hands supported her elbows.

"Thank you," Charlotte said without looking at Paul.

She strode over to Charlie. "What do you want me to do?"

"Grab the firewood from the boot under the wagon. We'll get the coffee goin', and then I'll rustle up some grub."

Charlie turned to Paul. "How long we stayin' here, Boss?"

Paul scanned the meadow. "Several hours. This is good feed for the horses. I'll unhitch the team and let them graze too, then I'll head back and check on the boys and the herd."

Charlie dug a shallow pit and placed a tripod over it. He showed Charlotte how to get the campfire started. She filled the galvanized coffeepot with water from the stream and hung it on the tripod hook. Charlie unlocked the chuck box, and the lid became his worktable. Charlotte checked on Emma and then watched as Charlie mixed up the ingredients for biscuits, greased the Dutch oven and set it on the hot embers. He shoveled a few scoops of burning wood on top.

"Have you always been a cook, Charlie?"

"No. Had my own little place in Texas. Left it to come to the goldfields in California. Got tired of mining and started cowboyin' for ranches, but the grub was so bad, I decided to learn how to cook. Besides, cookin' pays better than cowboyin' and I get to boss those boys around now and then." Charlie's dark eyes twinkled, and his mustache curled up. Charlotte grinned at him.

Horse hooves thundered, and manes and tails flew high in the air as the horses blasted onto the field.

Chapter Five

Paul stared at Charlotte. Again. He found it difficult to keep his eyes off her. He smiled to himself. He was fascinated by her actions. She always included Emma when she helped Charlie set up for supper and with other tasks. Everything was done with joy, and sometimes she hummed a tune.

As Emma searched for firewood, Charlotte teased her about how strong she was to carry huge sticks. They hauled buckets of water from the creek to refill the barrel on the side of the wagon and picked dozens of wildflowers. Emma scrunched the flowers into a little bouquet while Charlotte fetched a cup of water to put them in. Paul heard Charlotte ask Charlie to name them. She was like a sponge soaking up information. Everything fascinated her. Too bad she couldn't stay. *She's good for Emma*, he mused. *Not for me, though.*

She had a dream, and he'd promised to release her. Anyway, she was opinionated and sassy. Kind of stirred his blood, though. He liked a challenge. This one he could handle for thirty days. But for a lifetime?

He strolled to the table where she and Emma worked.

"The flowers are nice." He pointed at the bouquet in the blue tin cup.

"Aren't they lovely? Charlie's helping me and Emma learn their names. See, this is a desert paintbrush, and this is a purple sage, and look at this beautiful evening primrose." She pulled out the white primrose and held it for him to smell. Her eyes sparkled.

It wasn't the scent of the primrose that left him breathless. It was her. Her smile. Her proximity.

He inhaled and steadied himself. "It's mighty nice."

Paul looked around at the others. Emma sat on the ground and drew with a stick. Prince was curled beside her, and her rag doll lay in her lap. Charlie and the boys stood over by the campfire with their coffee.

Paul swallowed a couple of times and wiped his brow.

"Charlotte." He waited until she looked at him.

"Sorry for being bossy with you. I like your idea about teaching Emma her letters. That wasn't part of our deal but thank you." He stared into her deep green eyes and hoped she'd forgive him.

She bit her lip and placed the primrose back in the cup. "I shouldn't have lost my temper. I'm sorry too." She nodded in the direction of three small fir trees. "Can we talk over there?"

"Sure." Paul turned to Emma. "Stay here, honey. Charlotte and I will be over there for a minute or two." He pointed to the trees.

Emma glanced up and nodded, then went back to drawing in the dirt.

Strolling with Charlotte felt familiar. Like they'd walked side by side for years. A sense of contentment flooded his heart, though he willed that feeling to move on and not to settle in. She wasn't staying. He couldn't afford to think about something that wouldn't be good for him.

When they were farther from camp, Charlotte stopped and said, "Emma's very bright. She follows directions well, and I know she understands even if she can't speak. I wondered if you would mind if I taught her sign language. It's like speaking with her hands. I took a summer class at college, and I remember the alphabet and some words."

Paul often got lost watching her and tuned out what she was actually saying. She was enchanting. Her eyes sparkled when she spoke, and her hands moved to emphasize what she said. But while he was grateful that she wanted to help Emma, he was confused about this sign language thing she spoke of.

He smiled at her, amused. "I have no idea what you're talking about. What is speaking with her hands? I've never heard of it."

Charlotte raised her hand and recited the alphabet as she moved her fingers. "See, if Emma could learn the movements that correspond to the letters, she could spell words." Charlotte moved her fingers and said, *"C."* Then she moved her hand into another position. *"A."* Moving her fingers again, she said, *"T. C-A-T.* Cat. Wasn't that easy?" Her eagerness excited him. He was astonished that letters had associated hand movements. He could have watched her make words until the sun came up.

"That's mighty interesting." He paused. Looking at her, Paul said, "Emma used to talk. But she hasn't said a word since the day her mother left."

He took off his hat and brushed it against his thigh. "I hoped it'd been long enough she'd talk again. It's a powerful hurt when your own ma leaves ya standing on the porch, weeping. I pray Emma's hurt will be healed, and one of these days, she'll speak again."

His blue eyes filled with agony. He felt so much sorrow for his little girl. He'd known the ache of losing parents and he never wanted that for his Emma. He'd felt guilty for choosing a woman who would abandon her child for another man and then go and get herself killed. Paul sighed.

Charlotte gasped. "I... I had no idea. That's wonderful. I think it won't be long until she speaks again." She tipped her head to the side. Her eyebrows arched, and her mouth turned down. "Oh, dear. Sometimes I don't think before I speak. I meant I am happy she can talk but very, very sorry about her mother. It's a heartache for sure. I lost my own mother and father when I was young." Charlotte reached out to touch Paul's arm. "She's blessed to have someone to love her like you do, Paul."

He stared at the small, smooth hand on his arm. Delicate yet strong. His pulse quickened at the sweet way she said his name. Like the taste of warm honey on buttered toast. Heat spread up and down his spine. He stood very still so she wouldn't move. Could she hear his heart thumping?

"Thank you, Charlotte."

She pulled her hand away. "Guess we'd better get back to camp."

They walked in silence. Charlotte stopped at the wagon to retrieve her Bible and then joined the others at the campfire. Emma climbed onto her papa's lap. Bernie played several tunes on the harmonica while Charlotte read by the light of the fire.

Charlie cleared his throat. "Miz Charlotte, would you read us some verses out of the Good Book?"

She looked around. The men smiled and shook their heads in agreement. Paul gazed at her. "I'd like that."

Charlotte chose the Book of Joshua, ending with the verse, "'Have not I commanded thee? Be strong and of a good courage; be not afraid, neither be thou dismayed: for the Lord thy God is with thee whithersoever thou goest.'"

"Amen," Charlie said. He got up and threw out the remains of his coffee. "I'm turnin' in, boys. Mornin' comes early." He chuckled as he walked to the chuck wagon and grabbed his bedroll. Bernie and Zeke followed.

Paul stood. Emma was still wrapped in his arms. "You and Emma can sleep inside the wagon." He nodded at Charlotte. "There should be enough room. It'll be warmer and not so many crawly critters to deal with."

Charlotte frowned. "I despise bugs."

He grinned. "I'll be right close if you need me."

While Charlotte hurried to get their quarters ready, Paul stepped into the wagon and gently slid Emma onto the bedroll and covered her. He brushed against Charlotte's arm as he jumped down. His heart thumped, and his pulse quickened once more.

"Thanks again for taking good care of Emma today. Sleep well." Paul turned and hurried back to the campfire for one more cup of coffee. He had to quiet his thundering heartbeat. Was she edging her way over that fence and into his heart? He couldn't risk more sorrow. He had to stop this—he'd keep his distance. Her idea of friendship might not be doable. *Oh, Lord, please help me.*

It was still dark outside when Charlotte heard the rustle of pots and pans. She peered out from the slit of the wagon bonnet. Charlie lit the fire under the coffee-pot. Hurrying, she pulled on her skirt and blouse from yesterday, and her jacket. She ran the brush through her hair and then quickly tied it back with a ribbon.

Charlotte slid out of the wagon. She found her cloth and washed her face. The cold water and cool morning air pricked at her skin. She shivered and glanced at the horses grazing in the dew-covered meadow. Steam flared from their nostrils.

As she walked toward Charlie, she asked, "What can I do to help?"

Charlie looked at her. "You're up mighty early, ma'am."

She smiled. "Yes. I wanted to talk to you without anyone around."

He cocked his head. "Wanna cuppa coffee first?" Charlie handed her a tin cup and sipped from his.

Charlotte tasted the warm, strong brew and felt her mind clearing. She watched the cook pinch a bit of dough from a small crock and add flour and milk from a can.

"I'll keep on workin' here. Gotta have breakfast for the boys before daylight."

She wasn't sure how to ask Charlie if he would teach her to cook. Would he wonder why Paul married a woman who couldn't cook? She hoped he wouldn't question her.

"Well, Charlie, um—I can't cook. I don't know anything about cooking."

He looked up from his mixing bowl. "I kinda wondered about that."

"Could you give me a few lessons while we're on this journey?"

He chuckled and turned to glance at her. "I'd be right proud to help ya any way I can. I ain't no fancy cook, though." He shook his head.

"Thank you. I love to learn new things. I've already mastered making coffee, washing dishes and clothes and building a fire." Charlotte knew her voice held pride she couldn't contain.

Charlie set the biscuits inside the Dutch oven to rise and pulled out a slab of salt pork. "Here. Slice some of this for the fryin' pan." Charlie handed her a huge knife.

Charlotte attempted to cut through the thick hunk of meat, but the knife wedged in the middle. She inhaled...leather and coffee. Before she turned around, she heard a familiar voice behind her.

"Here. Let me help you." Paul reached around her, brushing her arm. She jumped back and he took hold of the knife. "If you notch the skin side, it might work best for you. Won't take so much muscle to cut it." He flipped the meat over and pulled the sharp blade through the skin, leaving a carved trail. He handed her the knife. "Now you try."

Charlotte cut several slices, smiled and thanked him.

"Charlie's going to give me cooking lessons." She wrapped up the meat and handed it back to Charlie.

Paul poured coffee and winked at Charlie. "He's a fine cook. You'll have it mastered in no time."

He strolled to the back of the wagon and peeked in at Emma. "I'm riding on ahead this morning and I won't be here when Emma wakes up. Can you handle things with her by yourself?"

She smiled at him. "We'll be fine."

Bernie and Zeke sat up. "Mornin' really does come early, don't it, Boss?" Bernie said. He and Zeke rolled and tied their beds and set them by the chuck wagon to be loaded later. Each poured a cup of coffee and stood by the fire.

"Boys, I'll ride ahead this morning and find a good stopping place for tonight. You all help Charlie hitch the team and bring the horses on."

"Sure thing, Boss," Zeke said, pouring one more cup of coffee.

"Grub's on!" Charlie hollered.

They all grabbed a plate and loaded up on bacon, biscuits and gravy.

Once the horses were hitched to the wagon, Bernie and Zeke moved the herd on down the road.

Charlotte looked at Charlie. "Can you teach me to drive this team?"

He stared ahead, reins in his hands, seeming to ponder her request. "Well, that might be a right good idea. In case I needed to help them boys with somethin' on the trail." He flipped his big brimmed hat back and deliberated a little more. "Can you ride a horse?"

"I love to ride horseback. I rode sidesaddle back East but haven't tried a western saddle yet." Cantering her horse through fields and over fences had been fulfilling. Her aunt had been horrified when Charlotte galloped at breakneck speed to beat the stable hand back to the barn. An angry, critical lecture had followed with her aunt extracting a promise from her to never act so undignified again.

"You know about reinin' a horse, then?"

"Sure."

"Well, it's similar to drivin' a team. If you think of them two as one horse, it's a start." He handed the reins to her without stopping the pair. She'd seen how he'd put the straps over his fingers with his thumb on top. She adjusted the leather to fit comfortably in her hands.

"Be better if you wear gloves next time, ma'am. Your hands will get blistered and raw until you've done it awhile. Now, if you need to put both reins in one hand, this is how you do it." Charlie pulled them from her right hand and threaded them through her fingers on her left, with her thumb still on top.

Charlotte smiled. "Thanks, Charlie." The wagon bumped along. When a jackrabbit skittered in front of the horses and they picked up the pace, prancing a bit, Charlotte pulled back and tried to hand Charlie the reins.

"No, ma'am." He pushed her hands away. "You gotta learn to handle 'em under all circumstances. Talk to 'em. They need to hear your voice. Like this. Easy. Easy now,'" he sang out.

Jack and Belle slowed, and Charlie grinned. "See. Remember they're fraidy-cats. You gotta be brave for them."

"I'll try," Charlotte said, not feeling in the least bit courageous. "Easy now. Everything's gonna be okay. You're okay. Everything's fine," she crooned.

Charlie chuckled. "Just like a momma cooing to her baby. That's real good, Missy."

Paul galloped up beside the wagon and trotted alongside. "Charlie, I found a place to stop on up the road, in a grove of trees. Not a lot of grass, but a nice watering hole for the horses."

Charlie nodded. Charlotte didn't glance his way but kept her eyes on the trail ahead.

Paul looked over at her. "I didn't know you could drive a team."

"Charlie's teaching me." She smiled.

Charlie winked at Paul. "Thought it might come in handy, havin' another driver. You know, in case I need to ride a horse once in a while to get you boys outta trouble."

Paul chuckled.

"Hey, Boss, how about you take a turn helpin' her. I'd like to sit a different position." Charlie asked Charlotte to stop the team so he and Paul could trade places.

"Whoa. Whoa!" she shouted, pulling back on the reins. Charlie laughed and stood up when the wagon stopped. Paul looked unsure. He and Charlie swapped places.

"Thanks, Boss. I'm gonna enjoy this." Charlie chuckled and trotted off on Buck. Paul sat down next to Charlotte and nodded.

"Are you ready to go?" she asked.

"Yeah…we can start anytime." Paul grumbled.

"Go team! Get going. Jack, Belle, go!" Charlotte squawked, but the team didn't move. She turned to Paul. "What's wrong with them? Why won't they go? Are they stuck? Is something wrong with the wagon?"

Paul's deep blue eyes gazed at her for a few moments. "What in the world did Charlie teach you?"

The team didn't move, but her pulse accelerated. There he was, making her jittery again. Charlotte titled her head, raised her chin and said, "He told me to think of the two of them as one horse, and he showed me how to hold the reins in both hands or one hand. And he said they were—"

"That's all? You didn't practice starting or backing the team?" Paul shook his head. "I think Charlie pulled one over on me if all you know is how to hold the reins."

"And when would we have had time to do those things you're talking about? We've been trying to keep up with you and your fast-moving herd of horses." Charlotte glared at him. She was in no mood for his displeasure.

"Don't get riled up." Paul reached over her, placing his hands around hers, and gave the reins a gentle snap. He hollered, "Hup, Belle! Hiya, Jack! Get up!" The horses leaned into their harness, and the wagon moved forward, down the road. On the way to the next stopping place.

Sometimes he was the most aggravating man. She had to remind herself it was only one month. It was going to be a very long twenty-six more days, though. It couldn't go fast enough for Charlotte. She'd celebrate the day they annulled their marriage. He made her too edgy.

She couldn't wait to not be Mrs. Paul Harrison. She harrumphed under her breath to punctuate the thought, but for some reason her stomach somersaulted.

Chapter Six

Paul glanced up at the sky. "Look at those clouds. We've got to get to the meadow and unhitch these horses. Get 'em going," he ordered Charlotte.

Thunder snapped. Charlotte screamed and almost dropped the reins when the team reared and lurched forward, all but bolting out of their harnesses. Emma's eyes got big and Paul gave her a hug. Prince yipped at the thunder.

"Hang on to the reins! Pull them back!" Paul shouted. Loud noises crackled and boomed in the sky. Charlotte squealed as she tried to halt the running horses. "Help me!" she cried to Paul. Water poured down on them like a thousand buckets had been tipped from heaven.

Paul set Emma inside the wagon on top of the bedrolls and put his arms around Charlotte. He gripped her hands. "You can do this. Keep 'em steady—talk to them." He circled her hands with his but offered no assistance. "Pull, Charlotte."

She yanked and shouted, "Whoa! Whoa now!"

As they came hurtling into the clearing, the horses

slowed to a trot. The team had calmed enough to once again be directed by the bits in their mouths. Paul didn't let go of her hands.

"Get Jack to circle. Pull the left rein, gently. Let up a bit on the right rein so Belle can follow his lead!" he hollered. His hands still didn't leave hers. She tugged the leather to the left. Jack stepped that direction and Belle kept pace. The wagon started to turn. When the horses stopped, Paul took the straps from her and hopped out of the wagon. "Get Emma."

Charlotte snatched the child from inside and handed her down to Paul. "Stay beside me, Emma." The little girl bowed her head and stood next to her father. "Throw out some bedrolls," he commanded Charlotte. She grabbed two and threw them to the ground, then handed Prince down to him. He reached up for her. Charlotte toppled into his arms. He gave her a gentle hug and lifted her face so she was looking at him.

"Get to the middle of the meadow. Unroll the canvas and squat down on it. Keep Emma close to you. Put your heads down. I've gotta unhitch the horses. Don't get off the bedrolls. Get goin'—I'll be there!" Paul shouted into the deafening sounds from the air that muffled his words. Lightning flashed again and touched the ground somewhere close by. A crackling sound swept through the patch of trees. The horses stomped and pranced in place while Paul worked to get them unhitched.

Charlotte huddled on the bedroll and held Emma close. She covered the child's ears and her head as best she could while Prince shivered in the rain. Paul joined them on the canvas and a torrential waterfall spilled from the sky as they nestled together. The horses scattered into the woods.

Paul reached for Charlotte's trembling hand and held tight. Was it his touch or the frightful storm pummeling them that caused her to shake? With his other arm, Paul cradled his daughter to his chest and covered her with his coat, whispering something Charlotte couldn't hear.

When the thunder and lightning stopped, Paul pointed at the wagon. "Get inside." He picked up Emma and, pulling Charlotte by the hand, ran through the pelting rain to the wagon, Prince bounding beside them. Settled inside, Paul found several blankets and wrapped Emma and Prince in one, handed one to Charlotte and draped one around his shoulders. He set his Stetson out on the bench seat where the water poured off it in rivulets.

Charlotte handed her straw hat to him with a frown. "We've got to find Emma a bonnet of some sort. She needs one to keep the sun and rain off her head and face." She wished she'd known Emma didn't have a hat at home; she would have bought one at Beiber's store that first day in Cedar Grove.

Paul nodded. "Next town we come to we'll get her one." Emma snuggled into Paul's chest. He wrapped the blanket tighter and used the edge to wipe droplets from her hair.

"Wow. I've never been out in anything like this rainstorm. It's fearsome. Why didn't we get under a tree? Seems like we'd be less soaked." Charlotte stared into Paul's deep blue eyes.

He ran his fingers through his wet hair. Took a deep breath and looked into her eyes. "Are you okay?"

She nodded. "I'm fine. Really wet, but fine."

"It's dangerous to be under trees in a lightning storm. A tree could be struck and drive a bolt right to you or fall and hit you. It's dangerous to be near anything that could send the current toward you, especially anything tall or big…even the ground can carry the electricity. That's why we used the bedroll and squatted out in the open."

"I'll file that information away. I might need it again when I start teaching school in this rural area and you aren't around to help me." She smiled up at him.

Charlotte thought of something else then and tilted her head and raised her eyebrows. "Why didn't you take the reins? I was scared. I wasn't sure the horses would stop for me."

Paul stared at her for a moment. "If you're going to drive a team, you've got to know how to handle them in any situation. I was right there. I wouldn't have let anything happen. You did good." He smiled at her.

Paul peered out from the canvas cover and perused the meadow and beyond. A sinking sun turned the trees into shadowy giants.

"Soon as the rain stops, we'll build a fire and dry everything out. Looks like we'll camp here for the night. Wonder how the boys fared."

"They were ahead of us, weren't they?"

"Yeah. The thunder and lightning probably scattered the herd. Hope everybody's safe." His jaw clenched and his voice sounded ragged.

"We could pray for them," Charlotte suggested with a smile. When Paul prayed in the evening after she read a passage from the Bible it seemed to bring a sense of peace and settle everyone for the night.

He glanced at her. "Fine idea." He bowed his head, took her hand and Emma's, and closed his eyes. "Lord, we pray for the protection of our men and the well-being of our herd. Thank You for keeping the three of us safe. Amen."

When Paul took Charlotte's hand to pray, an electrifying current that had nothing to do with the storm surged through his veins. If only he could get away… go somewhere quiet to think and calm his chaotic emotions.

His chest tightened. He was stuck right now. He couldn't leave Emma and Charlotte with rain hammering the canvas as if it would burst through at any moment. Tranquility sidestepped him. Confined to this small space inside the wagon with his daughter and this woman, this enchanting lovely woman, his heart thrashed and his mind whirled. He fought to regain control of his emotions. When Rachel left them, he'd vowed no woman would ever again trespass in his heart or mind. He wouldn't allow it.

Less than thirty days. Paul bowed his head again and quietly begged God for help.

Bernie galloped into camp, leading Paul's horse with Charlie slumped over in the saddle, barely hanging on. Bernie shouted, "Boss, Boss! Charlie's hurt!"

Zeke followed close behind. Paul jumped out of the wagon and pulled Charlie out of the saddle. "Get him inside." The men lifted and dragged Charlie until he was under the canvas covering. He was unconscious.

Charlotte and Emma moved as far back as they could to make room for the man. Charlotte pawed through the bedrolls and found blankets to cover him.

Zeke, Bernie and Paul hovered over the wagon seat. "What happened?" Paul asked.

Bernie took off his hat and shook the water from it before putting it back on his head. "When that thunder cracked, Buck threw him and he hit his head on a rock. He mumbled somethin' afore he passed out. Me and Zeke got him back here. The herd scattered, Boss. Sorry." Bernie's head drooped.

Paul looked at his men, soaked to their bones. He sighed. "I'm grateful you were around to help Charlie. We'll gather the herd when this gully washer quits. You boys take your bedrolls and get under the wagon, out of this rain."

Charlotte handed each of them a bedroll with extra blankets. Looking at Charlie, she asked, "How can we help him, Paul?"

"We'll get him as dry as we can and keep him warm. Help me get some of his wet clothes off." Paul unbuttoned Charlie's heavy coat and lifted him. Charlotte tugged on the sleeves, and together they pulled it off. Paul examined Charlie's shoulder, pressing down. "He might have broken his collar bone. Find me a couple of towels."

She located two. Paul rolled them and placed them under his arm. "We need to make a sling. Hand me one of Emma's dresses."

Emma found her suitcase and handed it to Charlotte.

"Why do you need one of her outfits? What are you doing?" Charlotte asked before she opened the valise.

"I'm going to tear one up to make the sling."

Charlotte glanced at Emma. A tear slid down the child's cheek, but she quickly brushed it away. Her lips turned down and her eyes were full of sadness.

"No, Paul."

He looked at Charlotte's flashing eyes. There she was again. Challenging him. She always had an opinion and it usually opposed his—and her timing stunk.

"I have to make a sling. Give me one of my shirts, then." He scowled at her.

She leveled her gaze. "Emma's clothes supply is limited and so is yours. I have two petticoats. I'll tear off some cloth from this one." Her cheeks flushed. She turned her back to him, lifted her skirt and ripped a length of material from her slip.

He shook his head but took the scrap and worked with it until the sling held Charlie's arm supported by the towel rolls. They wrapped a blanket tight around his chest and put several more on top of him. "Now we wait. And pray," Paul said with his head bowed and eyes closed.

Sunrays settled on the canvas, and light exploded inside the wagon. Emma, with a big smile, grabbed Charlotte's shoulder and shook it, pointing upward.

"Paul, look," Charlotte whispered, gesturing toward the sun shining on the canvas. Paul opened his eyes to see the happy face of his little girl and the sparkling green eyes of his wife. *No.* Not his wife. The temporary caretaker of his daughter, he corrected himself.

"At last," he said, and jumped out of the wagon. "Come on, we'll start a fire, get some breakfast and dry out all the wet things."

Zeke and Bernie stood at the end of the wagon, both frowning. Bernie said, "Boss, we don't know where the coffeepot is."

Charlotte and Emma picked their way around Charlie and waited for Paul to help Emma down. Charlotte handed him Prince and began to alight herself when Paul grasped her waist, lifted and twirled her around. She grabbed his shoulders. He smiled and looked into her eyes. "Storm's over," he said, releasing her.

Charlotte stared at him, then backed away. "I'll make the coffee and see what Charlie has for breakfast." She expertly lowered the table.

Paul started a fire. Bernie and Zeke strung a rope from tree to tree and hung all the wet blankets and bedrolls. Charlotte hooked the coffeepot on the tripod over the fire, then ground the coffee beans and tossed them in when the water bubbled.

Like a bear in a cage, Charlie growled from inside the wagon, "Get outta my chuck box," they heard him groan. Paul, Zeke and Bernie climbed up and assisted Charlie down.

Leaning against the wagon, Charlie asked what had happened. When they told him and he tried to move his arm, his face flinched in pain. "Guess I ain't gonna be cookin' much for a while, Boss." He hung his head.

Charlotte strode to his side. "It's a good thing you were teaching me to cook. You can give me instructions and I'll learn by doing. Maybe this worked out for the best," she chirped and patted his arm.

Charlie's eyes widened, his eyebrows arched and he shook his head. "You're the most confounded woman I ever met." He paused and looked around. "Guess we don't got much choice. Hadn't counted on havin' no Little Mary along on this trip." Charlie glanced up at Paul with a questioning look. "Boss, you okay with this?"

Paul, Zeke and Bernie tried hard to smother their laughter.

Paul winked at him. "Charlie, you and Charlotte make a fine team." He turned to the others. "We better find our horses after we finish our coffee. Who knows? Some of them might wander back into camp."

Charlotte smiled at Emma. "Let's get you into some dry clothes." Emma started to climb up the wagon wheel when Paul lifted her. She scrambled over the bench seat and waited for Charlotte. Paul put his strong hands around Charlotte's waist and drank in her rose scent. He shook his head. If only she didn't make his pulse quicken. He gave her a boost up and sped off, muttering about women and broken fences and wounded hearts and not getting what he'd bargained for.

"Boss!" Bernie shouted. "Look there. It's Jack." He pointed to the horse grazing at the edge of a clump of trees.

Paul retrieved a rope from the side of the wagon. "Maybe Belle's close by. Let's catch Jack." Zeke and Bernie found a couple of cords and edged quietly toward the sorrel, Prince walking behind them the way he'd stalk a pheasant.

Charlotte gathered Emma's wet clothes along with hers. She shoved their suitcases to the side of the wagon and pushed them down hard. A clang rang out. Surprised, Charlotte reached to the floor of the wagon, wiggled her hand under all the bedrolls and extra blankets and pulled out a big bell tied to a leather belt.

"Emma, look. This must be Sassy's bell. Your daddy's going to be very happy. Let's go give it to him." Charlotte climbed over the wagon seat and waited for Emma. She worked her way down the wheel and motioned for Emma. The child toppled into her uplifted arms. Charlotte caught her, stumbled a little and tumbled to the ground with Emma on top of her. Emma rolled off Charlotte, her eyes wide, eyebrows raised and a fearful look in her eyes. Charlotte sat up and laughed and gave her a hug.

"That was funny, wasn't it Emma?" Charlotte stood and dusted off her dark blue skirt and gray blouse. She reached out her hand for Emma, who'd dusted off her brown-striped dress with vigor. "Let's take this bell to your daddy."

Emma hesitantly put her tiny hand in Charlotte's, and together they strolled toward the men who had a rope around one of the wagon-team horses.

Charlotte called over her shoulder, "Charlie, we'll be back to fix breakfast as soon as we deliver this bell!" She gave it a hearty jerk, and it rang out loud and clear.

Paul whipped around at the sound. Charlotte held Emma's hand and strode toward him. His gaze drank in the sight of that beautiful woman, with her radiant smile and sparkling green eyes, and his sweet little girl skipping beside her. His mouth went dry, his heart bumping hard against his chest.

Could a woman love a child not born to her? Was this what a true mother's love looked like? Paul didn't know. He couldn't remember his own, and Rachel had never looked happy about her daughter.

What about his little girl? Would she accept another woman as a parent? He hadn't thought Emma was too attached to Rachel, but when she quit speaking, he reasoned he'd not understood the depth of his child's feelings for her detached mother.

Why did his heart feel so unguarded? This woman who came from the East and was now his wife—it felt like she was dismantling the fence around his heart. Her smile, her laugh, her sweetness with Emma—her desire to learn, her eyes that danced with delight or pierced him with intensity…she unintentionally kicked at the barrier he'd carefully constructed. And that troubled him.

She isn't staying. It's only one month. Reinforce that fence, he admonished himself.

Chapter Seven

Charlotte glanced up from the mixing bowl to revel in the beauty of the afternoon. Sunrays streamed through the treetops, lighting up leaves, and the tall grass in the meadow looked as if someone had skipped through haphazardly scattering diamonds. No manicured park in Boston could match this wild and crazy, beautiful country. She smiled, breathing in that right-after-a-rain fresh clean smell. Her fingers squeezed the dough over and over. She tilted her head up to watch small cloud flurries zigzagging across the light blue sky.

"Not too rough, now." Charlie stood over her shoulder. "Add a bit more flour."

Charlotte reached for the flour container and filled her hand. "This much?" She showed Charlie.

"Looks good."

She tossed it in the bowl. Charlie coughed and stepped back. Puffs of particles rose, then settled on her cheeks. She swiped her forehead, leaving a wide white trail. Emma glanced up, giggled and pointed at Charlotte's face.

Charlotte smiled at her. "So you think this is funny?" With a gleam in her eyes, Charlotte dipped her hand in the flour once more and moved toward Emma. Emma dashed away and then twirled to see if Charlotte followed.

They circled the wagon once before Charlie shouted, "These biscuits ain't never gonna get made if you two keep up these shenanigans!"

Charlotte trotted back to the mixing bowl. Emma skipped beside her, and Prince pranced along behind, wagging his tail. Setting the biscuits aside to rise, she cut the meat the way Paul had shown her. Carefully following Charlie's detailed instructions, she made the gravy. No lumps. Nice and smooth. She rolled the biscuits real easy, exactly the way Charlie told her to.

"Emma, come help me with the biscuits." Charlotte dragged over a round stump and lifted Emma up to stand on it. She brushed her hands on the apron Charlie insisted she wear and handed Emma the biscuit cutter. Round circles were stuffed into the Dutch oven until it was full.

Emma reached up and pulled on Charlotte's sleeve, pointing to the center of the meadow. Two shiny black horses trotted into the pasture, then stopped, plunked their noses into the tall grass and munched side by side.

"The horses are coming back, Emma. Oh, your papa will be very happy when he gets here." Emma smiled at her.

Charlotte glanced again at the grazing horses. Beyond them, in the woods, she spotted a plume of dust. Movement. Three riders. They didn't look like Paul,

Zeke or Bernie. Her skin tingled and she felt her body tense.

She grabbed Charlie's arm and shook it. "Charlie. Charlie. Look over there." She pointed to the riders. He grunted.

Her hands shook as she led Emma to the front wagon wheel. Charlotte knelt down and turned Emma's chin toward her, then smiled at the little girl.

"Emma, you must get in the wagon and hide under the bedrolls. Don't make a sound. No matter what." She took Emma's shoulders and pulled her close and then looked into her eyes again. "Wait until I come get you or your papa does. Do you understand?"

The child's blue eyes widened, but she nodded. Charlotte boosted her into the wagon and watched until she was safe inside. Prince yipped to be picked up, but Charlotte ignored him. "You'll give her away. You stay with me, boy." She reached down and patted his head.

Charlie growled for her to come stand beside him at the worktable. "Keep on with your cookin'. We'll check out who they are. Let's you and me make an apple pie." He grinned and nodded toward the fruit. She rinsed out the mixing bowl and waited for instructions. Prince sat down by her heels.

"Start peelin' them apples."

Charlotte found the knife while keeping her eyes on the riders coming their way.

"Should I offer them coffee?"

"That'd be neighborly," Charlie answered, but his eyes also tracked the horses loping through the trees.

She gathered three galvanized cups and set them

in front of her. Charlotte then picked up an apple and worked the knife round and round the sphere.

"You know how to shoot?" Charlie asked.

"No. Never had an occasion to use a gun." Charlotte's heart raced. The knife trembled in her hand. She took a deep breath to regain control. "Do you think there'll be shooting?"

"Never know when ya might need to fire a gun. I'll talk to the boss about it. Maybe he can teach you to use it." Charlie stepped away and pulled a rifle from the side of the wagon. He laid it on the worktable and covered it with dishcloths.

"Who do you think they are?"

Charlie patted her shoulder. "Probably men travelin' through. Don't you worry none. Keep peelin' them apples. The boys'll be happy there's pie this evening."

The men were close enough to describe. The one in front was chunky. He wore a brown jacket, tan shirt and a chocolate-colored hat. His reddish hair and beard made Charlotte think of a crimson bear riding a horse. Silver conchos surrounded the hatband of the rider on the left. His vest flapped as he rode. A dark blue scarf circled his throat. The third man looked older and hunched over as he sat his saddle. Gray hairs peeked out from his tattered hat. His dirty blue-denim jacket was ripped. A frothy white foam covered all three horses.

"They been pushin' them horses hard," Charlie whispered as the men rode into camp. A swirl of dust spiraled in the air behind them when they reined in their mounts.

The one in the brown jacket walked his horse up to the fire, the others staying behind him.

"Hi folks." His smile revealed stained teeth. "Can we trouble ya for a cuppa coffee?"

"Sure," Charlie said and nodded at Charlotte. She picked up three cups as the men dismounted. Prince followed her to the fire. Handing them coffee, she noted the cheeks of the man with the fancy hat were peppered with tiny cervices, pockmarked. Maybe he'd had chicken pox and picked at the scabs. The old man's grizzled beard barely covered a thin scar extending from his ear to his jaw line. Had he tripped and fallen against a sharp object? Or was that wound the outcome of a knife fight? Her hands trembled.

"Where you boys headed?" Charlie asked from the chuck wagon worktable. He motioned for Charlotte to come back beside him. She scooted close to Charlie, picked up her knife and an apple.

"Nowheres in particular," said the crimson bear with a lopsided grin. "We been travelin' around some. Lookin' for work here and there." He sipped but kept his eyes on Charlie. "You all got any work? Need help tendin' them there horses?" He cocked his head toward the two black horses in the meadow. The other two men separated from the one talking.

Charlie's dark eyes locked with the red-haired man's rigid gaze. "Nope. We're doin' fine. Thanks all the same." He snaked his hand under the dishcloths, ready to grip the rifle. Before he could pull it out, the man in the vest threw his cup to the ground, drew his revolver and aimed it at Charlie.

Charlie shoved Charlotte behind him, muttering, "Get down, under the wagon." Charlotte flopped to the ground and crawled out of sight. The minute she rolled onto her stomach, she glanced up to see the old man sneak behind Charlie and jab his gun in Charlie's back. She grabbed the growling dog and pulled him close to her, then clapped her other hand over her own mouth, smothering a scream.

"Okay, boys, get what you can and let's get outta here," barked the redheaded man. They grabbed sacks of beans, rice, coffee and flour, then yanked out the chuck box drawers until one of them shouted, "Found the money!"

Their leader snarled at Charlie. "You tell your boss he better just head back. He ain't gonna make it in time to sell that band of ponies." He turned to the others. "Let's get goin'." They mounted their horses and galloped back into the woods.

Charlotte's heart pounded and her body trembled as she dragged herself from under the wagon and let go of Prince. "Forgive me, you poor sweet dog—I nearly smothered you."

She stood next to Charlie. His eyes were moist. "Are you okay, Missy? I'm sorry they got the jump on me. I'm getting kinda old, I guess." His head slumped and he wandered over to a log and sat down.

"I'll be back," Charlotte promised, then stumbled to the front of the wagon. She heaved her shaking legs onto the wheel, then pushed herself over the bench and inside.

"Emma, Emma." When the little girl crawled from beneath a pile of the bedrolls, Charlotte lurched and wrapped her arms around her, crying, "Oh, Emma, Emma, thank the Lord you are safe." She rocked her back and forth, stroking her hair and uttering her name over and over, tears streaming down her cheeks.

Paul, Bernie and Zeke halted at the rim of the meadow and stared at the campsite. Paul pinched the clapper on Sassy's bell and the clanging stopped.

A breeze rustled tree leaves and rippled the tall grasses like an ocean wave.

"Somethin' ain't right, Boss," Bernie whispered. "Look there at the coffeepot."

The pot hung on the tripod over a circle of smoldering ashes. "Charlie wouldn't let that there fire go out."

Silence floated in the summery air like low-lying clouds. No aroma of coffee drifted their way.

Something was out of order.

"I don't see Emma or Charlotte," Paul said. There was no movement. Anywhere.

Nothing. Paul's heart slammed into his chest. *Where's my daughter? Where is Charlotte?* Worst-case scenarios taunted his imagination.

Pointing at the two black horses, Zeke muttered, "Looks like a couple of horses made it back to camp."

They dismounted, undid their holster ties, drew their revolvers and edged quietly toward the chuck wagon. When Bernie spotted Charlie sitting slumped over next to the pup curled up in a ball, he charged forward. Paul and Zeke sprinted to the wagon.

Paul bellowed, "Emma! Charlotte! Where are you?"

He heard Charlotte's muffled cries: "Emma, Emma, oh, Emma."

His chest tightened. Sweat beaded on his forehead. He gulped air and gripped the side of the wagon, steadying his faltering steps. Was his precious daughter injured? What was wrong?

He bolted inside, slid beside Charlotte, seized her shoulders and saw Emma tucked into the young woman, her little arms draped around Charlotte's neck. Emma tilted her head. When she saw it was her father, she smiled.

"Oh, thank God, Emma, you're okay." Paul tugged her into his arms. He gazed at Charlotte. Her eyes were puffy and red from the tears rolling down her cheeks. Her lovely blond hair hung loose and wild; her dress was covered in dust. Paul moved Emma to his left knee, reached for Charlotte with his right arm and enveloped her in a strong embrace. She buried her head in his chest and sobbed uncontrollably.

He rested his head on hers, stroked her hair and murmured, "It's okay now." Paul's heart walloped his chest. It's a good thing they were all sitting. He felt Charlotte's body trembling. He knew he couldn't stand. His legs felt like jelly spread over a warm biscuit.

"Charlotte," he whispered, "are you and Emma okay? What happened?"

She pushed away from him, looked into his eyes and blinked back more tears. Her mouth moved, but no words came out. With his fingertips he brushed hair from her eyes.

"We'll talk in a minute. Don't worry. I'm grateful to find you and Emma." He inhaled her scent. He had to get out of this wagon. He needed to move away from her. She was too much in need of comfort. He straightened up, let go of Charlotte's hand and lifted Emma onto the bench. He held out his hands for Char-

lotte, not able to look into her beautiful emerald eyes.
He'd regret it if he did. He might do something fool-
ish. Might squeeze her to himself. Might kiss her tears
away. Might beg her to stay when the month was over.

And ask her to become his real wife.

Stop. Stop it now, he scolded his treacherous heart.

"Let's find out how Charlie is," he mumbled.

She stood but wobbled, and Paul wrapped his arm
around her waist. He helped her down from the wagon
and then stretched up his arms for his daughter. When
he had Emma safely in his embrace, he couldn't put
her down. He hugged his daughter close. She was all
he had. This trip was for her. Something awful had
happened here, and he didn't know what yet, but he'd
find out soon.

He carried Emma and held Charlotte's hand as they
walked to the back of the wagon. Drawers from the
chuck box had been dumped and scattered. Bags of
supplies were missing. He dropped Charlotte's hand
and stopped for a moment. He turned over one of the
smallest drawers and searched inside. Those thieves
had found his money. He pounded his fist on the table,
kicked the dirt and then reached for Charlotte's trembling hand.

They watched Bernie help Charlie get his arm back
in the sling.

"Now, boys, don't need to worry none about me. I'm
just thankin' the Man Upstairs for protecting our little
ladies." He grinned and nodded.

Zeke patted Charlie's shoulder. Emma squirmed out
of her daddy's arms and dashed for Prince.

Paul turned to Charlie, concern in his voice. "You gonna be okay? Should I go for a doc?"

Charlie tried to shake his head but squinted in pain. "No doc. Soon as my head quits poundin' I'll be good as new." He paused. "Well, 'ceptin' for this shoulder." Charlie grimaced when he raised his head to look at Paul. "Those low-down good-for-nothin' snakes… Wait'll I catch up to them."

He glanced at Charlotte, his eyes full of admiration. "Glad you and the little one are safe." He nodded with a big smile. "You done a right good thing, Missy, hidin' that babe in the wagon 'fore those scoundrels rode into camp."

Paul dropped Charlotte's hand, put his arm around her shoulder and pulled her close.

"She's a smart one." Paul smiled down at her. He knew no words could adequately express his gratitude to Charlotte for protecting his precious daughter.

Paul looked at Charlie. "Can ya tell me what happened?"

Charlie took a deep breath. "Miz Charlotte saw the men a comin' from them woods over there." He pointed in the direction they'd approached from. "She quick-like got Emma inside the wagon. Then them three varmints rode into camp. We offered 'em coffee. They had a cup. Then they drawed their weapons and stole our provisions."

Charlie hung his head. "Sorry, Boss."

Paul stared at him for several moments. He'd not given a thought to riding off to hunt for his scattered herd with the boys. He'd left his darling daughter, a young city gal and a hurt old man to deal with good-for-nothing scoundrels.

Paul rubbed the back of his neck. He'd been careless. What was wrong with him? He knew better. This wasn't the ranch. This was open country where bandits looked for easy pickings. He slapped his hat on his thigh and cleared his throat.

"Charlie, Charlotte, I apologize to you both." He glanced at her. "I never should have left you all alone. I wasn't thinking clearly. It won't happen again. Where's the rifle?"

"They done stole that too." Charlie's face reddened and he stared at the ground. "I was goin' for it, when one of 'em snuck up behind me and poked his gun in my back."

Paul looked around at his crew. "They took a fair amount of our food supply. They didn't find all our money, so we can buy more provisions and another rifle in the next town. Let's get the fire going, have a bite, then we'll get back to runnin' down the rest of the herd."

He turned around to grab a bundle of firewood.

"Boss," Charlie called, trying to stand. He staggered and sat back down.

"Hey. You stay right there. We'll take care of this," Paul assured him.

"I wanna talk to ya about somethin' else." Charlie motioned for Paul to come closer. "Maybe ya should give some thought to teachin' Miz Charlotte how to handle a rifle and a revolver." Charlie raised his eyebrows. "I'm only thinkin', if there's a next time, she might need to be doin' some defendin'."

Paul jerked on his hat. His forehead wrinkled. He gawked at Charlie.

He'd hugged Charlotte today. And held her hand. He'd wanted to kiss her. He was so grateful and relieved that she and Emma weren't hurt. They had all been frightened. His aim was to reassure Charlotte that everything was under control now that he was back in camp.

But…he'd come close to kissing her. He'd wanted to kiss her. He'd had to fight with himself not to snatch her into his arms and smother her with kisses and lingering hugs. He was sure it was because he was relieved and grateful. Surely it was nothing more? The worst, though, was he'd almost begged her to stay with him and Emma. To tear up their agreement and remain his wife. For real.

If he had to teach her to shoot, he'd have to get close to her. Mighty close. As close as a noose around his neck.

He might have to put his arms around her to show her where to put her hands on the gun. Help her hold the rifle at shoulder level. He could feel his pulse racing with the thought of being that close to her again.

He took a deep breath.

He had promised to cherish and protect her. And he was a man of his word.

Plus, it might be a good thing if she knew how to handle a gun.

Paul coughed. "I'll think about it, Charlie."

He hustled back to the campfire.

Chapter Eight

Bernie and Zeke hitched Belle and Jack to the wagon after the noon meal and handed Charlotte the reins. Emma nestled between Charlotte and Charlie, patting her rag doll's yellow yarn hair. She glanced back now and then at Prince lying on top of a bedroll inside the wagon.

Charlie smiled at Charlotte. "Dinner's over and daylight's burnin', Missy. Get this team movin'."

Charlotte grinned, lifted the reins in her gloved hands and, lightly tapping the leather on their broad rumps, shouted, "Get up, Belle! Hup, Jack!" The horses stepped forward at the same time. The sight of those big beautiful animals striving together to pull their load thrilled Charlotte every time.

She decided that's what a good marriage must look like. If two people were going to wed, they should work together. Like a harnessed team of horses with a common purpose. Of course, love for one another and the Lord would be necessary. Matrimony wouldn't have to be the way her suffragette friends described a traditional marriage. They'd bombarded her with the notion that a ring on her finger meant a woman became her husband's property. Her friends rattled on and on about overbearing husbands. Charlotte had had enough of her domineering aunt to last a lifetime. She wanted no husband to boss her about, give her orders and expect her to jump with never a thought or an opinion of her own.

No. She had no inclination to stay married to Paul. She wanted freedom to make her own decisions, to pursue her dreams. She'd waste no time annulling their marriage.

Her stomach seesawed. She'd miss sweet little Emma, though. And…him.

She rolled her eyes. *Humph. Driving this wagon day after day gives me too much time to ponder*, she scolded herself. Why was matrimony even a topic on her mind, let alone how one could make a marriage work? She hadn't changed her thinking on the subject. She wanted no part of that prison sentence. She enjoyed working with Paul, except when he was bossy with her. But being a schoolteacher was her dream. Not marriage.

She visualized expanding her students' view of the world. She'd encourage them to want to learn more. She hoped to promote a vision for young women in her class that allowed them to dream beyond society's expectations about their role.

Distracting herself, Charlotte turned her attention to the band of horses. They ambled along as if they hadn't a care in the world. Zeke and Bernie had taught her the colors of horses: sorrel, bay, brown, black, dun, buckskin and palomino.

"Did they find most of the herd, Charlie?" she asked.

She gazed at Paul trailing alongside Sassy, her bell clanging in time with the clip-clop of her strides. Paul was like no other man she'd ever known. All the men she'd met at college and at her aunt's social events were immaculately dressed, not a hair out of place, with soft hands that resembled her own. They spent their days at leisure activities requiring lots of money, and their only purpose was defeating their opponents and impressing their friends.

Paul was ruggedly handsome, tough, strong, bullheaded, decisive and competent. With his Stetson cocked to one side, his strong legs gripping the side of the horse, he was a picture of power and control. No wonder he bossed people around—he was clearly a man used to being in charge.

She bristled and straightened her shoulders. That was no excuse for bossing *her* around, though. She'd make sure he understood she'd take no more orders from him. He could ask politely from now on if he wanted something from her. When it came to his daughter, though, he was tender and sweet, a bowl of sugared mush. He was definitely the most compelling man Charlotte had ever encountered.

"They found all but three," Charlie answered. "Those still might hear Sassy's bell and join up. Horses like to stay with those they growed up with. They're familiar with their own herd rules. They don't hardly ever seek another group, 'lessen it's a stud colt. Those little boys go off and start their own herd. But Mr. Paul, he only has geldings and mares in this here band he's sellin'."

Paul galloped to the wagon and Charlotte halted the team.

"Hi, Paul. Everything okay?" She looked him in the

eyes and smiled. That leather-and-coffee scent wafted her way. Her stomach churned. Had she eaten something that didn't sit well with her? Had Charlie added anything different at mealtime?

Paul tugged at his hat, his deep blue eyes searching hers. Connecting. He smiled.

"Doing great. We'll be stopping in Adin. There's a general store there. We can pick up supplies."

Paul caught Emma's eyes. "Hey, sweet one. You doing okay with these two?"

Emma nodded and gave her daddy a big grin.

Charlie asked, "Who's stayin' with the horses while we're in town?"

"Bernie and Zeke will switch off. Everybody needs a trip to town now and then." Paul chuckled and trotted back to the herd.

Town? Oh, no. Charlotte bit her lip.

"Charlie, will we stop before we get to Adin?"

He cocked his head and raised his brows. "Not sure. What's the matter?"

Charlotte focused straight ahead. She swallowed several times and blinked, feeling the heat in her cheeks.

"I… I don't want to seem vain." Pausing, she turned to look over Emma's head and whispered, "I… I must look a mess. I'd like time to freshen up before we get to town. And I need to get a little trail dust off Emma too."

One of the wagon wheels thumped over a rock half-buried in the road. Charlotte and Emma bounced in their seat and knocked against one another. "Guess I better watch the road." She cringed.

"Cleanin' up sounds like a mighty good idea. For all of us." Charlie reached down and grabbed the stick with a red bandana tied at the end. "Let me get the boss back over here." He handed it to Emma. "Wanna signal your papa?" She nodded and took the flag.

"Swing it back and forth nice and easy–like until he sees ya. Not too hard, ya don't wanna spook Jack and Belle."

When Paul spotted the waving scarf, he trotted over. "What's up?"

Charlie met his eyes. "We'll be needin' to stop and freshen up 'fore we head into town. Let's find a campin' spot by a crick."

Paul started to protest, but Charlie's furrowed brows and glare let him know this stop wasn't negotiable.

Paul grinned. "I'll ride ahead and pick out a good place."

After he galloped away, Charlotte thanked Charlie. She was excited to be going into a town. She missed people. The thought of perusing store merchandise made her smile. Maybe she'd find Emma a hat and perhaps a few new dresses. New stockings too.

Wagon tracks cut deep into the road ahead. Charlie advised her to stay in the ruts; it was easier on the team and more comfortable for those in the wagon. Not so much jerking and bouncing around. Paul had instructed Charlie and Charlotte to keep the wagon on local roads as much as possible. He trailed the band of horses alongside at a distance off the main thoroughfares.

Charlotte marveled at the miles and miles of wide-open grassland. No fences. No buildings. The sky waltzed across the base of rounded hills and lingered for stunning, colorful moments. Jagged, steep mountains with snowy tops pointed to the sky behind the bare hilltops. Wooded areas cropped up around huge stacked boulders.

Looking toward the peaks, she said to Charlie, "The view from that height must be glorious. What kinds of animals inhabit such a place?"

"Well now, all kinds of deer, bears, mountain lions and rabbits. Badgers and coyotes make their homes in the mountains too."

"Do people live that high up?"

"There's a few settlements. Trappers and home-steaders have homes up there. Some ranchers maintain shacks for their line riders."

Charlotte shifted the reins into her left hand and pointed to a village squeezed between two forested hills. "Look, Emma. That must be Adin."

Paul motioned for them to head the wagon toward him. Charlotte turned the horses off the road and trotted them up a slight incline where he waited. "There's a stream near those willows. We'll camp there tonight. We won't unhitch the team until we get back from town."

"Don't stop the wagon too close to the stream." Charlie pointed to a shady area a good distance from the creek. "If there comes a summer squall, the crick might rise and the wagon could float away."

Was he teasing her? "Charlie," she said, trying to sound exasperated.

He grinned. "I seen it happen."

Once a campfire was started, Charlotte hung the coffeepot on the tripod, and then she and Emma filled the bucket at the creek to heat water for washing up and for laundry.

They all scrubbed up and changed into clean clothes. Charlotte threw their garments in the washtub and added hot water and soap.

"The clothes can soak while we're in town and I'll wash them when we get back," she explained to Emma and Charlie as she drove the wagon away from camp. Paul and Bernie trotted alongside the wagon. Zeke hung around the fire, sipping his cup of coffee, and waved goodbye until they were out of sight.

At the Adin General Store, Charlotte and Paul chose a small straw hat with a blue-ribbon tie for Emma, some black stockings and colorful ribbons for her hair. There were no ready-made dresses, and since Charlotte didn't sew, they didn't choose fabric. Paul ordered the replacement supplies in between naming candies in big glass jars that Emma kept pointing to. Charlotte admired a feathered hat displayed in the window.

Suddenly she gasped and stepped backward, knocking several bolts of cloth to the floor. Paul strode up behind her. He set Emma down.

"What's wrong?" He glanced out the window over her shoulder. Charlotte had not turned nor taken her eyes from the glass.

Her lungs felt like they'd shrunk and collapsed on one another. Her mouth was dry. Her thoughts blurred in a whirlwind, and her ears numbed to outside sounds. Her body trembled and she stumbled into Paul.

"What is it? You're white as a full moon. What's wrong, Charlotte?" Paul turned her around and gave her a gentle shake. He stared into her eyes, which she knew must be big and round like a panicked critter.

She pointed with her gloved finger out the window to a sandy-haired man across the street in front of the barbershop. "It's him," she stammered. "It's one—one of the men—who robbed us." She collapsed into Paul's arms.

Paul pulled her close and patted her back. It pained him to see Charlotte terrified. Grateful she'd thought to protect his Emma, he'd promised to protect the caretaker of his daughter from those brutes. He bowed his head, closed his eyes and prayed.

He leaned away from her. "Don't worry. The boys and I will take care of it." He needed to find Charlie and Bernie.

"You and Emma go to the cafe down the street and get something to eat. I'll be along to fetch you later. Don't leave the restaurant until I come to get you. Understand?"

Charlotte nodded, took Emma's hand and walked out the door toward Sally's Home Café without a word. Paul marveled at her silence. She offered no rebuttal. She spoke no second opinion. If the situation weren't reprehensible, he would have chuckled at her uncharacteristic, docile behavior.

He gathered their purchases and stepped out the door. Bernie lugged a bulging burlap bag toward the wagon at the feed store. His best friend had arrived at the orphanage a year after Paul. Bernie was a small kid some of the bigger boys had delighted in tormenting. After Paul walloped the toughest, oldest boy and warned him never to bother Bernie again, Bernie had shadowed Paul and taken to calling him Boss. When Paul ran away a couple years later, Bernie had followed. They'd lived a western version of Tom Sawyer and Huck Finn until Paul decided to settle down, get a real job and get married.

Paul sprinted to the feed store, stuffed the packages under the bench seat and helped Bernie load the last sack. "We gotta find Charlie. Charlotte spotted one of the thieves," Paul uttered.

Bernie frowned at Paul. "Charlie's at the post office. What are we gonna do?"

"Not sure. I need to make sure he's okay."

Paul and Bernie hurried across the street. Charlie stood on the wooden-plank walk in the doorway of the post office, smiling at them. "Hiya, boys," he called. Abruptly, his smile faded, his mustache twitched and his eyes shifted from cheer to rage.

When Paul and Bernie stood next to him, Charlie said in a controlled growl, "Over there's one of them skunks that robbed us."

Paul nodded. "Yeah. Charlotte noticed him too."

"Boss, what are we gonna do?" Bernie asked without taking his eyes off the man on the other side of the street.

"How about we go talk to the sheriff? He could arrest that fellow," Paul said, looking for the jailhouse.

Charlie rubbed his shoulder and scowled. "If it weren't for my bad arm, I'd give him a whoppin' and make him tell us where our stuff is. But, guess it's best to let the sheriff handle it."

Paul tipped his head. "Sheriff's office is that way."

A few strides later they flung open the door. A gray-haired, leather-faced old man sat hunched over a desk. He glanced up when they burst inside.

"Can I help you boys with somethin'?"

"You bet you can." Charlie pushed his way in front of Paul and Bernie. He stopped. "You the law?" He squinted at the man wearing the deputy badge.

"Yep. Deputy Willis. Sheriff's outta town. Be back this afternoon." The old man peered at Charlie and the others. "Do I know you?"

Charlie grabbed Paul's arm, yanked him back a step or two and tilted the brim of his hat downward. "No. We never seen ya. Lost a few horses in a thunderstorm the other night. Wonderin' if anyone reported findin' any strays. Brand is the Bar H."

"Nobody's said anything. If somebody brings 'em in, where can we find ya?" The old man glared.

Charlie turned to leave, looked back and said, "They'll turn up. We'll check at the livery. Thanks." He pushed Bernie and Paul out the door.

In the middle of the street, Paul stopped. "Charlie, what was all that about missin' horses?"

"True, ain't it?" Charlie asked.

"Yeah…but…" They continued to cross the road.

Bernie interrupted, "Was that another one of them thieves?"

Charlie nodded as they stepped up onto the board-walk.

Paul led the way to Sally's Home Café. "Let's get the girls. We'll talk, but not in front of Charlotte and Emma. Don't wanna scare them."

"Should I ride out and let Zeke come into town?" Bernie asked.

"No, we've got to get out of here. I don't want to be anywhere near this town. They might look for us again. That old deputy might figure out who Charlie is after he thinks on it awhile."

Paul saw Emma and Charlotte seated by a window and waved for them to come out.

Charlotte looked peaceful again. Paul smiled. "You're not so pale now. What'd you have to eat?"

"Blackberry pie and a nice cold glass of milk. It's been a while since Emma's had any. She loved it. Me too." Charlotte grinned.

"We've got to get going," Paul muttered.

Charlotte stopped and knelt down to adjust Emma's new straw hat. She started to tie the ribbon, but Paul lifted her elbow.

His eyes flashed. "Now. Tie it later." He stomped toward the wagon. She was the most aggravating woman sometimes. Hadn't she heard him? They needed to leave Adin. At once. Before those thieves figured out who they were. It wasn't good that one was a deputy.

On the wagon ride back to camp, Charlie didn't say one word. He stared straight ahead, like he was mulling over a new recipe. Emma held her little doll and played with the ribbon under her chin. Charlotte didn't ask about what had happened in town.

Paul heard Charlotte say, "Perhaps we should sing." Charlie grunted. Charlotte sang out, "Rock of ages, cleft for me…"

Emma smiled and tapped her foot.

When they arrived at camp, Zeke looked puzzled. "Hey, Boss. You're back early. Everything okay?"

Paul dismounted and helped Charlotte and Emma down. Charlie and Bernie stood beside him.

"Turns out this is not a good spot to camp. Pack up. We need to get back on the road. If we don't dilly-dally, we'll find a better place before dark. Let's get movin'."

Charlotte looked confused. "But you all didn't have your supper. Did you even get a cup of coffee?"

Zeke pointed at the pot. "There's plenty."

"Drink it up so we don't waste it." Charlie said, then grabbed the vessel and poured everyone a cup. He dumped the grounds and handed the coffeepot to Charlotte.

"Oh no! I forgot about the clothes I put on to soak." She hurried to the tub.

Paul hollered, "Dump the water! You can rinse them later. Get Prince loaded too." At the sound of his name the pint-size dog wagged his tail.

Paul was surprised Charlotte didn't bristle at his commands. He hoped she sensed the urgency of their situation. He didn't want to deal with a confrontation now—they needed to skedaddle.

Emma trailed Charlotte like a puppy. They squeezed out the clothes and wrapped them in a towel. Charlotte hung the washtub on the side of the wagon and hurried to the stream to rinse out the coffeepot.

While Charlotte and Emma were at the creek, Paul explained, "One of the men who robbed us is in town. Another one of those crooks is a deputy sheriff. We've got to get out of here quick. They might come looking for us.

"Bernie, you and Zeke start the herd moving. Get them into those woods up ahead. It'll be harder, but it will offer us more protection than being out in the open." He paused. "I don't want Charlotte and Emma alarmed. I'll help Charlie finish up with camp. We'll catch up."

Bernie and Zeke trotted across the meadow. Calmly, they herded the horses forward. Some of the horses rebelled against moving by stopping to snatch bites of tall grass. Stems hung from their mouths like stringy green noodles.

Charlie climbed into the wagon, despondent. Paul lifted Emma up. Charlie took her hand and helped her onto the bench seat. She reached back inside the bonnet to give Prince a reassuring pat. When Paul put his hands on Charlotte's waist to help her up, she turned to him and whispered, "Why are we really leaving this campsite? What happened in Adin?"

He leaned close, put his lips near her ear and breathed in her rose scent again. His breath caught. He had to protect her. And his precious daughter. "I promise I'll tell you tonight after Emma's in bed." She nodded, put her foot on the wheel and didn't resist when Paul gave her a boost.

"This time," he said, "keep the wagon off the main road. Follow the herd into that grove of trees." He pointed to a wooded area. "Be careful. I'll watch in case you need me. Use the flag."

Paul rode away, looked back and waved. He asked the Lord to protect his loved ones and to help him find a safe place to camp far away from those treacherous thieves.

A canopy of leaves blocked the orange-and-pink sky. The setting sun streaking through the trees created a golden haze hovering close to the ground. Charlotte kept the team at a steady pace. Paul watched her lean forward like she was struggling to see where they were going in the evening shadows.

He rode back to the wagon and directed Charlotte to a spot in the woods with room for it to be out of sight of the main road. He unhitched the horses and tied them to a line strung between two trees. Jack and Belle found tufts of grass to munch while waiting for their grain.

"I'll help the boys settle the herd. We'll be back in a bit. Keep an eye out." He tipped his Stetson and trotted off on Buck.

Charlie and Charlotte set up camp in the twilight. They had coffee, biscuits and hot leftover stew ready for the crew's return. Charlotte sat on a log and drew letters in the dirt, naming them for Emma. She wrote Emma's name and said the letters for her. Emma, holding Prince in her lap, watched and smiled but didn't speak.

Charlotte stood. "I need a few moments alone, Charlie. Can you please keep an eye on Emma?"

He nodded. "Sure. Be careful Missy."

Chapter Nine

Charlotte took a lantern and zigzagged around trees. Shadows danced playfully from the top of the trees to the leaf-covered ground. She marveled at the Lord's creation as she plopped down on a fallen log. The woods were enchanting in the lamplight. She would never forget this journey. All the chores and skills she had mastered. The joy she'd found taking care of Emma. The opportunity to make mistakes and learn without reprimand. The freedom she'd experienced with Paul, to be entirely herself without criticism.

Charlotte took a deep breath. "Better get back to camp before they send out a search party," she muttered and smiled.

She turned to go. Where was the campfire and wagon? Nothing shone in the darkness but her own lamplight. She stepped up on the log and turned round and round and round. No horses. No fire. No camp. Uh-oh. She'd wandered too far.

She was lost.

Her heart leaped. Would a mountain lion pounce on

her from a tree branch? If she shouted for help, it might frighten Emma if she heard her. Or if she yelled, she could give away her whereabouts to a waiting coyote.

She had to find her way back to camp. Charlotte shivered. She vowed not to panic. She gripped the lantern handle and swallowed several times. The wagon couldn't be that far. She had been reminiscing and not paying attention where she was walking. Maybe she could locate the band of horses and call to Zeke or Bernie or whoever had the night watch. Striding forward, she shuddered and pulled her jacket tighter.

Spirals of smoke ahead indicated a campfire. She dug in her heels and slowly proceeded down the slight incline. Charlotte refused to let herself tumble down the hill into the men's midst. When she stopped behind a tree to shake the dust from her skirt, she noticed there was no tripod with a coffeepot hanging over the fire.

This was not her camp.

Three men in heavy jackets sat on the ground. Who were these men so close to her own site? Were they friends? Enemies? After the robbery all strangers were suspect.

Charlotte stashed her lantern in the scrub brush and crept closer. Crouching behind a huge boulder, she strained to hear their conversation.

"Looky here, Coop… Shorty, we can take that whole herd of horses." Charlotte recognized the speaker. He was the red-haired man who had robbed them and the one she'd seen in town.

He pushed to a stand, grabbed a piece of wood and threw it on the fire. It crackled, and sparks jumped outside the rock boundary, lighting up the darkness.

"Let's round 'em up and drive 'em to Dry Wash Canyon. Then we sell 'em off one or two at a time. Why settle for a few measly dollars to scatter the herd and take a chance on those folks recognizing us? We could gather all those horses and make hundreds of dollars. Those yahoos would never know what hit 'em." He cackled.

The old man in the tattered hat rubbed his chin. The vested one sipped coffee from a tin cup. Both seemed deep in thought.

The vested one spoke. "There ain't no water in Dry Wash. Not too much feed, neither. How we gonna keep 'em healthy? It's bound to take months to sell off that many horses."

Tattered Hat bowed his head then stared off into the distance. "They all got brands. What're ya aimin' to do about that?"

The red-haired man turned to the old man. "Shorty, you know we can change a brand. We done it a hundred times. And we ain't never been caught yet." He sneered. The old man's name was Shorty. Charlotte filed that information. She might need it—when she identified them for the sheriff.

The vested one stood and paced around the campfire. "That'll take time. I got to do my sheriffin' job. And Shorty, you're deputy now. Can't be runnin' off on a whim. Won't look right to the folks in town. Boss said we're to play this one right. You heared him, Dusty. We was supposed to harass that Harrison fellow. Slow 'em down so they don't get to Lyonsville on time." He stopped and glared at the red-haired man. Charlotte would remember that name too. His hair looked like red dust. The other one must be Coop, Charlotte decided.

Coop continued, "We could be in a bad situation a robbin' those folks. We was only supposed to scatter the herd. If the boss finds out what we really done, he's gonna be hoppin' mad. But keepin' the herd is big. Boss wouldn't like it none at t'all."

Dusty sauntered over to Coop and faced him. "We don't have to tell him what we're doin'. Like we didn't tell him about our last job." He paused. He glanced at Shorty and back to Coop.

He folded his arms over his chest. "Ain't you boys tired a bein' told what to do? Doin' the boss's dirty work all the time and gettin' chicken feed for our trouble? I say we handle this ourselves. It's one less cut of the money when we sell the horses. We can take care of the brandin' and findin' water and feed in our spare time. We won't be in no rush."

Charlotte had heard enough. She had to find Paul and warn him. She quietly worked her way back to her lantern and scrambled up the slope. With her lantern held high she hurried, tiptoeing and hopping to avoid snapping sticks and crunching leaves. She didn't want those criminals to follow her. She had to get to Paul.

Charlotte vaulted over fallen logs and pushed through the brush. When her breath came so fast it made her head spin, she plopped on the nearest stump for a rest. She bowed her head and begged God to help her find her own camp. Paul had to be told about those bandits.

Her eyes scanned the woods. She glanced up. Pockets of stars shone through the dark veil of leaves, but she couldn't discern any of the constellations. Not that it would do any good. She'd failed to look for identifying landmarks during her walk out there.

All of a sudden, a hand closed over her mouth and an arm gripped her and lifted her off the ground, dragging her away. Her heart sputtered. Had one of the robbers followed her? She tried wiggling free. Her captor clamped down tighter. She kicked the air. Tried to scream but no sound came. She mustn't lead them to Emma.

Her teeth sank hard into the hand covering her lips. Her assailant growled. She inhaled a scent of leather.

A deep voice blurted, "Ouch." He twisted his hand but still held it over her mouth. A pause. His grasp was firm.

The whispering in her ear burst through her confused thoughts. She heard her name. "Charlotte."

Did this foe know her?

"Charlotte. Stop. Stop struggling. It's me. Paul." He paused. "Don't scream." The hand didn't move from her mouth. His arms pinned her close to his body. He let her feet drop to the ground, then turned her until she faced him, his fingers still covering her lips.

"Charlotte. It's Paul. When I take my hand away, don't scream. Don't run. Nod if you understand."

She nodded and took a deep breath. Paul gently pulled his hand away, shook it and mumbled about teeth marks implanted in his skin forever.

"Are you okay?" His eyes filled with concern.

"I'm fine."

"What happened to you? You scared us half to death. Where in tarnation have you been? We've searched for hours. Why did you take off like that? In the dark?

You could have been hurt—could've fallen down a hillside. You're so small a mountain lion could have hauled you off. We might never have found you. You could have been kidnapped. This isn't the city—it's dangerous country. You can't wander around, especially—"

Charlotte threw her hands in the air, locked eyes with Paul, stomped her foot, pursed her lips and commanded, "Be quiet, Paul!"

He stepped back. His eyes widened and his brows lifted. He pushed his hat back on his head and stared at her.

She swallowed. Bit her bottom lip. And took a deep breath. She'd done it again. Confronted him. With loud, direct words. This wasn't her. She didn't challenge people. What was happening to her?

"Sorry. I loathe opposing you. Paul, I'm grateful you found me. I have something important to tell you. I need you to focus and listen carefully." Charlotte drew another deep breath. He waited. "Nod if you understand."

She couldn't resist. Her lips curled into a big grin. In the lamplight she watched his eyes transform from anger to bewilderment to amusement. He gave her that boyish, teasing smile that made her heart beat at twice its normal rate.

Paul laughed and nodded. "Okay. Tell me."

"I stumbled onto the camp of those fellows who robbed us. You know, that redheaded man I saw in Adin? All three of them were together. The same ones. Their camp is over there. Down the hill a ways." She stepped forward and pointed, and he glanced in that direction.

"I overheard them talking about stealing your herd.

And hiding the horses in a canyon—Dry Water or Dry Wash Canyon. That's what I think they said. Dry something. They have a boss, but he doesn't know they robbed us. They did that on their own. Their boss is not in on their plan to capture your horses either. He wants them to slow us down by scattering the herd."

She hesitated. "What are we going to do?"

She looked up at him with her big, beautiful eyes and waited for an answer. His pulse loped through his veins. His mouth was dry. He felt trapped, like he was tangled in underbrush. Indescribable outcomes twisted and turned in his mind with no clear way out of this perilous snare.

A slight breeze rippled the air. Charlotte shivered. Paul removed his jacket and draped it around her shoulders. She pulled it close and waited.

Relief. He should be relieved. She was here. She was safe. Her skirt was torn at the hem, her blouse sleeve ripped, her face splattered with dust, and her hair had that wild, messy look he adored. But…she wasn't hurt. She hadn't been attacked by a wild animal or captured by the robbers. Those bandits hadn't discovered her listening to their conversation. If so, that could have been quite a fracas. He smiled and glanced at the bite marks still showing on his hand.

God had answered his prayers to keep his wife safe. His temporary wife, he reminded himself again.

She didn't comprehend, though. She didn't understand how close she'd come to being in terrible danger or how close he'd come to losing his mind. When Charlie told him she'd been gone for over an hour he'd panicked. He was determined to get her safely back to Cedar Grove so she could accept her teaching position. He'd promised her, and he was a man of his word. How could she do this to him?

Paul glared at her and spoke with a quiet firmness. "We? There is no *we* here, Charlotte. *We* aren't doing anything."

Charlotte's eyebrows rose in unison. "What? We have to stop them. You can't pay off the debt on your ranch if they steal your horses. We have to thwart them. We have to do something."

Paul wanted her to realize he was serious about keeping Emma out of danger and keeping her safe. He could not bear another heartache, for himself or for Emma. He was through being polite.

"Look at me, Charlotte," Paul said with a steely coldness, cupping her chin and waiting until her eyes met his. "You will not involve yourself in my business. You are here to take care of Emma. That's your job. Your only job. That's why I hired you. That's why you're on this journey. When the month is over and the marriage is annulled, you are free to get tangled up in whatever you choose. But until then, Emma is your only responsibility."

He watched tears well up in her eyes. She bit her bottom lip and bowed her head.

His heart ached. He despised hurting her. It took everything in him to stand there holding her face and let her cry. Once or twice he almost pulled her to him. He wanted to kiss those tears away. He had to convince Charlotte not to care about him or his ranch. He wanted her to understand that taking care of his daughter for three more weeks was her only job. She wasn't staying. She'd move on. Her dream was to teach. No use encouraging any attachments. Nothing could last with a beautiful woman anyway. The truth was the truth.

He let go of her. Charlotte looked like she'd been punched. She stepped backward. Her eyes were red and puffy.

He had to concentrate. Focus.

"The men and I will decide what to do about those men. It's not your problem. Is that understood?"

He couldn't let her wander any further into his heart or mind.

"I'll take you back. Don't stray again." He took her hand in his and marched to camp.

Emma ran to her and threw her arms around her legs. Charlotte knelt and hugged her close. "Emma, I'm sorry. I got lost and couldn't find my way back. I'm grateful your papa came to find me."

Emma nodded and gave Charlotte's neck one more squeeze.

"Charlotte, please get Emma to bed. I need to talk to my men." Paul dismissed her. Charlotte turned to confront him but changed her mind after opening her mouth. She took Emma's hand and stomped toward the wagon.

Zeke, Bernie and Charlie followed Paul. He pointed at the coffeepot and sat down on a log near the fire. "Let's have a cup."

When he shared Charlotte's report, they were astonished. Charlie rose and picked up the coffeepot again. With his back to Paul, he mumbled, "That's some kinda wife you got there, Boss." Bernie and Zeke chuckled and nodded in agreement. Paul shook his head. His heart and mind twisted into a knotty mess when he thought about Charlotte.

"Y'all got any ideas about how to get our herd back?" Paul asked. Opinions jumped between them, like grass-hoppers looking for food. At last they devised a plan. Paul left to speak with Charlotte. Zeke and Bernie tight-ened the cinches on the saddled horses.

Paul stood at the end of the wagon and called Char-lotte's name. She crawled to the edge and started to climb out.

Paul took off his hat. "No need to come down. I wanted you to know Charlie is staying here with you and Emma. Me and the boys are going after those three. I'd appreciate your prayers." He nodded, shoved his hat on his head and turned to leave.

"Wait, Paul." She clambered out of the wagon. Pull-ing her jacket tight around her chest, she looked at him. "I want to apologize for getting lost, for causing you worry and for endangering everyone. I thought I was helping when I stayed to investigate those scoundrels, but I see there could have been serious consequences. Can you forgive me?" Charlotte lowered her eyes.

"It's done—over. We'll go on from here. You and Emma stay safe. Sorry to leave the two of you again. Charlie has my other rifle." He strode to his waiting horse.

How could he tell her he'd been in sheer agony the moment Charlie told him she hadn't come back to camp? The thought of losing her stabbed at his heart. He'd let his feelings bust through that flimsy fence he'd built around himself. He had to stop this. That broken barrier desperately needed mending. Quickly. He'd pray harder.

She was leaving. Nothing was permanent about their relationship. He'd be polite, but no more thinking about things that couldn't be. He'd let that happen with Rachel, but he'd not risk it a second time. Charlotte would say goodbye in a few weeks. *Remember she's not staying*, he reprimanded himself.

Paul swung into the saddle. "Now, boys, let's go lasso some thieves."

Chapter Ten

By the time the sun reached its midday position in the cloudless blue sky, Charlotte paced again. Round and round the wagon. Her feet stayed in step with her thoughts.

Where are they?
What's happened to them?
Why aren't they back by now?
Did they find the thieves?
Are they okay?

She, Emma and Charlie had proceeded with their normal morning camp routine. Wash up, get dressed, make breakfast, eat, clean up, take water and grain to Jack and Belle, stake them out to graze.

She washed clothes and hung them on the line Charlie stretched for her.

Still Paul and the boys had not returned. Charlotte fought her apprehensions. Every time a worrisome thought popped into her head, she prayed. She guessed that was what the verse "pray without ceasing" meant.

Charlie set out apples, sugar and flour.

"Miz Charlotte, you and the little one come on over here. Let's make an apple pie."

"Oh, Charlie. I can't concentrate. If you show me now, you'll just have to teach me all over again." Charlotte sighed.

"Now, Missy, they'll be back by-and-by. Don't ya be worryin' none. They'll take care a one 'nother." He held up the apples and a knife.

Charlotte took the fruit. "Emma, come, let's wash these up." Emma trotted over. Charlotte rolled her log stool to the table and set it up. Emma wiped the apples, and Charlotte peeled and sliced. No one spoke.

Charlie smiled. "There 'tis. Those boys will be mighty happy to celebrate with some apple pie."

Charlotte nodded absently.

"Missy, can ya carry the Dutch oven over to the fire for me? My shoulder's still achy."

Charlotte set the oven to the side of the fire and heaped coals on top. She checked the coffeepot. Full. The mugs were set out. Everything was ready for their return—anytime now.

Charlotte meandered around the wagon again. And again.

Charlie rubbed his chin and said, "Missy, just 'cause we got a little trouble here don't mean we have to invite it to be sittin' and visitin' with us. Maybe you and the babe could do some writin'."

Charlotte nodded, climbed into the wagon, unpacked Emma's tablet and grabbed the book she'd been reading to her. She wrote letters for Emma, naming them, then asked Emma to write the letters in the dirt and helped her form their shapes with a stick.

Under the tarp Bernie and Zeke had rigged up, she wrote words on the tablet paper and let Emma draw pictures to go with them. She made up a sweet story about a butterfly that befriended a girl named Emma and her dog, Prince, and followed them wherever they traveled. Emma giggled.

Charlie whittled.

Opening the book, she read several chapters out loud. Emma leaned against Charlotte, and Prince sat in Emma's lap.

Charlotte felt like she was going to pop. No use talking to Charlie about their companions. She'd had multiple conversations with him already and they all sounded the same.

She'd quizzed him on what he thought might be going on. Did he think something was wrong? Did he think they were safe?

His answer for every question was, "They're taking care of business. They know what they're a doin'."

She'd say, "Don't you think they should be back by now? They've been gone all night."

He'd say, "They'll be back shortly, Miz Charlotte."

Why wasn't Charlie worried? Did he know something she didn't? Sometimes when Emma wasn't around, she asked him. But his answer remained the same.

There was no laundry left to do. All their clothes had been washed and dried, folded and put back in the proper suitcases. The bedrolls were stacked. The inside of the wagon was organized.

They'd gathered enough firewood for dinner, breakfast, tomorrow's supper and extra to store in the boot below the wagon.

Prince curled up by Emma's feet, content to lie beside the child and sleep.

Charlotte closed the book. Stood to stretch and check their surroundings again.

"Look at those wildflowers." She pointed in the direction of a rotted log.

"Charlie, Emma and I are going to pick some wildflowers." She reached out her hand for Emma and pulled her up. Prince immediately got to his feet to follow behind them.

"Don't get out of my sight, Missy," Charlie called after them. Charlotte bit her lip and wanted to snap back with an unkind remark. She knew he was following Paul's orders, though. It wasn't his fault Paul didn't trust her. Her last escapade had created that doubt.

She reached for a purple flower. "Emma, let's make watercolor paints for you with these flowers." Charlotte twirled and Emma imitated her. They gathered handfuls of flowers and trotted back to the wagon.

Charlotte set the wildflowers in the middle of the camp worktable. She found the knife and lopped off the blooms. Each color group went into a separate cup.

"Charlie, do you have a small pot I can heat water in?" Charlotte rummaged through the cookware, not finding anything suitable.

"Here ya go." Charlie handed her a pint-size pot.

She smiled up at him. "Thanks. That's perfect. Can we use a piece of this section of the worktable for our paints?"

"Yeah. That'd be okay. When they come back, I gotta

be fixin' dinner, though." He brushed the ends of his mustache up with his finger.

"I know. We'll clean up and help, of course." Charlotte filled the little pot and put it on the fire.

She motioned for Emma to come to the table. Charlotte helped her onto her stool. Charlie had graciously packed up and hauled that log stool ever since Charlotte had Emma helping her with meal preparations.

"We're going to crush these blooms to make paint." She proceeded to show Emma how to smash the petals and put them in a cup. "We'll add a tiny bit of hot water to bring out the colors and then we can use them." Charlotte smiled and Emma returned her grin.

"Hmm…we don't have any paintbrushes."

Emma jumped off her stool and ran to pick up the stick she'd been drawing with in the dirt. The end of it was frayed and resembled a brush.

Charlotte hugged her. "Emma, that's great. We can make more of these so we don't mix the colors." They gathered sticks and Charlie helped them separate the ends. He went to the chuck box and pulled out a drawer.

Handing Charlotte a pure white feather, he asked, "Could ya use one of these?"

She stared at him. "This is beautiful. We don't want to accidentally dye it."

He smiled. "I can get another one. Let's see how it works."

Charlotte used a knife to cut pieces of paper into four squares. They each took one and picked up their sticks. Charlie held his feather.

"Let's paint."

"Wait," Charlie said. "We need a brown color. How

'bout we use a little coffee? You know how it stains everything." He poured a tiny bit of coffee in one of the tin cups and set it next to the other colors.

Emma worked on a butterfly while Charlotte painted wildflowers in the corners of her paper and designed an elegant *E* in the middle. An initial for Emma. Charlie used both ends of his feather to draw and paint a chuck wagon and a campfire.

Absorbed in their work, no one heard the horses galloping until they got close.

"Hello to the camp!" Paul shouted. Zeke and Bernie waved their hats.

Charlotte dropped her brush and rushed to Paul. Emma followed. The minute he dismounted, Charlotte threw her arms around his neck and buried her head in his chest. "I've been so worried. I didn't know if you'd come back. Charlie wouldn't talk to me. He wouldn't tell me anything. I've been beside myself. Oh, thank God you are all right." A tear slid down her cheek. Paul pulled her close and laid his head next to hers. She felt his breath on her hair.

What had she just done? Charlotte pushed away from Paul, feeling heat rise in her cheeks.

Her emotions leaped away from her again—fear that something had happened to them propelled her actions. She shouldn't be so familiar with Paul.

Emma embraced her daddy's knees. He knelt and picked her up, gave her a hug and kissed her cheek.

Charlotte's legs wobbled. Paul had made himself clear last night: her only job was Emma's care. He had no interest in her. She'd let her feelings overcome her once again. At the sight of him and the sound of his voice, her heart had soared. His harsh words from the night before had vanished from her mind.

How could she have thrown herself at him like that? And spoken her feelings? He must be very tired of her impulsiveness. *He'll be happy to get rid of me*, she thought, straightening her blouse.

Back East, her unladylike enthusiasm in speech and manners often had resulted in Aunt Arilla's shrill scolding. "Charlotte, your hair is always a mess. Look at your blouse. It's rumpled and not tucked in. Can't you slow down and think before you throw yourself into something? Men don't like such openly expressive behavior in a woman. No wonder we're having trouble finding you a husband."

This marriage she had gotten herself into would be undone in less than twenty-one days. She'd no longer be a worry or a bother to Paul. Her fervent desire at this moment was for the ground to open up and swallow her.

How she yearned to be on her own. No one to please anymore. No critical aunt, no reproachful husband. She'd be free from feeling like she'd done something wrong again or like she could have done it better. Surely her students would appreciate her eagerness and knowledge. Yes, she looked forward to moving ahead with her teaching career and ending this pretend marriage.

"Emma and I are very happy you've returned. I apologize for my exuberant greeting. Please forgive me." Charlotte turned and walked back to help Charlie clean off the worktable and start the evening meal. She didn't wait for a response from Paul. She couldn't bear to see his disapproving look.

* * *

Paul stared after her. With each step, the hairpins holding her golden-haired bun at the back of her head threatened to come undone. Her light blue skirt swished, and her brown boots sent puffs of dust trailing behind her. She rolled her small, strong shoulders more than once as she walked away.

She was by far the most exasperating woman he'd ever known. Hot and cold. Like a flash flood. He couldn't guess which way her mood was coming or which way it was going. One minute she was throwing her arms around his neck, carrying on about how frightened she was, and the next minute she was pushing him away like he had smallpox. Her emotions sure kept her busy. He smiled.

Paul set Emma on the ground. "Emmy, I have to unsaddle Buck and water him. I'll be back real soon." He ran his hand down her hair. "Run on over and help Charlotte and Charlie."

Emma skipped back to camp. Her cascading red curls flipped in the air as she pranced away from him. Paul's heart overflowed with gratitude. His little girl was doing much better. Though she still wasn't speaking, her eyes lit up and she exhibited joy. That was because of Charlotte's attention to Emma. The child blossomed with Charlotte. An aggravating woman for him yet full of life and fun and perfect for Emma. Charlotte brought out the best in everyone but him. Old Charlie was like a lamb around her. Always eager to give her advice or help her with cooking or driving a team of horses. Even Zeke and Bernie talked with more expression and minded their manners when she was around.

Yet he remained on guard with her. What was it about her that riled him up? Why did she always want to fight him? On every single thing. He rubbed the back of his neck as he led Buck out to graze.

Charlie had the evening meal ready by the time they'd unsaddled, watered and grained their horses. When Charlie announced there was apple pie for dessert, Zeke let out a loud, "Hooray!"

Bernie started to mention how they'd captured the outlaws, but Paul raised his brows and nodded toward Emma. Paul looked at Charlotte. "Charlotte, I think it's Emma's bedtime. We'll be gettin' an early start in the morning."

Without a word, Charlotte rose and took Emma's hand. Paul smiled at his daughter. "I'll come say prayers with you in a minute."

Paul could hear Charlotte talking to his daughter as she helped Emma into her nightgown, handed her the rag doll and settled Prince next to her. He pictured her tucking her in under the pink quilt as she said, "We had a lot of fun today. Your butterfly painting is beautiful. When you get back home, you can hang it in your room. Your daddy will be here soon. Sweet dreams little one."

Paul halted as he came around the wagon. He'd held his breath when he heard Charlotte's words. She was so kind to Emma. Gentle and sweet. Emma would miss her very much. And he was torn up about that.

Charlotte placed her foot on the wheel, and he caught her around the waist and lifted her down. Her rose scent filled his nostrils. She was so small. So strong. So fearless. So feisty. Her neck invited kisses. He leaned closer and breathed deep, tightening his grip.

She slapped his hands away. "I don't need your help." She hopped to the ground.

"Charlotte, please. Let's try to be friends. Like you suggested." He grinned at her as he shoved his hands in his pockets.

Her emerald eyes were like daggers aimed at his heart. "You have no idea how to be a friend. What you do know is how to order people around and find fault with what they do." She glanced at the worktable. "I have to help Charlie."

After dinner the men sat around the campfire with their pie and coffee. Charlie asked what had happened. Charlotte refused to join the circle, choosing to sit on a log by the worktable, under a lantern with her book.

Zeke swallowed a bite of pie and grinned. "Never had better apple pie." He beamed at Charlie, who nodded his acceptance of the compliment.

Bernie stood to get more coffee. "We found those snakes where Miz Charlotte said they'd be. Two whoops and holler from us. They were hunkerin' round their campfire, drinkin' their coffee, still plannin' on how to steal the boss's herd. We sneaked down on 'em and lassoed 'em. They never knowed what hit 'em." He chortled.

Charlie grinned. His mustache turned up at the ends and his eyes were full of merriment. "You mean you actually roped those scoundrels."

"We sure did. They was sittin' under a ledge. We just leaned over and throwed our ropes on 'em. Why, it was easy as eatin' pie." Zeke chuckled and forked another bite.

"And then what'd ya do?" Charlie asked.

Paul lifted his chin. "We tied them up and hauled them into town. They squawked a lot about how their boss would get them out. About how no jail cell could hold them. 'Course, since two of them were a deputy sheriffs, we had to go find the mayor to lock them up. Mayor said the US Marshall was coming through in a week and he'd haul them to the circuit judge. They won't be bothering us or any other travelers for a long time."

Paul pushed his hat back on his head and glanced at Charlotte. She refused to look up from her book, but he believed she'd heard the conversation.

In the lantern light, her hair gleamed and her skin glowed. He wished she'd smile. He delighted in her smile and laughter, when her green eyes appeared to be dancing.

A lasso tugged and tightened around his heart. He knew this loop wouldn't be tied. There was no holding on to this woman, even if he wanted to find out if he cared enough to suggest they stay married. She had her mind made up about what she wanted, and it didn't include him. Or Emma.

He remembered what he wanted. No wife, just a plain, middle-aged woman to care for his Emma and their home. Not this woman. A relationship with Charlotte would require tearing down that fence around his heart, becoming vulnerable and risking heartache. He wasn't ready to trust again.

Paul wished to thank her for helping them capture

those robbers, but he was afraid she'd mistake his gratitude for approval of her actions last night and she might
get careless again. He couldn't afford for anything to
happen to her. Not on this trip. He needed her—for
Emma's sake.

He rubbed the back of his neck and walked toward
her. He wanted to talk to her about something else tonight.

When Charlotte saw him striding toward her, she
grabbed her book and hurried away from camp. Into
the woods.

Paul followed. "Hey, didn't I tell you not to go too
far from the wagon?" Paul shouted at her, picking up
his pace.

When she spun around, her skirt twirled and her eyes
challenged him. "Well, since you're right by my side,
I didn't think I was in any danger." Her hands flew to
her waist, her head cocked to one side. "Is there something you want, Paul?"

Her lips quivered but her expression, other than those
piercing eyes, was unreadable. "Have I done something
else to displease you? Again? Is Emma not properly
cared for? Are there more improvements I should make?
Do you have more complaints to add to your list?" She
squared her small shoulders, tilted her chin, raised her
eyebrows and waited. He could see she fought to hold
back the tears welling up in her eyes.

He stared at her. His heart felt like it'd been sliced
in half. No one, except himself, had taken better care
of Emma. Had he not expressed his pleasure with how
she was handling his daughter? Emma's face and hair
were always clean. Charlotte either braided her locks or

put it in two ponytails or tied a colorful ribbon around the child's head. Her clothes were spotless at the beginning of the day. Emma skipped and smiled and giggled on occasion. He was amazed at her progress in what seemed like two shakes of a lamb's tail.

This evening, before he'd prayed with Emma, she'd shown him her watercolor butterfly, carefully stowed away with the drawing tablet. His eyes misted and his heart tugged at his daughter's lovely creation.

Charlotte had confronted him about that tablet. She'd insisted on bringing it. She'd done something she detested—challenging someone—for Emma's sake. Because she'd realized Emma could draw. She'd recognized her ability those first days and wanted to encourage it. And somehow, she'd found a way for Emma to color her drawings.

He knew then that Charlotte was more like a mother than a caretaker. She'd managed to reach inside his daughter's hurting heart and pull out beauty. He was amazed and grateful for her wonderful care of his beloved daughter.

Paul reached up and took off his hat. He stared at the ground, kicked the dirt and raked his hand through his hair before locking eyes with her. "I… I want to thank you. Emma showed me her butterfly."

There was so much more he wanted to say, to talk with her about, but the words stuck and sank back in his throat like a cow trapped in knee-high quicksand. He slapped his hat on his head and strode back to camp. He'd wanted to ask her about friendship. What did that look like between a man and a woman?

He was alarmed. He felt something for her, but his

thoughts were all jumbled up in his mind. Was he enamored with Charlotte because she nurtured Emma the way he imagined a good mother would? Certainly, her maternal abilities far outweighed her wifely skills. He smiled.

She was attractive…but he'd been trapped by that unreliable trait before and was on guard. He was perplexed with how he looked forward to getting back to camp after his long days with the herd just so he could be around her. He liked to watch her, to listen to her, to talk with her—he even enjoyed arguing with her.

What in the world was this feeling? Was it friendship…or something more?

Chapter Eleven

Charlie frowned at Paul standing by the fire in the early dawn. "You don't look so good this morning, Boss. Have another cuppa coffee."

Paul took the tin cup Charlie handed him and poured in the hot, dark and steaming liquid.

He'd tossed and turned all night. His mind wrestled with thoughts of Charlotte. How could he make her understand he wasn't disappointed in her? What could he say to convince her she'd been exceptional when it came to caring for Emma? Every time he tried to express his feelings to Charlotte, he felt like a schoolboy talking to a girl for the first time.

He tried praying. He asked the Lord for help and tried to remember verses he'd had to learn in the orphanage Sunday school services but couldn't recall any that helped with his situation. Except one. Something about trusting. He'd had to memorize it and finally was able to recall it.

"Trust in the Lord with all thine heart and lean not unto thine own understanding." He'd repeated it over and over in the darkness until the first rays of sunlight flooded across the sky. He'd have to trust the Lord with his thoughts regarding Charlotte. He couldn't allow his heart to long for what couldn't be. He couldn't hope. Weren't beautiful women treacherous? Maybe not middle-aged plain women... He wasn't sure about that. Rachel had been beautiful and smart, but unable to attach for a long-term commitment. Was Charlotte different?

Zeke and Bernie slapped their rumpled hats on their heads and joined Paul at the campfire with their coffee. Coats on, they waited for the morning sun to rise and shine. They mumbled, "Hey, Boss," swallowed their coffee and kicked the dirt without further conversation.

Paul hadn't heard Charlotte. He didn't know the girls were awake until he felt his daughter tugging at his coat hem. He leaned down and kissed the top of her head. Her cape had been fastened in a neat bow, and her hair was brushed up into a ponytail and secured with a yellow ribbon to match her yellow-striped dress. Her brown boots were laced and tied. Once again, he marveled at Charlotte's attention to details where Emma was concerned.

"Good morning, Emmy, my gingersnap. You're up early." He smiled at her, glancing around for Charlotte. She stood beside Charlie.

"Ready for breakfast?" He took Emma's hand and walked to the worktable.

"Morning, Charlotte." He tilted his head toward her. She nodded but didn't speak.

"Biscuits are ready to go," she said to Charlie and grabbed the cast-iron Dutch oven with both hands. Paul stepped in front of her and took hold of the handle.

She held tight, pulled back. With her head bowed, she hissed, "I don't need your help." Elbowing past him, she set the oven deep in the coals and shoveled more on top.

Charlie picked up the big skillet loaded with salt pork and carried it and the eggs to the fire. He stirred the eggs in the skillet and said to Charlotte, "I'll keep an eye on the biscuits and Emma. You and your husband go talk." He said it without glancing at her, but Paul knew she'd take his advice.

Charlotte strode back to Paul. Biting her lip, she looked up at him, "Charlie thinks we should talk."

Paul glanced over at Charlie squatting by the fire. Did Charlie guess they weren't really married? In the traditional sense? Oh well, he wanted to speak to Charlotte anyway. Paul walked to the fire. Without a word to Charlie, he filled two coffee cups and ambled back to Charlotte.

"Let's check on Belle and Jack." They meandered toward the two horses staked out to graze a brief distance from camp. The morning light thrust sunbeams through the canopy of leaves, creating a sparkling white stairway from the clouds to the ground. Basking in the sunrays, neither of them spoke for several minutes. Paul turned and faced Charlotte. He didn't want trouble or a shouting match. He'd try to be gentle.

"I want us to be friends, Charlotte. You are right. I don't know much about friendship. Bernie is the only one I've had since childhood, but he thinks I saved him, so he won't let us have an equal standing. He always defers to me."

She watched him. "What about your wife? Wasn't she your friend?" With a sudden gasp, Charlotte slapped her hand to her mouth. "I'm sorry, Paul. That was improper. I don't want to pry and it's none of my business."

He sipped his coffee. He'd never thought about Rachel as his friend. She definitely wasn't loyal. Maybe he didn't know what Charlotte thought being a friend meant.

He looked at the ground. "Guess I never thought about marriage that way. Do you think a husband and wife can be best friends?" He felt curious to seek her opinion on this subject. He'd had no one to discuss things with before. Rachel rarely conversed with him. She never wanted to talk about Emma or the ranch. She didn't share news about the people they knew at church. She never wanted to chat about the pastor's sermon after Sunday services.

The only thing Rachel went on about were all the things Paul couldn't afford to give her and how disappointed she was with her life. So he'd quit listening to her. He'd shut her out 'cause it hurt too much to know he'd failed her time after time.

And Bernie, the only one Paul called a friend, was more like a puppy dog. He didn't have opinions. He wanted Paul to tell him what to do and he was always happy to do it.

Charlotte stepped next to a tree and leaned against it. She curled her fingers around her cup and sipped.

"Are you really interested in my thoughts, or are you trying to appease me for the sake of appearances? Don't you think Charlie knows we're not really married?"

Paul looked into her deep green eyes. Her sun-kissed hair hung below her shoulders. A pink ribbon held it back from her face. Her sand-colored blouse was neatly tucked into her dark brown skirt. A leather belt surrounded her small waist. She was beautiful. And kind. And courageous. And really good with Emma. Why hadn't she married some man back East who understood what women like her wanted? Why did she want to teach school so far from her Boston home? When he looked at her, his heart raced like a jackrabbit trying to outrun a coyote.

"Do you have to make this hard?"

Charlotte's eyebrows rose in unison. Her lips almost curled into a smile.

"No one but my professors and Charlie have been interested in what I think."

Paul shook his head. She didn't trust him. But could he blame her? He hadn't talked to her much. He'd given her orders and stated what he wanted done. Occasionally, she'd expressed her views in a heated moment and he'd listened. Did he care about her thoughts?

He took a deep breath. Would her opinions be critical judgments like Rachel's? Did he want to hear about his failures? He needed to make peace with Charlotte. In the time they had left together perhaps the remainder of the trip could be more pleasant if they gave friendship a try. Again, he knew he'd have to trust the Lord.

"I am interested in what you think." His eyes met hers. She stared at him a long while. Was she thinking about whether to trust him? He stilled, like he was waiting for a wild horse to work up the nerve to surrender. Some things couldn't be hurried.

She took a deep breath, bit her lip and said, "Well, then, if you want to know, I think if a man and woman do not build a marriage on a foundation of friendship and respect, it cannot be very happy."

Paul considered her words. He pushed his Stetson back on his head. "What does friendship look like?"

Charlotte stared at her shoes, at the dirt, at the sun streaming through the trees, at the wildflowers popping up in little bunches by the tree trunks.

Finally, she smiled at him. Her emerald eyes danced. "The truth is I'm not sure. I never had a devoted friend growing up. There were the girls I went to school with and participated in activities with, but there was never anyone I confided in or shared special moments with. I was always afraid it would get back to my aunt and that would add to her disappointments in me."

Paul stared at her, then grinned and chuckled. "Well, aren't we a pair? Trying to be friends when we don't know what that means."

She laughed. "Maybe we'll have to think on it awhile."

"Let's do that. We can talk about it another day. Today we need to head up Split Rock Pass. It's already daylight."

He wanted to reach out and hold her hand as they strolled back to camp. Was that something a friend would do? Since he wasn't sure, he kept pace walking with her, and they stayed side by side.

Charlie smiled as they approached. He held out a plate of food for each of them. His big black mustache curled into a grin when he asked, "So, Boss, what are we doin' today?"

Charlotte held the reins in her trembling, gloved hands and took a deep breath. She looked over at Charlie sitting on the other side of Emma. His weathered hat sat cockeyed on his head. He focused on the steep, curvy grade ahead.

She scanned the mountainside. "I'll need a lot of help getting this wagon up and over that pass."

The dirt road zigzagged up the steep peak. In some places the path wasn't visible because of the trees and brush. "I don't know if I can do it." Her voice wobbled.

Charlie leaned over and touched her shoulder. With a big smile that turned up the ends of his bushy mustache and his dark eyes shining, he said, "Missy, you can do anything you set your mind to. I been watchin'. You got grit."

Charlotte was grateful for his confidence but didn't feel as positive. A few weeks ago, she hadn't known how to drive the team. She felt brave enough on flat land and trotting them up small inclines and also crossing small creeks, but this mountain pass was way outside her experience and abilities.

"Paul said to wait here until they get the horses started up the pass. I can hear Sassy's bell, but I can't see any of them. When do you think we should get under way?"

They both searched the road for any sign of the herd. Emma raised her arm and pointed at a sleek black horse emerging from the trees.

"Thanks, Emma. Guess we'll get going now." She bowed her head and silently prayed to keep a steady hand and a watchful eye. She asked the Lord to help her and to also keep everyone safe.

"Hup, Jack! Belle, get up!" she commanded with an authoritative shout. The team heaved forward.

The climb was steep. Jack and Belle puffed and

snorted as they came to the first curve in the road. Charlie tapped Charlotte's shoulder. "Pull 'em over to rest a bit. There's a bend." He pointed to a wide place in the road next to the mountainside. Charlotte guided them over and stopped the team.

"Get the horses some water. Not too much, though. I'll hold the reins."

Charlotte climbed down and found a basin. She ladled water into it from the barrel and held it for Jack and then Belle. When their breathing had quieted, she climbed back into the wagon.

She looked at Charlie. "Shall we go on now?"

"Yep. You're doin' fine, Missy. But next time ya water the team, use a bucket, not my dishpan." He chided her with a big grin.

By the time they'd conquered four switchbacks, the sizzling, August noonday sun had unleashed its fierceness in full force, and Charlotte felt like hot molasses. Belle and Jack were lathered up. She'd poured water over their backs and rubbed it into their skin, trying to cool them down. Her hands hurt from the tight grip she kept on the reins. Her legs felt like jelly from climbing up and down out of the wagon and hauling water to the horses. Her soaked blouse stuck to her skin, and sweat dripped from her forehead. She took off her hat, held the full ladle over her head and tipped it, drenching herself.

When she hung the bucket back on the side of the wagon, Charlotte turned to see Paul's teasing eyes staring at her. She felt heat in her cheeks and her pulse pounded. She knew she looked a sight. Water dripped from her head onto her shoulders.

"You—you snuck up on me," she said accusingly.

"I wouldn't have missed this sight for all the gold in California." He chuckled.

Charlotte flounced to the wagon, climbed up and yanked the reins from Charlie's hands.

"Hey, Boss. You sure gotta knack for aggravatin' your wife!" Charlie chuckled.

Paul nodded. He sure did. Before Charlotte started the team, he hollered, "Hold on a minute, Charlotte!" She held the reins, stared ahead and waited.

"I came to help you out. The horses are on the other side of Split Rock Pass. They're grazing in a meadow. I'll drive the team the rest of the way up the mountain. You can rest. There's only about two more hairpin turns, and then we'll be at the top."

Paul tied Buck to the back of the wagon and hopped up on the wheel. Emma bounded off the bench seat into the back of the wagon. Charlotte handed the reins to Paul as he sat down beside her. She glanced at Charlie. His eyes sparkled and a grin stretched across his face.

For the first time since they'd started up the mountain, Charlotte allowed herself the luxury of a view other than the horses' rumps and the road in front of her eyes.

The hillside was covered in scrub trees and brush. The pond shimmered when sunrays caressed the water. A single road at the bottom of the mountain cut through hayfields and hillsides. Puffy white clouds floated in a glistening blue sky. It was spectacular, dream-like. Charlotte took a deep breath and prepared to relax for the next leg of the trip.

Suddenly a deer leaped out of the undergrowth and onto the road, brushing the horse's noses. Jack and

Belle reared. Charlotte jolted back with a scream. The horses snorted and charged off like a locomotive at full speed. Paul tugged hard on the reins yelling, "Whoa, whoa!" Their hooves pounding on the hardened ground drowned out Paul's shouting.

The wagon careened, thundering ever closer to the edge of the road where one misstep would plunge them all over the cliff. Emma tumbled backward away from the wagon seat and onto the pile of bedrolls. Paul yanked harder and hollered louder, but Jack and Belle didn't slow. Terrified, Charlotte shrieked when the team took a turn at breakneck speed. Pieces of the road pummeled by the wagon wheels plummeted down the steep incline. Charlotte buried her head in her hands, too scared to scream, too scared to watch, too scared to pray.

At last the team slowed and finally halted. One wagon wheel teetered on the crumbling edge of the road. Paul heaved a sigh of relief and spoke softly. "Charlie, help Charlotte and Emma get out of the wagon. Then see if you can get Buck untied from the back."

Charlie gently let himself down. Charlotte handed Emma to him and then made her way to the ground. They moved to the bend in the road. Huddled together, Charlotte struggled to comfort Emma.

Charlie approached Buck with soft reassuring words. The horse was braced, nearly sitting on his haunches. He looked ready to jerk backward at the slightest provocation. "Hang on, Buck. I'm gonna get ya outta this here mess," Charlie crooned to the trembling horse. Carefully he worked the knot on the lead rope until it came undone. Then he led the buckskin over to Charlotte. "Hold him, please," he said with a nod and walked back to the wagon.

"Boss!" Charlie called. "Shall I get behind and push?"

Paul raised his bowed head. "Too dangerous, Charlie. Might slide back onto you. I think the team can pull the wagon off this ledge. I'll take it slow and easy. Could you get ahold of Buck and stay with Emma and Charlotte?"

Charlie nodded, then sauntered over and took Buck's lead rope from Charlotte. He patted her shoulder. "Don't worry Missy. Paul's one of the best teamsters I've seen."

She nodded, unwilling to look anywhere but at Paul and the wagon hovering on the brink of the cliff.

Paul eased his grip on the reins and spoke to the horses lathered in layers of frothy white foam. "Belle, Jack, easy now. Easy." The team stepped forward. The wheel rolled along the edge, thrusting more dirt clods downhill.

"Easy, now…come on…" He directed them at a slight angle toward the mountainside. Slow and steady, the team inched the wagon wheel onto solid ground away from the ledge. Paul guided them to a small turnout in the road and halted the hard-breathing horses. He dropped his head and rubbed his forehead with one shaky hand.

Charlie, Charlotte and Emma walked over to him. Paul gathered the reins and looped them around the brake. He hopped down. Emma rushed to him and hugged his legs until he swung her into his arms. He buried his head in her red curls, whispering, "Thankfully, you're all right. Thank the Lord we are all okay."

Charlotte's knees buckled and she slid to the ground.

Tears spilled down her cheeks. She didn't bother to brush them away. Her thoughts swirled. What if she'd been driving? They'd all be lying at the bottom of the ravine.

Paul set Emma down and walked slowly to Charlotte. He knelt. With both hands he tipped her face to meet his eyes. "It's okay now. We made it."

He lifted her, pulling her close, and tightened his arms around her. She buried her face in his chest and collapsed into his embrace, sobbing.

"Go ahead. Cry as much as you need to. I'm here," he whispered, stroking her hair.

Reassured by his touch, a great peace filled her heart and mind. She thanked God Paul was her husband. Maybe she wouldn't be grateful tomorrow, but right now, in this moment, there wasn't anyone she'd rather be with. To her he was like a warrior guarding his kingdom. If the whole world crumbled, she knew Paul Harrison would still be standing, protecting his daughter, his wife and all those he loved and cared about.

"Paul... I... I..." She looked up at him. "Thank you. Thank you for coming to drive the team. Thank you for saving us. I am so grateful to you. We could have been..."

He smiled. "The Lord is good. We're all fine. Let's go find Bernie and Zeke." He took her hand and led her to the wagon.

Chapter Twelve

The idyllic meadow stretched the whole width of Split Rock Valley. Wildflowers clumped in scattered bunches. A forest of tall cedar trees lined the perimeter. The herd of horses grazed peacefully, a medley of their shimmering colors peppering the pasture. Charlotte caught sight of Belle and Jack side by side, enjoying their knee-deep feed. One lone log house and barn flanked the forest near the meandering creek. Smoke billowed from the chimney. An older woman with a yellow scarf tied around her hair stepped onto her porch, carrying a pail. She ambled to a well, centered between the house and the barn.

Charlotte found Paul. His strong arms held a heavy bucket, and his hands dripped with an oozing black goo. That's what she'd called it when she watched Paul and Bernie grease the wagon axles earlier on the trip. Beads of sweat lined the brim of his forehead under his hat. Oily splotches dotted his face. He stopped when he saw her. Looked up at her and grinned. His radiant blue eyes teased her.

Charlotte's heart skittered. She caught her breath and then smiled at him and pointed to the cabin. "I'd like to take Emma and visit the old woman in the log house. Is that okay with you?"

His eyes followed to where she pointed. "That's fine. Looks like whoever lives there could use some help with repairs. Tell her we'll be over to see what we can do after we finish with our chores here. You two ladies have fun."

Emma tried to tie her bonnet's blue ribbon into a bow under her chin, but her fingers wouldn't cooperate, and she let Charlotte finish it. She skipped and twirled through the tall grass. Swinging her arms, Charlotte followed behind Emma, delighted to be off the dusty trail for the day. Prince was left in the care of Charlie, who actually had time to sit down and have a cup of coffee after breakfast.

Emma giggled and danced ahead of her.

"We'll pick flowers on the way back to camp. Maybe we can do some more watercolors this evening after supper. You can show your papa how to paint with a stick brush!" Charlotte shouted to her.

Worn, splintered boards creaked as they stepped onto the porch to knock at the door. A petite woman with wrinkles and a big smile greeted them.

"Hello. I was hoping someone would come to visit from your camp." She opened her door wide. "Come on in and sit a spell."

The little home was neat and tidy. One big space included a round rag rug covering the floor near the fireplace with two wooden rocking chairs facing the hearth. An enamel pitcher with wildflowers sat on the dining table. White lace curtains hung from the windows, and there were several embroidered pieces hanging on the walls. Not unlike Paul's home in Cedar Grove. Charlotte sighed when she remembered she'd spent only two days in a real house since coming west.

"Thank you, ma'am. We're traveling through on our way to Lyonsville to sell that band of horses grazing in the meadow. My name is Charlotte Carpenter, I mean, Harrison. This is Emma, Emma Harrison, my…" Charlotte almost said *my daughter*, but instead she extended her hand.

The older woman's well-worn brown apron covered her yellow-striped dress. She removed the scarf from her silver-streaked hair and greeted Charlotte.

"This is a wonderful treat to have visitors. My name's Hattie McClain. My husband, Earl, passed on about a year ago. Been kinda lonesome out here by myself."

She pointed at the chairs surrounding the small round table.

"Sit down. Can I fix ya a cuppa tea or coffee?"

Charlotte smiled. "I haven't had tea since I left Boston. I'd love some. May Emma have a cup also?" Emma smiled at Charlotte.

Hattie filled the kettle, put it on the stove and stoked the fire. She ambled over to sit with them at the table. "So, you're from Boston. What're ya doin' way out here?"

"It's a long story. I came to teach school, but things happened that were beyond my control. I married Emma's father, Paul, and we're on this journey to sell those horses in the meadow. I've been teaching Emma her letters and to write her name."

The kettle sang out. Emma clapped and smiled. Hattie took a Blue Willow teapot and three cups and saucers down from a shelf. She tossed tea leaves into the vessel and added hot water.

Hattie poured the liquid amber into each cup.

She set a matching Blue Willow cream pitcher and sugar bowl in the center of the table. "Help yourself. I don't have much occasion to use my nice china."

Hattie sipped her tea. "We didn't have no schools close here in the valley. I taught our little girl at home." Hattie's eyes misted. Charlotte wasn't sure if the tears were from happy memories or from some kind of sadness. Hattie rose and went to a shelf by one of the rockers. "Yes, sir. I sent all the way back East for these McGuffey Readers." She ran her fingers across the row of books.

Charlotte followed her. "What a wonderful set. May I look at one?" Hattie nodded, and Charlotte pulled one out and thumbed through the pages. "These are brand new books."

"Well, practically new. Our little Alice died shortly after they came in the mail." Hattie wiped tears from her eyes with a corner of her apron.

Charlotte touched her arm. "I'm so very sorry. You must miss her very much."

Hattie's hazel eyes gazed out the window. "I do miss her. I've missed her every day for over thirty years. That pretty little one reminds me of her." Hattie glanced at Emma. "Our little Alice didn't have no red hair. But she had them big blue eyes and rosy cheeks."

They returned to the table, and Hattie poured more

tea. Emma smiled as she sipped from the teacup and munched her sweet molasses cookie.

"Say, I have somethin' in the barn I bet little Emma would like to see."

They followed Hattie out to the barn, where a cacophony of yipping greeted the visitors. Hattie opened a stall door where three puppies sat on a bed of straw—two solid black ones and one black-and-white-spotted one. When Hattie came near, they waddled to her, wagging their fluffy little tails. "I been feedin' 'em since their momma got kilt by a mountain lion. They're about eight weeks old now. Would you like to have one, Emma?"

Before Charlotte could protest, Emma scooped up the black-and-white pup and said, "Oh, yes, please."

Charlotte's breath caught. She froze. Her mouth opened, but no words came out. Tears streamed down her cheeks. Hattie glanced up.

"Charlotte, what's wrong?" Hattie put her arm around her.

Nothing in Charlotte's body cooperated with her mind. Her heart felt like it was skidding down a steep slope. She couldn't breathe. Couldn't think. Couldn't speak. Finally, she shook her head in disbelief as if to clear her foggy mind. She leaned down and whispered to Hattie, "Emma's daddy says it's been over a year since she's spoken any words at all. I'm astonished. I'm overjoyed." She knelt to hug Emma and the puppy. Then she took Emma by the shoulders and looked into her eyes.

"Emma, I'm happy to hear you speaking again. That

is a joy. But we must ask your daddy before we can commit to keeping the puppy."

"I'm going to name him Spots. Look at all his spots." She beamed and her eyes sparkled.

"We still have to get your daddy's permission," Charlotte insisted. "We can take him with us, but if your papa says no, we'll have to bring him back to Mrs. McClain. Okay?"

Emma nodded and snuggled the pup in a protective hug.

Hattie said, "I have something for you too, Charlotte. Let's go back to the house."

Inside, Mrs. McClain gathered the set of McGuffey Readers from the shelf and carried them to the table.

"I want you to have these readers, Charlotte."

"Oh, Hattie. I couldn't. They hold special memories for you."

"Yes, yes they do," she murmured. "But you bein' a teacher and all, you'll have more use for 'em than me. And I got nobody to leave them to when I die. I want you to take 'em. Please. It'd make my heart real happy knowin' Alice's books was bein' used by such a sweet one as Emma and maybe others who want to learn to read." She stacked them on the table, found some twine and tied them into a bundle for Charlotte to carry.

As they stepped off the porch to go back to camp, Charlotte said, "Paul and the boys will come on over when they finish their chores and see what they can do to be of help to you while we're here."

"That'd be right friendly. Stop by and say goodbye on your way outta the valley." Hattie waved to them from her door.

* * *

Paul scrubbed the gooey grease from his hands and face and tossed his dirty shirt into the burlap sack Charlotte had designated as his laundry bag. She'd informed him dresses and jeans should not be washed together. How she came by that knowledge he wasn't sure, since she hadn't known one thing about how to wash clothes when they married over two weeks ago. He chuckled, picturing her dunk-and-swirl approach to cleaning clothes. He suspected Charlie had advised her, but in order to keep their current state of peaceful existence, he complied without comment.

He watched Emma skip through the meadow toward him, a big smile on her face, her red curls bouncing under her new straw sunbonnet. She carried a furry bundle in her arms. Charlotte trotted behind her, toting her own package.

Emma had blossomed in such a short time with a full-time caretaker. Why hadn't he thought of this before? Widow Miller had seen that Emma was fed and watched over, but Emma had not thrived. Except with Charlotte. Could anyone have accomplished this transition? Or was it that Charlotte was more like a mother than just a caretaker?

By the time the two of them stood in front of him, Charlotte's cheeks were glowing pink and her breath came in spurts. She opened her mouth to speak, inhaling with each word. "Paul… Mrs. McClain…offered… Emma a—a puppy…" She stopped to catch her breath.

She was a beauty right now, standing next to him. Close enough to touch. To hold. To— His insides jolted. *Friends. We're friends.*

Paul jerked his head to focus. He looked closely at the bundle cradled in Emma's arms. A small, fat, round black-and-white puppy.

"No." He shook his head. "No siree. We don't need one more mouth to feed or one more thing to look after on this journey."

Emma's eyes pooled with wetness. Paul knelt beside her. "It's a cute puppy, Emma, but we can't keep it. We'll have to take it back."

"His name is Spots, Papa."

Paul's heart stalled. His stomach somersaulted. Every muscle in his body went rigid. His mouth flew open. His eyebrows rose, and his eyes stung with salty moisture. He felt like he'd been hit over the head with Charlie's frying pan. Did he hear Emma, or did he only imagine her voice? He'd prayed so long for this moment. Yearned for it. He couldn't believe it yet.

He stared at Emma and stammered in a hushed voice, "What…what did you say?"

Emma smiled up at him. "Papa, his name is Spots. Please, may I keep him?" Her big blue eyes begged him to say yes.

His daughter had spoken for the first time in over a year. He looked at Charlotte for one moment, then pulled Emma to his chest in a tight embrace. He wept. When the puppy squealed, Paul released his hold. He gazed up at Charlotte again and mouthed "thank you." She shrugged and shook her head.

He stood. In his most serious voice he said, "Emma, you'll have to take care of both Spots and Prince if we keep him. If you're old enough to have your own puppy, then you have to be responsible to take care of it. Can you do that?"

Emma turned a solemn face to him. "Yes, Papa. I'll take good care of Spots, and Prince too. I'll make sure they have food and water and I'll brush them. I promise."

Paul patted her shoulders. "Good girl, Emma. Why don't you introduce Spots to Prince? I'm sure they're going to be best friends."

"Take off your bonnet. Lay it on the worktable!" Charlotte called after her.

Emma managed to untie the bow with one hand, then slipped off her hat and tossed it onto the table. She strode to Prince, who lay next to a stump, and sat down beside him. She gathered him into her lap next to the puppy. Prince sniffed the little dog all over. The puppy tried to lick Prince. Emma talked to Prince in a gentle whisper, presumably explaining this was his new brother.

Paul reached for the bundle of books Charlotte was still holding. "Here, let me get that for you."

"Isn't it wonderful that Emma is talking again?" Charlotte looked at him. "We were looking at those puppies, and Mrs. McClain said she could have one and then she spoke."

Paul gazed at her. "It's an answer to my prayers. I'm very grateful to you, Charlotte, for the care you're giving Emma. I know you've been a comfort to her."

He carried the books to a stump near the worktable. "What are these?"

"Mrs. McClain gave me her set of McGuffey Readers for Emma and the other school children, when I start teaching. It was the saddest story about how she came to have them and why she gave them to me. I'm so excited, though. I can start teaching Emma to read now."

Paul stared in wonder at this woman. She was excited to have books to teach his Emma. How he wished she could teach him to read also. His heartbeat quickened. He took a step toward her. He wanted to hold her, to express his gratitude for her love and care of his beloved daughter. He longed to share his desire to learn with her, but could she respect a man who didn't know his letters?

"Let's get a cup of coffee, and you can tell me about your adventures with the old lady—and more about how you got Emma to talk." His hand went to the small of her back to guide her. Charlotte stepped away from his touch, removed her hat and set it next to Emma's.

They took their coffee and sat down on a log, watching Emma play with her dogs. Charlotte told him what she knew of Hattie McClain's story. His eyes filled with sympathy when Charlotte mentioned the loss of her little daughter, Alice. She told him she didn't understand how or why Emma had started talking again after all this time.

"Me and the boys will ride over and see what we can do before dinner. Maybe we can invite her tonight for supper? I'll check with Charlie. Sounds like she doesn't get many visitors."

Paul looked for Bernie and Zeke. He strolled over to speak with Charlie and found him dozing with a torn shirt in his lap and a threaded needle in his hand.

He walked back to Charlotte. "Charlie needs the rest. You let him know what we're doin'. Ring that bell when dinner's ready and we'll come a runnin'." Paul rounded up the others. Barely seated in their saddles they galloped off like they were in a race to the log house.

Before Paul dismounted, he perused the corrals, the house and outbuildings. One side of the huge barn door hung on by one hinge. The chicken house looked to be in fair shape. He'd better ask Mrs. McClain what her first choices for repairs might be, in case they weren't able to finish all her projects. He knocked on the door and introduced himself, Zeke and Bernie.

"Thank you for comin', Mr. Harrison. I had a good visit with your wife and little girl. She's one special child. Reminds me of my sweet Alice." Tears threatened to flow, but she quickly dabbed her eyes with her apron.

"Now, that Miz Charlotte is quite a woman. You done good when you picked her, Mr. Harrison. What a good momma she is to Emma." She grinned at him and patted his arm with a wink.

He smiled, feeling heat rise up his neck. "Yes, ma'am. Thank you."

A momma to Emma? Did others see Charlotte in that way? Mrs. McClain's words took root in his heart.

Looking at the porch's rotten boards, he wondered how bad the roofs were. "Shall we check your roof? Maybe the barn roof too?" He pointed to the porch floor. "We could replace these bad boards if you have any extra wood someplace."

Hattie's eyes filled with tears. "I don't know how to thank ya, Mr. Harrison. The good Lord must've sent you. I been prayin' for help." She locked eyes with Paul. "Ain't nobody 'round here been this nice to me since my Earl died. I'm not a regular church-goin' woman, but I read my Bible ever night and I pray hard. I was a worryin' about my roof. Winter's comin' on." She beamed. "You must be sent by God. I'll show ya where the new boards are."

In a barn stall, lumber was stacked high. She said, "Earl got the fixin' materials. Then he up and died. It's been a sittin' here waitin'. Hammers and nails are in the tack room." She pointed to a door.

Bernie grabbed a ladder and headed for the house. Zeke climbed up to the barn loft. Paul carried several pieces of lumber to the porch. When they'd finished for the day, Paul invited Mrs. McClain to join them for the evening meal. She gladly accepted and brought a delicious frosted chocolate cake. For Charlotte and Emma, Hattie brought her nice china teapot, cups and saucers and tea, all bundled in dishtowels for the trek across the meadow.

Paul watched as Charlotte and Hattie chatted with Emma and sipped tea. Charlotte complimented Emma on how well she handled the cup and saucer. He'd always wondered what a woman's gathering looked like. Charlotte offered so much for Emma: a chance to connect in social situations, a way to participate in normal activities.

Things he'd never had. He'd had no one to teach him proper behavior or the correct way to talk. He'd watched and imitated those he admired. He learned their speech and how they acted. The orphanage had hired him out many times to kind ranchers nearby. He worked hard, listened and learned. When he and Bernie left the home for good, he'd continued the practice of learning from others, keeping the good and discarding the bad.

He wanted more for Emma, but he couldn't ask Charlotte to stay on as Emma's mother. She didn't want a husband or a family. She'd made that clear the first day they met. He knew her dream was to teach school and live independent of a husband. He'd promised to help her fulfill that dream, and he was a man of his word.

Maybe Charlotte would consider tutoring Emma in the social graces after their marriage was annulled? He might persuade Charlotte that a little extra money for lessons could come in handy. If they remained friends, he'd have a better chance at pleading his case. So he'd work hard to build their friendship. For Emma's sake, he told himself.

Chapter Thirteen

A horrifying screech blasted through the meadow. Charlotte ripped off her covers, leaped up and tried to focus inside the pitch-dark wagon. Her heart raced like there was no finish line. She put her shaking hands over her mouth to stifle the scream threatening to force its way out of her mouth.

Loud, frightened neighing and high-pitched whinnying permeated the darkness. The ground shook with the sound of stampeding hooves. She leaned over and checked on Emma, who was snuggled with Prince on one side and Spots on the other.

Charlotte grabbed her boots and jacket and vaulted down from the wagon into the moonlit night. She looked around, trying to identify where the sounds came from. Paul, Zeke and Bernie charged on foot toward the scattering horses.

A full moon lit up the meadow. Horses reared, stomped and tossed their heads. With their manes and tails flying, they kicked at an invisible intruder and galloped off at full speed.

Charlie came to her side. "Don't worry Missy, the boys will take care of whatever is out there." He glanced in the direction of the chaos.

"What do you think it is? What's upsetting the horses?" Charlotte strained to see something, anything, yet she saw nothing but fleeing, frightened horses.

"Somethin's got 'em spooked. The boss will take care of it," Charlie reassured her. "Let's stand over by the fire and wait." Charlie led the way and then tossed on an extra hunk of wood.

Suspended like a perfect giant snowball, the moon illuminated the twinkling stars sprinkled in the coal-black sky. The world stood still, poised in those mysterious moments between darkness and daylight. It was perplexing and intimidating. Charlotte trembled and edged closer to the fire.

One single shot ricocheted, silencing the bloodcurdling shrieks. Horses scrambled from one end of the meadow to the other, Sassy's bell clanging with every step she took.

"It's okay, Miz Charlotte. It's all over now." Charlie patted her shoulder, bowed his head and stared into the crackling fire.

Paul, Bernie and Zeke tramped back carrying something strung out between them. Charlotte heard a heavy thump at the edge of camp.

"Let's wait for the morning light and round up the horses that scattered. We'll have a better chance when we can see what we're doin'. Thanks, boys," Paul said in a hoarse voice.

"Okay, Boss." Bernie nodded and headed to his bedroll. Zeke and Charlie ambled back to their beds too.

Paul set his rifle against the worktable and went to stand near the fire next to Charlotte, who shivered and pulled her jacket even tighter around her shoulders. She wished she'd thought to get a blanket.

Paul's face was drawn. His tousled hair gave him a carefree, boyish look. A light stubble outlined his strong jaw line and chin. His shirt hung loose over his denim jeans. He was handsome and strong in every way. Her stomach hurt again. Was it Charlie's cooking? Maybe it was her cooking?

He shook his head and sighed as if he were disappointed.

Charlotte gazed into the flickering embers. "What happened?"

"A mountain lion killed one of the young fillies. Attacked another mare and almost got one of my best geldings. Sassy went after it. She's a might scratched up too. We'll have to doctor the injured ones and bury the little filly when it's daylight." He sighed again and rubbed his hand on the back of his neck.

She put her hand on his arm. "Oh, Paul. I'm so sorry. Not only for the loss of the little horse but for the drastic way in which it happened."

"Yeah. It's a shame. Life is tough." He shook his head. A log shifted, sending bits of lit embers into the night air.

"It's a wonder Emma and the puppies slept through all the noise and commotion." Charlotte turned to look toward the wagon.

"Can't believe those dogs didn't start howling and cause another ruckus." He smiled and looked into her eyes, staring for a long moment. "I can see the moon in your eyes." He paused. With his teasing gaze and dimpled grin, he said, "I'm gonna call you Lottie Moon."

Charlotte pushed his arm. "That's a strange name."

He reclaimed her arm and looped it through his, sending a shiver bounding up and down her spine. Paul snuggled closer to her. "I heard about Lottie Moon at church. She was a rich girl who gave up everything to become a missionary in China. They say she was kind of a spirited and outspoken young woman. Kind of like you, I guess." His blue eyes sparkled. "Yeah, you're my spunky Lottie Moon." He chuckled and patted her hand.

The cool night breeze rustled the flames into a midnight dance. She unhooked her arm from his and stepped sideways. "Morning comes early around here, and nobody likes breakfast to be late. Good night, Paul." Charlotte turned to go.

Paul took hold of her elbow. "Wait a minute, Lottie Moon. I need to talk to you about something."

Since he was grinning, he probably wasn't about to criticize her. Perhaps he wanted to discuss the amicable way they were getting along lately? A pleasant thought. Becoming a friend was easier to learn than being a wife or mother. She felt she was really struggling there.

Friendship with Paul would be difficult, though. Every nerve in her body reacted to his presence. If she thought about him, she forgot her task at hand. Anyway, he didn't want to be married to her. She wasn't what he'd expected. He'd married her because he was desperate for help with his beloved daughter. And for the sake of her own reputation. Focusing on a friend relationship was her idea.

If only they could transform their alliance. Then,

when they got back to Cedar Grove, she could go on with her dream to teach school, have her freedom and visit Paul and Emma once in a while.

Paul lifted her chin to face him. Their eyes locked. She held her breath and waited.

"Lottie, you need to learn to shoot."

Startled by his words, she backed up and stumbled. He caught her and held her. He wanted to talk about shooting? He was thinking about guns at a time like this? He didn't want to talk about being friends? The man was impossible.

"I know nothing about guns. I don't like them, and besides, I couldn't kill anything." She pushed away from him again.

With a serious gleam in his eye, he said in a husky voice, "This is the second or third time when it would have been good if you'd had a gun for self-defense. You may need to protect Emma." He stood in front of her, his feet apart, arms crossed over his chest. "I want you to learn to shoot as part of your job of taking care of Emma."

She would not be intimidated.

Hands on her hips, she scowled at him, clenched her jaw and said, "Don't you give me orders. I am not one of your hired hands, remember? I don't like being bullied. I do not wish to learn to use a firearm. I will not be forced to do something against my will." She stomped her foot and tossed her head, her hair swirling in front of her face.

Suddenly Paul grabbed her to him, enveloping her. Both arms around her, he held her close to his chest and mumbled, "Oh, Lottie, my Lottie Moon."

She tried to push away, to kick at him…but she felt safe. Protected. She longed to stay in the shelter of his strong arms.

She swallowed. Couldn't speak.

He leaned in close, his lips near hers. His gaze held her, his chest heaving. He hesitated. His blue eyes weren't teasing or playful, weren't serious or angry—just wistful.

"Please Charlotte. For Emma's sake. It isn't hard to learn. You've already mastered so many new skills on this trip. I need to feel at peace when I ride away from camp. I need for you to be safe. For Emma to be safe. If you could shoot, I'd feel better when I have to leave you for a while. I'll teach you myself."

He paused. "After all, what are friends for?" Now his blue eyes sparkled. That dazzling, dimpled smile melted her resolve.

"Paul, I'll never get this. I can't shoot this rifle." She took the gun down from her shoulder. "It's too hard to use the sight." Charlotte's eyes dropped and her mouth turned down. "Let's quit for today. How many more branches can I aim at and miss? It's embarrassing."

He chuckled. "You've just started. You need more practice. That's all. Can't learn it in a day. You're a teacher, so you know that."

Paul strolled over and stood beside her. "You know mastering a new skill like reading or writing doesn't happen on the first try. Come on, Lottie…a few more shots? Then we'll call it quits for today." He patted her shoulder, remembering trying to learn to read. If he'd had more time to practice, that would've helped. But the teachers hadn't liked him disrupting their classes. The orphanage had started hiring him out after he learned to write his name.

"It's hot out here," she groused. "Isn't there a shady spot to practice?" she asked, glancing around. With one hand on the gun, she used her other hand to wipe her brow with the kerchief she pulled from her skirt pocket. "I'm parched. I need a drink."

Paul retrieved the canteen from a low-hanging branch and handed it to her. She swallowed a few drops, poured a little on her kerchief and scrubbed at her neck. "That feels good."

Charlotte squared her shoulders and hoisted the rifle again. She put her hands on the firearm the way Paul had instructed. She closed one eye and tried to see the tree limb he pointed to as her target.

He stepped behind her. Her arms quivered.

"Are you nervous?" He stared into the long hair hanging loose over her back. He liked that she wore it down once in a while now.

She started to move. With a light touch he rested his hands on her shoulders. "Don't turn around. Are you afraid? You're trembling."

"No. I'm not scared." She paused. "I'm not used to holding this kind of weight at this angle. I'm not strong enough to keep the gun steady."

He moved closer. "I'll help you. It takes some getting used to."

He inhaled that rose scent. She sure wasn't what he'd expected. When she stepped off that stage, shock and disappointment had flooded his heart and mind. She was beautiful. She unnerved him. It terrified him to think another captivating woman could rip his and Emma's life right in half.

The annulment agreement guaranteed they'd split when this journey ended. No wondering if he'd be fooled, no wondering if this relationship would last, no wondering if it could be more than it was. No broken hearts from an unanticipated departure. They both knew what would happen at the end of the month.

Friendship. Nothing more.

He slipped his hands under her arm and elbow. "Rest in my hands. I'll hold you steady."

Charlotte sucked in her breath and answered with a mumbled, "Okay."

"Lottie, open your eyes. How can you shoot with your eyes closed?" He chuckled. "Pretend I'm a fence post you're leaning the gun on."

She lifted her foot to kick back at him. He sidestepped but never let go.

"C'mon. Focus. You can do this. Take a deep breath, aim and fire." Paul leaned his head next to her face. "I'll help," he whispered in her ear. "Look at the target, get it sighted in, take a breath and then fire."

Charlotte found the branch and inhaled. His hands calmly tightened on her arm and elbow...then she pulled the trigger. The sharp bang zinged through the air, and in the next instant, a snap parted the leafed branch from the tree. She lowered the gun to her side, squealed with delight and faced Paul. "I did it! I did it! Did you see that? I shot the branch off the tree."

His arms circled her waist. He stared into her green eyes dancing with joy and leaned in. Should he kiss her to celebrate? Her lips were full and inviting.

He pushed her back a bit. Why risk upsetting her with his longing? *Friends,* he reminded himself. He smiled and dropped his hands.

"That was real good, Lottie. Let's end this lesson with a success." He took the gun from her. "Next time we make camp, we'll practice again."

"Oh, Paul, thank you. Thank you. It was your trusty fence-post stance that helped me. I believe I can learn to shoot that thing. Thank you so much. I can't wait to tell Charlie." She stood on her tiptoes, kissed his cheek, whirled and ran off to share her good news with Charlie and the boys.

His pulse bolted like a rabbit chased by a coyote. His breath stalled in his throat. His heart wouldn't stand still. His feet wanted to race after her, take her in his arms and have a real kiss.

Lots of them.

He stood for a long, long time, waiting for his weak knees to steady. He stared up at puffy white clouds slithering across the steel blue sky. Why had he insisted she learn to shoot? For his peace of mind? There was no peace in his mind at this moment. His mind was knotted. He felt like a colt who'd been tied too loose and the rope had tangled until the animal couldn't move. He was snared with thoughts of Charlotte.

Lord, help me. I'm baffled. I'm confused, Lord.

Once Paul had settled his thoughts and his knees had recovered, he meandered back to camp.

Charlie watched him amble over to the chuck wagon and put the rifle in its place. His mustache curled at the tips and his eyes sparkled. "So, Boss, how'd the shootin' lesson go?"

Paul cocked his head and stared at him. "You know somethin' I don't, Charlie?"

"Sounds like your little wife is a real Annie Oakley, to hear her tell it." Charlie chuckled. "And according to her, you're a mighty fine fence she can lean on. She demonstrated how you showed her to hit the target. I sure hope today's success ain't gonna mean she don't need no more lessons. I bet she's countin' on a lot more help." Charlie guffawed and winked at him. "We've got miles to go, Boss." He carried the coffeepot to the fire and hung it on the tripod.

Paul pulled his hat down and strode toward Buck. "I'm going to check on the herd, Charlie." A horseback ride was what he needed to sort out his thoughts and feelings. His current scattergun approach to dealing with Charlotte wasn't working. The turmoil hammering his heart jumbled his mind. He yearned for time with the Lord. Alone. He had to form a plan for all the upcoming miles he and Charlotte would be traveling together.

Chapter Fourteen

～

Charlie's eyes twinkled when he took the lid off the cast-iron Dutch oven and saw the *C-A-T* letter-shaped biscuits. He brushed his hands on his apron and shook his head. "Boy howdy, Missy. You sure know how to stir up a heap o' trouble. Those cowboys are gonna be fit to be tied." He chuckled and walked over to the coffeepot with his cup.

Charlotte smiled. "It's to help Emma with her letters. We're ready to start the first McGuffey Reader. I want to reinforce what she's learned so far."

With a folded corner of the apron Charlie had concocted for her, Charlotte lifted the heavy skillet of gravy and carried it to the table.

Plopping a spoon in the sauce, she called, "Emma, time for breakfast!" Emma ran to her, Spots and Prince close on her heels.

Emma squealed and pointed at the biscuits on her plate. "Look, a *C* biscuit and an *A*. There's the *T*."

Zeke strolled over and picked up his plate. He reached for a biscuit, then shoved his hat back on his head and hollered, "Charlie, what in tarnation do you call this here?" He pointed at the biscuits.

"Ask the boss's wife." Charlie grinned and sipped his coffee.

Charlotte smiled at Zeke. "It's biscuit letters. They're to help Emma remember her ABCs. They taste the same no matter their shape."

Bernie and Paul stood with their hands in their pockets, staring into the Dutch oven at the biscuits and listening as Charlotte explained again. Bernie's big brown eyes got wide and his bushy eyebrows arched high up on his forehead. His grin threatened to bust off his face by the time she finished talking. Paul chuckled, rubbing the back of his neck. "There's no one quite like you, Lottie Moon."

Emma looked up from her plate. "Papa, I can spell *cat*. Listen. *C-A-T. Cat.* Isn't that good? Look, here's the *C*." She held up the biscuit to show him. "And the *A*. This is the *T*, Papa." Emma was so excited it was hard for her to swallow.

Paul looked at his daughter. "That's great, Emmy." Keeping a close eye on her, he watched her pick up each letter and say its name. He repeated the letters over and over to himself, memorizing how to spell *cat* in case Emma asked him later. He took one letter biscuit each so he could make the word with her. He recognized the *A*. He had a couple of those in his name. Now he knew the letters *C* and *T* too. Maybe there was hope. Maybe he could learn to read after all.

"That's a right clever idea, Miz Charlotte. I might could learn to spell if I could eat the words later." Bernie laughed so hard food slid off his plate. Charlotte grinned.

While they drank the last of the breakfast coffee, Paul talked about crossing Rattlesnake Creek. "Problem is, it isn't a creek. It's a river. Bernie and I couldn't find a good flat place to cross with the wagon. About a mile up the road there's a slope heading into the current and a slight incline on the other side. Best we could find. It'll be tough for Jack and Belle. We'll need ropes to get the wagon to the shore. It's deeper than I thought."

"We're takin' the herd over first, right?" Zeke asked.

"Yeah. We'll get them across and come back and help with the wagon. You and Bernie take the side lines, I'll take the lead." He turned to Charlotte and Charlie. "We'll go on now with the herd. Meet us down at the river when you finish up here." He put his plate in the dishpan and went to hitch Jack and Belle to the wagon. Bernie and Zeke rode off to start the horses toward the fast-flowing water.

Once they were gone, Charlotte asked Charlie, "Is your shoulder healed enough yet to drive the team?"

He packed potatoes in a sack. "Missy, you can do this. I'll be right beside you, but you can do it."

"Thanks for your confidence. But I haven't had enough experience yet." She frowned. "Are there any special instructions for the best way to get across a river?"

"Charlotte, I can't tie my bow." Emma's little fingers were tangled in the blue streamers of her straw hat. Charlotte knelt and tied the ribbon and then lifted her into the wagon. She hoisted Prince and Spots to

Emma, who placed them with great care on top of the bedrolls inside.

Charlie stepped up into the wagon, took hold of the reins and stretched out his hand for Charlotte.

When she sat down, he said, "Here." Charlotte's gloved hands reached for the lines.

"When we get ready to cross, Emma best get in the back with the dogs and bedrolls. Don't want no possibility of her gettin' bounced out into the river if we hit a rock or somethin'." Charlie gave Emma's shoulders a squeeze.

"Hup, Jack! Get on up, Belle!" Charlotte called. In unison, the horses pulled forward and the wagon rolled. Charlotte marveled at how much she enjoyed driving the team and how much pleasure she took in brushing and feeding them. She wished she'd learned to drive a buggy or even a cart when she lived in Boston. Her aunt thought horseback riding was bad enough and had refused to entertain any notion of Charlotte driving herself anywhere.

"It isn't proper. In our social circle we must maintain a certain decorum," her aunt lectured constantly. Charlotte grinned, thinking of the hysterics Aunt Arilla would have if she could see her now: driving a team, sleeping in a chuck wagon, cooking with cast iron over an open campfire, washing clothes in a tub and shooting a gun. Her life had changed. Drastically. She'd learned new skills, discovered how to take care of Emma, and she'd had adventures working alongside her husband. Paul, her kind, strong, handsome husband—no, her friend, not husband. Her best friend.

She looked back at the log house in the meadow. She

wanted to remember this special place where Emma had spoken again and where she'd made her first female friend in the west.

Hattie stood on the porch and waved her yellow scarf. With her apron, she dabbed at the tears sliding down her cheeks. Charlotte lifted the reins to swipe the ones inching down her own cheeks. It was difficult to say farewell to Hattie McClain. Charlotte promised she'd write her a letter as soon as they got to Cedar Grove.

At the top of the slope Charlotte halted the team. The last group of horses plunged into the river. Bernie followed while Zeke waited on the other shore. Paul rode back and forth in the middle of the river, urging the horses to keep moving.

Suddenly two horses on the opposite bank squealed, reared and lunged out of the water, sprinting past the horses grazing nearby.

Zeke galloped over to investigate and yelled, "Rattlesnakes!"

He shot three times. Snakes skyrocketed into the air and into the river. Zeke eyeballed the bank, probably looking to see if more snakes were slithering out of their hidey-holes.

Paul hurried Buck to the other side, dismounted and inspected the spot. He waved and bellowed at Bernie, Charlie and Charlotte, "Stay there! We'll be back!"

An hour later they returned from trying to find the horses that had gotten bit. He told the others how, with revolvers drawn, they'd walked up and down the bank checking for more snake hideouts. Finding nothing, they'd crossed back to the chuck wagon.

Zeke and Bernie tied heavy ropes to the metal rings on each side of the wagon while Paul undid the lead ropes attached to Jack and Belle's halters.

"Emma, get in the back with the pups."

"Yes, Papa." Emma scrambled onto a bedroll placed where she could still look out.

Charlotte's heart thumped and her hands trembled. She kept one foot poised on the brake.

"Steady, Missy, keep a steady hand. Remember those two horses can feel what you're feelin' through them reins. Don't let 'em think there's anything to be afraid of. You can do this. I'm right here." He nodded, patting her shoulder.

Paul gazed at her. "Are we ready?"

Charlotte took a deep breath, smiled and nodded. "Ready."

"Hup, Belle. Get up, Jack." The horses started down the slope. Charlotte pressed lightly on the brake, slowing the wagon's descent into the river. Step by step, Paul urged Buck into the water. The current caused the wagon to sway. Charlotte watched Bernie and Zeke tighten their ropes to steady the wagon and keep it from tilting. The team trudged through the belly-deep flow.

Charlie pointed ahead. "When the horses hit the ground on the other side, get 'em movin' fast so they can haul this wagon out of the water and up that hill."

"Tell me when."

Buck stepped from the river and Paul turned to glance back at her.

"Now!" Charlie hollered.

"Hah, hah! Get up, come on, get up! Hah, hah!" Charlotte commanded and tapped the reins on the horses' backsides. They leaped forward, trotting up the hill. Bernie and Zeke pulled hard on the side ropes, helping propel the wagon up the incline.

When they stopped Charlie beamed. "You did it, Miz Charlotte. I couldn't have done it any better. You're a real teamster now."

"Oh, Charlie. Thank you. What would I have done without you?" Charlotte patted his shoulder, flashing a huge smile.

Paul attached the lead rope to Jack and Belle's halters again. Zeke and Bernie coiled the long ropes and hung them back on the wagon.

Paul urged Buck close to Charlotte's side of the chuck wagon and leaned toward her. Her heart pounded. Was it the aftershock of her first drive through a river or the closeness of the handsome cowboy seated on Buck, looking so in control? His smile let her know he was pleased. His beautiful blue eyes, full of admiration, held hers for several seconds.

"Is Emma okay?"

Charlotte nodded.

"Are you okay?" She smiled.

"Nicely done, Lottie. Nicely done."

He trotted off.

The band of horses meandered in the meadow. Paul wondered what it would be like to worry about nothing except the next bite of food. He sighed and prayed, troubled about the loss of another day while they waited for the snake-bit horses to get better.

There'd been the one extra day rounding up the scattered horses from the storm, and they'd stayed an extra day in the meadow to bury the dead filly and to doctor injured horses. Now they'd spend another day looking for the rattlesnake-bit horses and tend to them. He'd calculated enough time for unforeseen circumstances, though. He wondered if he'd make it in time to meet the buyer. Saving his ranch depended on him getting to Lyonsville on time.

He trotted Buck back to the camp they'd set up under a few shade trees. Charlie cut peeled potatoes and tossed them into a big pot. Hattie McClain had given them eggs and some fresh vegetables and fruits from her garden to thank them for all the work they'd done on her place. Paul had insisted on paying her for the canned peaches, apples, green beans, corn and the cheese. Charlie protected the dozens of cookies she'd baked like he was the deputy assigned to guard a gold shipment.

"Charlie, make us a berry cobbler with them left-over berries," Zeke begged. "They're gonna go bad if you don't use 'em up."

"I'm waitin' to teach Miz Charlotte how to make a cobbler."

Bernie hooted. "Tell 'er we don't want no ABC cobbler."

Charlotte raised her wooden spoon and shook it at Bernie as he and Zeke rode out of camp to check the herd.

Paul watched Emma smile as she named each letter of the alphabet. Charlotte wiped her hands on her apron, took out a reader and handed it to Emma.

His heart stilled. His daughter was reading. He might be more grateful to Charlotte for teaching his little girl than taking care of Emma so beautifully. Why didn't she want to be a mother? She was a natural, creative and fun. He admired her tenacity when learning new skills. He chuckled when he thought about those letter biscuits she'd made the other day. Even Zeke and Bernie had decided she wasn't plumb loco. They thought she was turning out to be a mighty fine cook, thanks to Charlie, even though her biscuits had odd shapes.

Paul watched from a distance but close enough to hear the lesson. He wished he could see what Charlotte pointed to. He yearned to read. Emma would find out soon he couldn't—and what would she think of her papa then?

Could he ask Charlotte to help him? As a friend? He'd pray about it.

Zeke tied up his horse, got his coffee and joined Paul. "Boss, looks like we got two horses with swelled-up legs. If we take it easy and don't move 'em too fast, they'll be fine in a day or two."

"Thanks, Zeke. Mare or gelding?"

"One of each."

After Bernie tied up his horse, he stood with his hands in his pockets.

"Boss, don't want to add none to your troubles, but there was a fresh-nicked horseshoe track off the road in the brush when I follered that snake-bit geldin'. Looked the same as one of them horses those varmints we took to jail the other day was ridin'."

Paul stared at Bernie. "You sure it belongs to one of those thieves?"

"Yup. I knowed the Marshall wasn't supposed to

be here yet, so maybe it ain't one of 'em. Wanted ya to know what I saw."

"Appreciate it, Bernie."

Were those thieves after his horses again? How'd they get out of jail? Did they think he had more money hidden somewhere in the wagon? He'd better talk with Charlie and Charlotte about being careful when he and the boys were out tending the herd.

Lottie needed another shooting lesson too. He smiled at the thought of being so close to her again. Then he frowned. She made him jittery. But since they had to wait at least a day to let the swelling go down from the snakebites, he'd set up some targets for her later.

Paul looked up from his coffee cup. "Boys, we're gonna keep a sharp eye out for those three thieves. Looks like they got out of jail. We're headed into the mountains where it'd be easier for them to pick us off. I'll mention to Charlie and Charlotte to be on the watch when we're not in camp. Why those yahoos trailed us this far, I don't know. Must want these horses pretty bad." Paul shook his head and rubbed his neck.

Bernie and Zeke nodded. Zeke pushed his hat back on his head. "Boss, I worked on a ranch not far from here. There's a purty waterfall a ways up Rattlesnake Creek. Sorta back in that rocky hill area." He pointed to a bluff not a mile away. "It'd be a nice picnickin' spot for you and the missus. Little Miss Emma would sure enjoy it too. Me and Bernie and Charlie can keep a lookout."

"Is it in walking distance?" Paul asked.

"Better to take a horse." Zeke smiled.

Bernie's eyes got wide and he mumbled how nice

it'd be to see a waterfall too, but Zeke kicked at his foot and scowled at him. Bernie looked away.

Paul knew Bernie longed for the old days, when it was the two of them. Bernie didn't care for Rachel. He remembered when she called Bernie a washed up wrangler. He'd been insulted and complained to Paul.

"Boss, ain't I more than just a hired man? Ain't I your best friend?" Bernie had asked him each time Rachel dismissed him.

The other day Bernie had rattled on about how much he liked Miz Charlotte. She was kind. And she was always doing something funny. She learned fast, though.

"And, Boss, she never complains about the work. Always has a smile and somethin' nice to say to folks. You picked out a good wife this time."

Paul thought a day of relaxation with his little girl and his wife—even though she wasn't his real wife— sounded good.

"Thanks, Zeke. I'll talk to Charlie about packin' up some food for a picnic."

Charlotte tagged after Paul. "I've only ridden side-saddle. I hope I can master the western saddle quickly. It might take me a little while."

"Missy, you can ride old Fred. He's gentle and don't spook easy. Give ya time to get used to ridin' again." Charlie grinned at her.

Emma was ecstatic about riding and the picnic but disappointed they couldn't take Prince and Spots.

Paul tied the blue-and-yellow quilt on the back of Charlotte's saddle and hung the canteen and the food bag from her saddle horn.

He gave Charlotte a hand up and noticed her cheeks

turned pink the moment he took hold of her foot. She looked away and straightened her blue-striped skirt.

Emma sat tall in Paul's saddle and looked down at him with her sparkling blue eyes. "Papa, I haven't ridden with you in a long, long time." She gave him a thankful smile as he swung up behind her.

He nodded to the boys. "Thanks for holding down the fort." Turning to Charlotte and giving Emma a squeeze, he said, "Now, ladies, let's go find us a waterfall."

Chapter Fifteen

Gentle Fred plodded along the dirt trail right behind
Buck. Emma chatted about the trees and the songbirds
and how much she liked riding horseback with her Papa
again. Paul hung on her every word and answered all
her questions with patience and sweet smiles.

Charlotte appreciated the western saddle, finding
she felt safer and like she had more control than when
she rode sidesaddle. Neck reining instead of direct reining was taking a bit longer to master. She longed for
her dark blue split skirt. How handy it would be. Skirts
and petticoats made horseback riding difficult. Maybe
there was a seamstress in Cedar Grove she could persuade to sew a new split skirt for her. Or maybe she
would order one from a catalog. She grinned, thinking
how flabbergasted and hysterical her aunt would be if
Charlotte ordered from a catalog—or worse, if her aunt
could see her riding astride.

Tall pines, oak trees and an abundance of scrub
brush lined the narrow trail winding down a gentle

slope. A warm summer breeze stirred memories of her cedar-lined closets in her bedroom at Aunt Arilla's.

They rode close enough to the hillside to touch the black volcanic rocks covered with shiny green moss. It looked like a scene from a fairy-tale garden in Alice in Wonderland.

Emma turned in the saddle and looked up at her daddy with her wondering wide eyes. "Papa, what is that loud noise?"

Paul grinned. "That is the rattle of Rattlesnake Falls. Sounds dangerous, doesn't it?" he teased. Emma giggled. He halted Buck and peered through the trees.

"Look, Emma, Charlotte, over there—the falls."

Charlotte urged Fred next to them.

"Can you see? It's magnificent," Paul said. He spoke with a reverence she'd heard when he prayed. "God's glorious creation. We are blessed to share in its beauty."

Charlotte gazed at Paul. He baffled her most of the time. Tough, strong, determined, bossy—yet tender and caring and a true worshipper of God, all wrapped up in one rugged, handsome cowboy. Her heart pounded. She swallowed and turned to feast on the most amazing sight she'd ever beheld.

Thundering fountains of water burst over the cliff, a torrent of white froth cascading into a swirling turquoise pool below. Voluminous streams sprayed from holes dotting the rock wall, adding to the downpour spilling into the little lake below. Charlotte held her breath. She was awestruck by God's amazing handiwork right before her eyes.

"Let's find a spot for our picnic, closer to the falls."

Paul clicked to Buck, and Fred followed without any coaxing from Charlotte.

The trees along the woodsy trail clumped closer and closer together and the chaparral grew thicker, blocking the daylight and making it appear as if it were twilight instead of midday. Charlotte shivered, not from a chill but from the volatile feel in the air.

The horses stepped out of the forest gloom and into the sunshine pouring into the wide basin at the bottom of the falls. Sunbeams streamed like arrows, piercing the ice-blue water and sending splashes of rainbow colors in all directions.

Emma clapped. Paul sighed and smiled. Shaking his head, he said, "It's beautiful."

Charlotte sucked in air and covered her mouth. She stared. No words would come. Soaking in the view, the smell and the sound, she commanded her mind to create a lasting memory.

At the edge of the water, big flat boulders squatted like guardians stationed around the lake. Back from the water, flatter ground stretched in a half circle surrounding the falls.

Paul dismounted and lifted Emma down. He tied Buck to a tree limb and strode to help Charlotte dismount. She had her foot in the stirrup and was leaning to lift her other leg over the saddle when Paul caught her by the waist and hoisted her to the ground, instantly pulling her to his chest with his strong arms. Pressed against him, her breath caught in her throat. Her knees wobbled. She closed her eyes for a moment, overwhelmed with an immense sense of security.

Emma tugged at the hem of Paul's jacket. "Papa,

Papa, let's have our picnic on one of those big fat rocks." Emma scampered away, picking her way over the smaller rocks and stones, her red curls bouncing. She found a huge one and tried to climb up on it.

She looked back at them. "This one. Is it good for a picnic table?"

Paul nodded. "We're coming." He took the canteen off the saddle horn and handed it to Charlotte. He carried the quilt and the sack with their food and utensils. He reached for Charlotte's hand to help her cross the stony path to the big rock Emma had picked out for them.

With the blanket spread out on the stone, Charlotte handed the plates and food to Paul and Emma.

"It's lovely here. Are these falls well-known?" Charlotte asked, stuffing a slice of chicken between the top and bottom of her biscuit.

"Look, they're playing chase." Emma pointed at two gray squirrels darting up a tree.

"Papa, look over there. It's that funny fat little bird with the wobbly topknot. Like the ones at home that come to eat bugs in the garden." A momma quail and four bitty ones scooted from one thick bush to another, their plumes bobbing back and forth.

Paul nodded at Emma and then looked at Charlotte. "I have heard of Rattlesnake Falls, but I've never been here. Word is that one of the pioneer wagon trains discovered it. Of course, the Native American tribes in this region knew about it. Most of the ranchers in the area and beyond are aware of the site. Beautiful waterfalls aren't common around here. Good thing Zeke remembered we were near."

He pointed to the black birds darting in and out of the falls. "Emma, those birds dashing around the falls are called black swifts, and that fat little bird with the babies are quail. And look up, way up there." He pointed toward the sky. "It's a bald eagle perched on that fir-tree limb." Emma strained to see the bird. Paul took her on his lap and guided her face with his hand.

"Oh, Papa, he's beautiful," she breathed.

Charlotte lifted her eyes and was struck by the majesty of the bird staring straight ahead, as if he couldn't be bothered to give any attention to the humans below.

"I'm so hot, Papa. Can I stick my toes in the water?" Emma pleaded.

Paul looked at Charlotte. "What do you think, Lottie? Want to wade in the water and cool off a bit before we start back on that dusty trail?"

Emma's hopeful eyes pleaded with her.

Charlotte stared at them. How could she refuse this adorable little lady?

"Let's wade in the water!" she declared.

Paul took off his boots and socks. Charlotte and Paul both helped Emma with her hat, shoes and stockings. Charlotte told them to go ahead, that she'd be right along. Turning her back and hiding behind a giant boulder, Charlotte peeled off her stockings and shoes and then tiptoed over the rocks into the cool, refreshing pool.

Giggling, Emma splashed her Papa over and over. Paul doused Charlotte with handfuls of water, and she retaliated.

"Hey, I'll get you two." He backed up, showering them again and again.

Charlotte stepped sideways to dodge the spray and sank below the surface. Her arms flailed and she kicked her feet. She raised her head, spit water and screamed, "Help!"

"Lottie!" Paul hollered. Paul strode to her, latched on to her hands and pulled her out of the water. She tried to take a step, lost her balance and collapsed against him.

He lifted her into his arms. She snuggled into his chest and tried to catch her breath.

"Thank the Lord," he murmured as he carried her to a huge flat rock. "Emma, come here. I don't want you to fall into one of those deep holes." Emma rushed to stand beside Charlotte, her eyes wide.

Charlotte saw the fear on Emma's face. She whispered, "I'm okay, honey. Thanks to your papa's quick action." She patted the child's hands, and Emma's worried look disappeared.

Paul pushed strands of wet hair away from Charlotte's eyes and took her face in his hands. "Are you okay now? Any scratches or bruises?" She shrugged. Her stomach churned.

He scanned her face and hands and then lifted each foot, examining her bare feet. "You have one cut near your ankle. Probably scraped it on a sharp rock when you went under."

Charlotte couldn't speak. His touch flooded her body with warmth, and she felt light-headed. Why had she panicked? She knew how to swim. Perhaps the weight of her clothes dragging her under had frightened her? When she swam in the ocean, she'd worn a proper bathing suit. Her training should have kicked in. Was it because she hadn't expected to swim?

Paul stepped back and looked at her. With a big smile and teasing eyes, he said, "I don't think you'll be comfortable riding back in those soaking-wet clothes, but we better start for camp before the sun goes down and it gets chilly. I don't want you to get sick."

He strode to their picnic boulder, retrieved the quilt and handed it to her. "Here. Wipe some of that water off and wrap up in this. Stand over there in the sunshine. You'll be warmer and you might dry out a little more while we pack up." Paul pointed to a grassy spot where the sun streamed down.

Charlotte used the quilt to dab water from her face and then flung it around her shoulders. She sat down on the flat rock and put on her socks and shoes.

Wandering over to the sunlit area, she said, "I hope this won't make us too late getting back to camp."

"We'll make it in time for dinner," Paul reassured her.

Emma handed Paul the leftover food and the utensils. He shoved everything into the saddlebags and heaved the pack onto Fred.

He glanced at Charlotte with a smile and chuckled.

"That quilt has never looked so lovely. Now we have one more memory to add to this fun day."

A slice of the bright yellow sun peeked over the dark mountaintops, and a crimson glow and golden clouds filled the night sky. At last they spotted their camp. Paul felt a tingling sensation run up and down his spine. Buck whinnied. He stopped the horse to let Charlotte and Fred catch up to him. He pushed his Stetson back on his head and pointed at the wagon and the tripod over the barren fire pit.

He whispered, "No fire. No lanterns lit yet. No dogs barking at us. Nobody standing around waiting for dinner. I don't like the looks of this." He hugged Emma's shoulders.

Buck whinnied again and pawed at the ground. Paul pulled back on the reins, speaking calmly. "Whoa, Buck, whoa. Easy."

"Charlotte, you take Emma." He lifted his daughter onto Charlotte's saddle. "Stay here until I signal it's okay to ride into camp. If anything happens, get Emma out of here. Don't look back. Ride to town and get the sheriff."

Charlotte started to protest. "I've never—"

"Just do what I tell you."

He didn't look at her, and she didn't argue. His eyes searched the camp for clues. He didn't hear Sassy's bell. He retrieved his revolver from the holster in his saddlebags. "Move over into those trees, Charlotte. Out of the way."

Without objecting, she clicked to Fred and guided him away from Buck into the grove.

Paul's mouth was dry. His heart slammed into his chest and his jaw clenched. He breathed deeply, then bowed his head and prayed, asking the Lord to protect Emma and Charlotte.

He held a tight rein on Buck and walked him toward the chuck wagon. Paul didn't call out. He glanced from side to side, hunting for signs of someone. Drawers had been emptied from the top part of the chuck box and the contents strewn on the ground. Mounds of white flour and sugar were heaped in piles near the wagon wheels, the empty sacks tossed on top. Paul circled the wagon but found no signs of Charlie, Bernie or Zeke. He rode away from the camp in the direction the horses had been grazing. No herd. Not one horse.

His entire band of horses had disappeared with no trace.

Chapter Sixteen

◣━◥

Paul scoured the camp and meadow for any signs of Charlie, Bernie, Zeke or his horses. The thieves had stolen Jack and Belle too. The wagon was stuck where it was until they could find the team.

Charlotte and Emma rode next to Paul. Fred seemed to sense he was to keep pace with Buck. Paul refused to leave his daughter or Charlotte alone at camp to go after the horses. Right now, he didn't want them out of his sight.

Charlotte wrapped an arm around Emma, who clung to the saddle horn in front of her. Paul stared into the open field. Charlotte glanced at his furrowed brow and set jaw. She recognized that look of concentration. She waited a moment and then patted his arm. "Paul, let's try again in the morning. It's too dark to find anything. Emma needs to have supper. Let's go back now."

"Papa, I am hungry. But we can keep looking if you want to." She gave him a hesitant half smile.

He nodded. "Lottie's right, honey. It's too dark now.

We'll go back." He led the way back to the wagon, keeping an eye out for signs of danger.

Deserted. Eerie. Charlotte's hands trembled as they rode close to the wagon. Her body felt weak. She needed to be strong. For Emma. For Paul. She missed Charlie's happy greeting when any one of them returned to camp. She missed Bernie with his big sad eyes and slow smile. He always kept a watch on Paul, and Charlotte had come to depend on his steadfast devotion to his boss.

Paul lifted Emma down and then helped Charlotte dismount. His quick embrace let her know she could count on him.

"I'll unsaddle and tie the horses and get them grain. You get a fire started and we'll fix supper." Paul led Buck and Fred to the other side of the wagon. He'd keep the horses close. He didn't want to lose their only means of transportation.

Charlotte and Emma gathered wood, and after the fire burned down to white coals, she hung the coffeepot on the tripod. Taking a quick inventory, Charlotte noted the essential items they'd need to replace.

Startled by crackling sounds, Charlotte spun around to stare at two puppies dashing toward camp. Prince and Spots raced round and round, barking and leaping up and down.

Emma squealed at the sight of them. "Charlotte, look. Here they are." She pointed at the dogs, plopped on the ground and called them to her. They leaped into her lap and snuggled close, licking her face and wagging their tails.

"They must have run off to look for us." Charlotte

wished the pups could lead them to Charlie, Bernie and Zeke. She found the sacks of fruit and vegetables Charlie had stored inside the wagon, along with the cheese Paul had purchased from Hattie McClain. The jar of pickled hard-boiled eggs Charlie had prepared the other day was sitting next to the cheese. Thankfully the thieves didn't take time to rummage around inside the wagon. At least they still had a bit of food for a few days.

Emma washed the carrots and radishes. Charlotte cut the vegetables and sliced the hard-boiled eggs, then some cheese and one apple.

Croaking frogs and singing crickets serenaded their meal, tempering the awkward silence.

After they ate, Charlotte took the lantern inside the wagon and read to Emma, Prince and Spots nestled at her side. Two chapters later Emma slept peacefully. Charlotte climbed down and strolled to the campfire.

Paul poured a cup of coffee and motioned for her to sit next to him. They watched the flames flicker and soar, vying to tap the hanging pot.

"I don't know what to think, Charlotte. What has become of my men? And my horses? Where are they? Common thieves couldn't get far with a herd of horses without being noticed. Those horses are all branded too. The horses couldn't be sold until the brand was changed on each horse. That would take time. They'd need a place to stash the herd for a while. And why take my men? I sure hope no harm has come to them." He took off his hat and rubbed his neck.

She felt helpless. What could she do? She prayed silently, asking how to help Paul. She laid a hand on his shoulder. "I know the Lord is faithful and I believe He will help you find the men and your herd. We can pray for their safety, if you'd like?"

Without a word, he clutched both her hands, bowed his head and closed his eyes, "Lord we ask You to keep Charlie, Bernie and Zeke safe in the palm of Your hand. We pray for wisdom in locating our horses. Please keep my wife and my daughter and myself safe too. Thank You, Lord." When Charlotte started to take her hands from his, he held on.

Charlotte, jittery from his touch, couldn't bring herself to pull away from Paul at that moment. She longed to comfort him—wished to hug him, run her hand through his sandy hair and whisper in his ear that all would be fine in time. But would it? She wasn't sure. It occurred to her she needed to trust the Lord in all things also.

Instead of hugging him, she leaned in and brushed against his shoulder. "It's too bad Zeke isn't around. Remember he said he worked on a ranch near here. Maybe he'd know where we could search for your horses and the men too." She touched his hand.

Paul leaned his cheek close to her head. Charlotte felt a quiet, rhythmic, powerful strength with each breath he took. Her stomach churned. Hmm, she hadn't eaten any of Charlie's cooking. Why were her insides in an uproar again?

Paul straightened his shoulders, then raised her hands to his lips and kissed them. He gazed at her, his breath coming in spurts. "Lottie, my Lottie. That might be our first clue." He grinned.

She raised her brows, shrugged and shook her head. "How can that be?"

He squeezed her hands, stood and pulled her up too. "My smart little Lottie Moon."

"Paul, what are you talking about?"

He faced her. "It's Zeke. Zeke knows something. Or maybe he has something to do with my missing horses. Zeke is the one who suggested we go to Rattlesnake Falls for a picnic. He knew how long it would take. Enough time to get the herd away from here before we got back. And if he worked in this area, he knows where to hide a band of horses. But why mess with Bernie and Charlie? That doesn't make sense." He frowned.

"Maybe he didn't take them. Do you think Charlie and Bernie could be part of the theft?"

Paul shook his head. "Not Bernie. He's been with me since our days at the orphanage. No one is more loyal. Charlie's reputation is outstanding in these parts. All the ranchers want him to come work for them."

He paused, running his fingers through his hair. "I don't think Charlie would be part of this. I hired Zeke about two days after I decided to take the herd south to sell. He's one of those drifter cowboys. Moves from ranch to ranch. County to county. Works awhile and then moves on. I needed one more man to help on this trip and Frank Kenny, the banker, said he knew a cow-boy who needed work. I don't think Zeke could pull off stealing the herd by himself, though. If it is him, I bet he's got partners."

Charlotte sighed and let go of Paul's hands. "Does a banker meet many temporary cowboys?" Charlotte tilted her head as she refilled her coffee cup and Paul's.

Paul frowned. "Come to think of it, it's mighty curious that Frank would be acquainted with a drifter. Those fellows don't use banks. They keep their money with 'em." He shook his head.

Charlotte wrapped her fingers around her cup. "What can we do? There are two of us and we can't endanger Emma. We'll have to go into town and find the sheriff."

"Next town is at the edge of the canyon. Pine Creek. We'll go there in the morning and talk to the sheriff. We'll report the missing men and horses."

Charlotte put her cup down. "We better turn in. Then we can get an earlier start." She took his hands in hers and looked into his sad blue eyes. "We'll find them. All of them. The men and the horses. We have to trust the Lord."

He nodded. "You're right. Thanks, Lottie."

Merchants unlocked their shops and opened their doors as Paul, Emma and Charlotte rode through town. Charlotte pointed to a mercantile store with dresses and hats in the window. "Do you think we could stop there after we visit the sheriff?"

Paul grinned. This woman liked to shop. It was a pleasure watching her face light up when she found something special. Usually it wasn't for herself. She was excited to get the new hat with the pretty blue ribbons for Emma. She was teaching Emma how to care for her bonnet and her clothes. He admired Charlotte's childlike trust in the Lord. He hadn't expressed his doubts last night when she'd assured him they had to trust God to find his men and his horses.

When Rachel ran off and left him with Emma, his trust in the Lord had plummeted. Why did God allow that to happen? Paul continued to go to church and pray, but doubts plagued him off and on. All those uncertainties had multiplied when Charlotte arrived. How could the Lord have sent him someone as beautiful and smart and caring as Charlotte? God knew his struggle with this type of woman. He had specifically prayed for a plain, middle-aged female to care for Emma. And why had God allowed Widow Miller to abandon him so he'd have to marry Charlotte to make this trip? How could the Lord have let his men and his horses disappear?

It felt like a cinch tightened around his chest. He yearned to trust God in all situations, but too many unanswered questions left him perplexed and doubtful.

Paul stopped Buck in front of the Sheriff's Office, dismounted and lifted Emma down. He tied Buck and then helped Charlotte, who straightened her hat and skirt. She fixed Emma's tilted bonnet and then walked with Paul through the door.

The sheriff sat hunched behind a large wooden desk. He'd looked up when the door opened. His silky white hair touched his ears and his white mustache curled up at the ends, like Charlie's black mustache. His dark eyes scrutinized his visitors.

"Hi there. I'm Sheriff Wylie. What can I do for you folks?"

Paul stepped forward and introduced all of them. He explained the situation with his missing men and herd of horses. Charlotte took Emma's hand and moved over to gaze at the wall lined with Wanted notices. So many desperados—there were even a few women.

Suddenly she threw one hand over her mouth to stifle the whoop about to escape. There she was! On a Wanted poster. Charlotte recognized the duplicate of the portrait her aunt had commissioned when she'd turned eighteen. Huge bold letters declared "WANTED: Charlotte Carpenter. Runaway. REWARD: $2,000. Contact local authorities if you see her."

She went quickly to Paul and touched his arm.

"Excuse me, Paul." He turned to her. "I'll take Emma to that shop we saw when we came into town. Meet us there when you're finished."

She turned to leave.

"Just a minute, Lottie."

She froze. Had he seen the poster too? She closed her eyes and took a deep breath, then pivoted and smiled at him.

"You'll need money." He chuckled and handed her several folded bills. She thanked him and hurried out the door, delighted he'd called her Lottie and not Charlotte.

"You know how women like to shop," Paul said.

"Yup. They sure do. One of my wife's favorite pastimes." The sheriff grinned.

Paul had noted Charlotte's panicked look when she spoke to him. He'd have to find out why later.

Sheriff Wylie took notes from Paul's descriptions. He asked questions, and his answers reflected he'd paid attention to Paul. "Rattlesnake Falls is a right nice place for a picnic. I have an idea where you might be camped." His fingers pulled at an invisible beard on his chin.

"Why don't you take a look at some of these Wanted posters." He pointed to the wall lined with notices. "See if you find anyone who looks like this Zeke fellow or any of those other men you mentioned. They might be wanted on some other charges. Could be using a different name now. I'll send a telegraph and notify the sheriff in the bordering counties to be on the lookout for stolen horses."

The sheriff plopped on his hat and opened the door to leave. "I'll do my best to help you, Mr. Harrison. I don't like these things happening in my territory." He walked out the door.

Paul studied the posters pinned on the wall. Not one looked like Zeke or the other rustlers they'd taken to jail. He noticed several with pictures of women and thought it was curious. He couldn't imagine a woman being a wanted person. Most of them looked wild or plain worn-out.

One poster of a beautiful young woman captured his attention. Her hair was piled on top of her head, the way Charlotte had worn her hair that first day and set off a whirlwind of emotions in his life. The woman's eyes looked a bit mischievous. Her dress was elegant with lacy sleeves. Several strands of pearls hung round her neck, and fancy earrings dangled from her ears. This was a high-society woman.

He leaned closer for a better look. This was…his Charlotte.

He couldn't read the words, but it was his Lottie. Why was her picture on a Wanted notice? What had she done? Was she a thief? Had she killed someone?

How had he put his beloved Emma in the hands of a

wanted person? Should he wait for the sheriff and ask him what the poster said? Was this why Charlotte had hurried out the door with that wild look in her eye?

Paul ripped the poster off the wall, folded it and stuffed it into his shirt pocket. Then he strode out the door, untied Buck and Fred and led them down Main Street to the mercantile. He needed to walk, to think, to clear his mind. He couldn't believe his Lottie was a wanted woman. She was kind and caring. So good with Emma. She tried hard to learn new things. He'd even begun to trust her—to open his heart to her. To care about her and to think about a friendship with her, even after they annulled their marriage. To hope she would continue tutoring Emma. Was a possible criminal teaching his daughter?

He kicked at a stone in the dirt road.

Maybe she'd reformed. Maybe this was from a long time ago and she'd quit her dishonest behavior?

Was he that bad a judge of character? All he had to do was remember he'd married Rachel.

Why had the Lord let him marry a lawbreaker? He'd prayed hard before deciding to hire a caretaker for Emma…and before marrying Charlotte. What kind of mess had he gotten himself into, trying to save his ranch for Emma's sake? Had he endangered all of them by marrying her and bringing her along on this trip?

Another alarming thought—did she have anything to do with the disappearance of his men and herd of horses? Had she purposely cast suspicion on Zeke and Charlie? She was smart and clever. Could she secretly be part of some gang? Was she like Belle Starr, the horse thief?

Chapter Seventeen

Paul looped Fred's and Buck's reins around the hitching rail in front of the mercantile. He strode up the steps and glanced in the window. A young man guided an older woman around barrels loaded with beans and rice. Charlotte, in her brown skirt and brown-striped blouse, with her gloved hands and plumed hat and silk reticule, was the most beautiful woman in the store. Right beside her was his darling Emma in her dark blue dress with the white collar and sash tied in a perfect bow. A little lady in the making. His heart swelled with pride.

He watched Charlotte hand the man at the counter several of the bills he'd given her. Two packages wrapped in the usual brown paper and tied with brown string sat on the counter.

She gathered the packages, took Emma's hand and walked out the door. She bit her lip when she saw him waiting. How could this lovely creature, this kind lady, be on a Wanted poster? She'd been honorable with him and Emma so far.

She'd acted with more decency than Emma's own

mother had. Charlotte was always thoughtful with Emma. She'd protected her on more than one occasion. Perhaps he should wait before he jumped to conclusions. Maybe her crime wasn't serious.

If she was his friend, like Bernie, what would his response be? Didn't a friend stick with you in the troublesome times as well as the good ones? He'd have to continue to trust Charlotte with his daughter, but he'd be on the lookout for any change in her behavior.

Emma rushed to Paul. He picked her up and swung her around, and she took her little hands and turned his face to hers. "Papa, Papa, Charlotte bought me a beautiful doll. It has real curly brown hair and brown eyes that close and a pretty yellow dress with a white bonnet, and she has black shoes too." She turned to Charlotte. "Can I show it to him?"

"Let's wait 'til we get back to camp, Emma," Paul answered. He carried Emma down the steps to the horses. He clutched Buck's reins as he lifted her onto the saddle and straightened her dark blue dress. He took the packages from Charlotte and held Fred's bridle while Charlotte mounted, and then handed her the bundle and the reins without saying one word. He needed time to think. And pray.

On the ride back to camp, Paul was aware that Charlotte once again had purchased something for Emma but nothing for herself. Rachel was never like that. Rachel would buy herself a new hat or gloves or a fancy comb for her hair but never think to get anything for Emma.

Did Charlotte pretend to be generous and kind as part of her masquerade? He shook his head. He knew

he wasn't a good judge of women. He glanced at her—
especially beautiful women.

He had been so wrong about Rachel. He'd thought
Rachel at least liked him. He'd known she didn't love
him. She'd told him so and he'd married her anyway.
She was very pretty and he'd felt incredibly grateful
that a man like him, an orphan without a family or con-
nections, could marry someone as beautiful as Rachel.

Emma came along the first year. After that, Rachel
wanted nothing more to do with him. He'd been hurt
by her rejection and all her complaining. He even practiced tuning her out. Since Emma captured his heart
from the moment she was born, he'd devoted himself
to her. She became his focus. He never dreamed Rachel would leave her own daughter. He had not seen
that one coming. He gazed at Charlotte again. Was he
wrong about this woman too?

Be logical, he told himself. *Look at the facts.* What
proof did he have that she was unreliable? What evidence could he examine? Charlotte's actions toward
Emma and him were honorable. There had never been
a hint of anything but kindness and thoughtfulness toward his little girl. In fact, he was real sure Charlotte
liked Emma a lot.

She didn't complain about things either. She hummed
or sang when doing chores and loved to include Emma
when it was appropriate.

Hmm. She did have a temper, though. Mostly directed at him. If she believed he was bossing her or bul-
lying her, she'd resist and spit out a whole slew of words
meant to stop him immediately. Some of the words he
understood, others he'd only guessed at their meaning.

Paul chuckled. Charlotte had strong opinions on marriage and men too. But still, her dealings with Emma and his men—and even the puppies—had all been kind. As a rule, she'd been considerate and sympathetic with him also.

Paul was confused. How could he sort this out without help? The Wanted poster was burning a hole in his pocket and resurrecting wounds in his heart.

Charlotte started to speak as they rode along. Paul said in a stern voice, "I don't want to talk now, Charlotte. I have a lot on my mind." He moved Buck well ahead of her and didn't look back to see her response.

He'd have to leave Emma in her care when they got back so he could search again for his horses and his men. He couldn't take Emma and further endanger her life if there were scoundrels to deal with. He'd trusted Charlotte until now and it had worked out. He wished he'd never seen that poster. It haunted him.

Had she stolen jewelry or money from someone back East? Had she repented and reformed since that poster went up? She was a praying woman, after all.

She had acted like she was escaping something, though. Running from someone. She hadn't shared much about her circumstances on her application. Widow Miller hadn't told Paul anything he should be aware of before he hired Charlotte and sent the money for the tickets. The school district had employed her also. They must have checked into her background as well as her college degree. He didn't feel so stupid. If he'd been fooled, the school officials had been too. And they could read.

When he rode into camp Paul breathed a sigh of relief. He dismounted, helped Emma down and tied Buck to the wagon. He took the packages from Charlotte but didn't assist her in dismounting from the horse. If she was surprised, she didn't react. She tied Fred next to Buck.

"Should I grain the horses or start on our noon meal?" she asked without looking at him. She untied Emma's bonnet and took off her own hat, laying them on the wagon bench seat.

"I'll take care of the horses. You get the meal." Paul strode to the grain sack and filled the feedbags. Charlotte and Emma gathered kindling and started a fire.

Paul pondered his situation while he unsaddled the horses, and he prayed. It was a three-day ride to Lyonsville. That was alone on horseback, not including a herd of horses, a wagon and a woman and child.

Now he didn't have a herd to take to Lyonsville. He sat on a log and dropped his head into his hands. Would he lose the ranch after all? He'd worked hard to save it. He'd even taken another wife—a beautiful woman—against his better judgment. He wanted Emma to have what he didn't have. Security. A home. Somewhere to belong and to feel loved every day. He'd taken a huge risk for Emma's security.

If he had no horses to sell, he couldn't pay the debt on his ranch. He had to find his herd. He'd have to trust Charlotte for a while longer—and he'd have to trust the Lord. He asked God to help him…for Emma's sake.

Paul walked to the worktable where Charlotte cut out biscuits. He watched her arrange them in the Dutch oven and set it aside. Emma was busy showing Prince and Spots her new doll.

Since none of the fellows were around, Paul decided to ask Charlotte about teaching him to read. He was desperate to understand that poster. He hated to admit he didn't know how, but since she wouldn't be his wife after the annulment, he thought she could at least teach him to read before they parted ways.

"Dinner's ready!" Charlotte called as she dished up the eggs, biscuits and bacon. Emma laid her doll on the log and came to get her plate.

Paul looked over at Charlotte. "I want to ask you something." She looked up at him, her expression unreadable. He knew she was confused by his grumpy behavior toward her.

Without a smile, she nodded. "Ask."

He shoved his hands deeper in his pockets and took a breath. "I can't read. Can you teach me?" He stared at her, his heart skipping a beat or two. A sweat broke out on his forehead and he pushed his hat back on his head.

"I never learned. I can write my name, but I don't know the names of all the letters in it. The orphanage started hiring me out when I was young. I was a stinker in the classroom, and the teachers couldn't make me behave. The other boys followed my example and then the whole group would get rowdy. I didn't go to school much. Guess it was easier on the teachers when I wasn't there. I was a good worker, and the home needed the money the ranchers paid for my labor." He bowed his head.

She wouldn't be his wife much longer, and he didn't know if they'd continue their friendship after they annulled this marriage. Right now, his desire to read that poster outweighed his embarrassment at not being able to.

* * *

Charlotte searched his deep blue eyes. This tough and tender cowboy couldn't read? He could sure do a lot of other things. He spoke well, unlike other cowboys—including Bernie and Charlie. She'd have to ask him about that. Was this why he'd acted so ornery? Was he having a hard time admitting he was illiterate? He wanted her help, but he'd been afraid to ask?

Relief. She almost smiled. He couldn't have read the Wanted poster in the sheriff's office even if he'd seen it. He wouldn't know she'd only run away, even though her aunt had implied she was a criminal. Like she'd stolen something or hurt someone. Her heart had almost stopped when she spotted the posters She'd been glad Paul didn't want to talk on the way home.

Every time Charlotte thought about Paul reading the notice, bile rose in her throat, choking her. Befuddled thoughts of how to respond to him when he questioned her about it had paced round and round in her mind since they'd left town.

She'd had no idea he couldn't read. He covered it up well. No wonder he knew how to do so many things—he'd been working since he was little. A piece of her heart ached for the little boy who'd never even had a chance to learn all the letters in his name. She'd make sure that didn't happen in her classroom. Everyone should be able to read.

Charlotte sipped her coffee. "I could do that. Do you want to study with Emma or have private lessons?"

"Since I'll be busy during the daytime, after the evening meal would be best. I wouldn't like the boys to know I'm having reading lessons. I've been ashamed my whole life." Paul glanced at the ground and then back at Charlotte.

"After Emma goes to bed we could take a lantern and go off by ourselves. They'd think it was 'cause we wanted to be alone as husband and wife." His face reddened at the mention of their situation.

"Sounds reasonable. Can you tell me what you do know?" Charlotte forked another bite of her eggs and bacon. She'd need to discern where to start with Paul.

"Like I said, I know how to write my name, and I know some of the letters."

"When do you want to start?"

"Tonight, when I get back from looking for my herd and my men."

He got up, strode to the wagon, put his dishes in the pan and walked around to untie Buck.

"I'm going out to search for the horses. I'll leave you the rifle. Don't hesitate to use it. Keep Emma safe." He took the firearm from the scabbard and handed it to her, mounted and rode off.

Charlotte laid the gun on the worktable and filled the pan with water, then she and Emma washed and dried the dishes.

"Emma, let's get the McGuffey Reader and practice. You can read to your new doll. What are you going to name her?"

The red-haired little girl smiled up at her. She held her new doll in the air and said, "Lucy. Isn't Lucy a cute name for this doll?"

"Lucy's a perfect name. I like it." Charlotte patted the doll's back.

She had Emma recite the alphabet and read some

words she wrote in the dirt, and then she took out the reader. Emma held it like an important object and proceeded to sound her way through several pages.

Charlotte heard movement in the brush outside their camp area, near the front of the wagon. It wasn't horse hooves. It was more like a critter crawling through scrub, trying to sneak up on them. Prince started to bark and dashed toward the noise. The puppy imitated him with loud yipping. Was it another mountain lion? Charlie had advised her to watch out for wild pigs too.

She hurried Emma to the wheel of the wagon and boosted her inside. "Keep hidden. Put some bedrolls in front of you. Be really quiet. You can play with your doll. Don't call out. Wait until your Papa or I come to get you. Understand?" Emma's eyes got big, but she nodded.

Charlotte went back and stood at the worktable next to the rifle. She peeled potatoes and watched the brush. Prince and Spots wouldn't quit barking. They ran in the direction of the noise and then back to her. Could it be a jackrabbit or a stray calf—or something else? Ever since the encounter with those thieves and the night of the mountain lion, she'd been suspicious of any unexpected company, human or beast.

A man dragged himself out from under the brush. Charlotte picked up the rifle and aimed it at him.

"Stop. Don't come any closer. Get on out of here. Go on!" she commanded in a loud, authoritative voice. The man didn't move. He lay in the dirt with his head on his arms.

A second man crawled from under the bushes and

fell beside the first man. Dust covered both men's faces. Their hair was matted and plastered to their scalps.

"Missy… Missy," a weak voice called. "It's us. Don't shoot."

One man pushed himself up. Dirt coated his shirt and pants and he wore no shoes. He bent down and lifted the other man up beside him. Arms draped around each other's shoulders, they stepped forward.

Charlotte's heart pounded. "Stop! I said stop!" she shouted, moving toward them with the gun aimed at their foreheads.

"Miz Charlotte…"

She paused and stared at the men.

"Charlie? Bernie?"

Charlotte set down the rifle and ran to them. Their faces were bruised and cut, and their clothes were filthy. Their bare feet were scratched.

"Oh, dear. Oh, my," she said, her arms wrapped around them as they staggered toward the wagon.

"Sit, sit here. Let me get you some water." She ran to the wagon and called, "Emma, come help me!"

Charlotte filled water cups, handing one to Emma and carrying one herself.

Bernie and Charlie gulped the water. In their haste, a lot dribbled down the front of their shirts. Charlotte refilled the vessels and wet two rags. She wiped at their faces and hands.

"What happened?"

Chapter Eighteen

Charlotte stared long and hard at the two of them. Bernie's shirtsleeves were torn at the shoulders and on the back side. His jeans were dirt stained; the rear pockets ripped. Maybe he'd tried to crawl under a barbed wire fence? The front of Charlie's red plaid shirt was ragged, like someone had grabbed hold at the collar and pulled hard enough to tear the buttons off.

She managed to wash most of the dirt from their faces and feet. Both of them had gashes on top of their heads.

"Maybe we should trim the hair around those cuts on your head, Bernie," Charlotte suggested. "It might need stitches."

"No. No, ma'am. I ain't gonna have no bald spot in the middle of my head. Put a little medicine on it. I'll be fine." He stared at the ground. Charlotte let it go for now. She'd talk to Paul later. He might have more influence with Bernie.

Charlie said, "I brought along some of that new Cloverine Salve. Those hooligans wrecked the chuck box again. I don't know where it is now. Maybe you could look for it, Miz Charlotte?" He shook his head, his eyes full of pain.

Charlotte searched through the demolished chuck box. In one of the bottom drawers she found the round tin and applied the soothing balm on their facial scrapes and scalps, but they insisted on doctoring their own feet.

Her eyes misted as she heaped beans and biscuits on two plates and got them cups of coffee. Emma trotted over and hugged Bernie's neck. "I'm sorry, Uncle Bernie. I hope you get better real soon. And you too, Mr. Charlie." The men teared up.

"We should wait for Paul before you tell us what happened. That way you can tell it once and save your energy." Charlotte raised her eyebrows toward Emma to let them know she didn't want the child frightened.

"Good idea, Miz Charlotte," Charlie whispered.

"More time for coffee and grub," Bernie agreed.

Their faces drooped when they handed her the plates and cups.

"You two rest until Paul comes back. Emma and I will get your bedrolls."

Charlotte wondered about Zeke. She was afraid to ask if he'd been too wounded to make it back to camp. Charlie and Bernie followed her to the shade tree without a word, grateful to lie down and close their eyes.

Taking Emma's hand, she said, "We'll have to be still and keep the puppies calm too. Quiet as deer in the forest. Okay?"

"I can hush, but Spots and Prince don't mind sometimes." Emma skipped along, holding tight to Charlotte's hand.

"We'll help them remember." Charlotte squeezed her hand. She marveled at the joy it gave her taking care of Emma. Why hadn't her aunt ever expressed pleasure in being part of Charlotte's life?

Her heart ached as she thought of the void that would be in her life when she and Paul parted company.

Humph. No use borrowing tomorrow's trouble. She wouldn't think about that right now.

"Emma, come roll out the biscuit dough," she called.

Charlotte finished peeling the potatoes, added carrots and the meat chunks, poured in the broth and hoisted the stewpot to the tripod hook. What had happened to Bernie and Charlie? Did they know where the horses were? Did they know where Zeke was? She had so many questions.

As she set the Dutch oven in the coals, Charlotte heard the sound of hooves and moved toward the rifle.

It was her husband. Paul. He and his horse moved as one. Tall and strong and handsome with that Stetson tipped a bit forward, hiding his deep blue eyes. Her heart skipped.

She hurried to him. As he dismounted, she whispered, "Bernie and Charlie are back. They're pretty beat up. They're resting over there in the shade." She pointed to the big oak tree.

Emma rushed to her daddy, her finger tapping her lips as she said, "Shh, shh." The dogs trailed behind her.

Paul glanced at the men, swung his daughter around and said, "Hello, gingersnap." He kissed the top of her head.

He looked at Charlotte as he asked, "What happened?"

"I don't know. I asked them to wait to tell us together." Charlotte nodded in Emma's direction. "Later."

"Yeah," Paul agreed.

"Supper's almost ready. I thought I'd let them sleep until it's time to eat. Did you find any sign of your horses?" she asked, strolling beside him toward the wagon.

"Yeah. I tracked them for a while, then I lost the trail. Since it's almost dark, I came back. Maybe the boys will have information that'll help me find the herd."

"Zeke isn't with them."

Paul's eyebrows arched and he frowned. "That's curious." He turned his attention to his daughter, still in his arms. "What did you do today, my sweet little dove?"

Emma smiled at him when he looked at her. He set her down and walked hand in hand with her to the washbasin. Charlotte's heart melted. Paul's love for his daughter was endearing. She'd never seen him lose his temper with her or criticize her. When she watched him brush her hair at night and listened to him recite the lyric about a hundred strokes, she almost cried.

She envied Emma's blessings, growing up with such loving kindness. Her aunt was not the doting type. She'd raised Charlotte out of a sense of duty and obligation. She'd never enjoyed Charlotte and she'd resented the time it took to raise her brother's child.

Emma's face lit up and her eyes twinkled. "We practiced my letters and some words, and I read in the reader. Charlotte says I'm doing good, Papa." Paul kissed her cheek.

Charlotte smiled at Paul. "She's very smart. She's

learned her letters quickly and is reading the primer very well."

Emma went on. "Then I hid in the wagon. I was real quiet, just like Charlotte told me to be. The doggies were bad, though. They kept barking. But Lucy and I were quiet."

"Lucy? Who's Lucy?" Paul's forehead wrinkled.

"My new doll, Papa. You remember. Charlotte bought her for me in town."

He nodded. "How could I forget?"

Paul stared at Charlotte with a quizzical look. "Why was she hiding in the wagon?"

Charlotte carried the stewpot to the worktable and retrieved the Dutch oven full of biscuits.

"Emma, will you please make sure Prince and Spots have food in their dish and that there is water in their pan?" Emma trotted off to take care of her chores.

"I heard movement in the brush, and I wanted Emma to be safe. So I had her hide like she did when the thieves came. But it was Bernie and Charlie who crawled out from under the bushes."

His blue eyes showed concern, but he didn't move near to comfort her. Not like he had in the past. "Thanks for taking care of Emma. You must have been scared."

She shivered. It was like a frigid breeze had followed them from town and enveloped them in an icy standoff. Perhaps he was overwrought about his missing men and horses. Or perhaps he realized, as she had, that in less than two weeks they'd no longer be together. No longer a family. He wouldn't be by her side. They wouldn't be husband and wife.

"Not as frightened as the other time. Since you

taught me to shoot, I feel more confident. Although I'm not proficient, I feel better equipped to handle some emergencies. Like, if it had been a mountain lion or a bear or a wild pig. Thank you for teaching me to shoot." She smiled at him.

"You're welcome." He turned and walked toward Bernie and Charlie.

He was still polite. He hadn't forgotten his manners. There was just a chilly wall between them. *Maybe this is easier*, Charlotte thought. They'd keep their distance. No more touching hands, no quick hugs, no lingering looks. Yes, this was better. She'd be leaving and she'd miss all of them. But she'd be on her way to fulfilling her dream.

She didn't want to be married. She didn't want a family, she reminded herself. She'd be busy setting up her classroom and would be teaching in no time. This rugged, handsome, caring cowboy with his adorable redheaded little daughter would no longer sidetrack her. She sighed and swiped at a tear gliding down her cheek.

After supper Emma and the puppies climbed into the wagon and dozed off before Charlotte could finish the story.

Paul took coffee to Bernie and Charlie, and Charlotte brought a bowl of hot rice pudding for each of them.

Paul yanked off his hat and ran his fingers through his hair as he sat down on one of the logs surrounding the campfire. "Boys, I'm sure sorry you got roughed up. What happened?"

Bernie's sad eyes drooped. He hung his head and coughed. "Boss, I wanna say I'm sorry I lost the herd and got captured by those scoundrels. That rattlesnake, Zeke, were part of 'em."

"Zeke?" Paul's head shot up. "What do you mean?"

"He helped 'em. He laughed about sending you and the missus and baby girl off on a picnic. Said it was perfect timing, and sure enough, in rode those three varmints. Right into camp. Zeke held us at gunpoint and ordered them crooks to get the herd to their hideout." Bernie shook his head and took a sip of coffee.

Charlie smiled at Charlotte. "Mighty fine rice puddin', Missy. Ya done good."

"You're a good teacher, Charlie." Charlotte grinned.

"Boss—" Charlie caught Paul's eyes "—those hooligans talked about somebody named Frank. Like they was doin' this so's they could get paid by that Frank fella. You know a Frank?" Charlie asked.

Paul got up, poured more coffee, and paced round and round the circle of logs. "I know only one Frank. Frank Kenny. The banker in Cedar Grove. They must be talking about a different Frank."

Charlotte picked up the empty plates and took them to the dishpan. "Do you boys know where the hideout is?"

"They blindfolded us," Charlie grumbled.

"We could hear the falls, though. It's gotta be somewhere near 'nough to hear the waterfall." Bernie smiled. "We could start at the falls and circle out until we maybe got a clue."

Paul looked earnestly at Bernie. "That's a good idea. Be a whole lot easier if we had more horses. Gonna make it harder when a couple of us have to be on foot."

He paused and stared at both of them. "How did you boys get away, anyway?"

Bernie frowned. "You wanna hear the whole kit and caboodle or just the particulars?"

"Let's start with the important facts," Paul stated. He hoped to quickly determine the degree of difficulty they'd overcome.

After Bernie and Charlie turned in for the night, Charlotte retrieved the big tablet and asked Paul if he wanted to start his reading lessons. He nodded, took a lantern and followed Charlotte several feet from the camp.

She sat down on a log and motioned for him to sit next to her. He hesitated. His mind grew jumbled when he got too close to her. He'd decided to keep his distance before he'd discovered the poster, but now he had to. Until he could read that flyer and find out why his wife was on it.

She'd written the alphabet for Emma on the tablet and asked him to read the letters he knew. When he finished, Charlotte pointed to them one at a time, said the names and showed him how each letter made a different sound. She wrote simple words for him that rhymed, like *run*, *sun*, *fun* and *gun*. Then she wrote an easy sentence using those words and asked him to read it. Before they called it quits, she asked him to read the letters and say their sounds once more. After, she mentioned that he'd learned six new letters in one lesson and she thought he'd be reading in no time.

On the way back to the wagon, Paul almost danced. He wanted to hug her. For the first time in his life, he'd been able to see the letters were different and remember their sounds. He'd been able to read a sentence—a small sentence, but he'd read it.

He felt like he could walk on clouds. He wanted to lift her in the air and swing her round and round…and kiss her.

No. Stop. No. Wait a minute. She was practically his former wife. Only a friend.

After he said good-night, Paul took the lantern under the wagon and wrote the letters he knew in the dirt. He wrote the words he'd learned too. Then he took out the poster in his pocket.

Studying it, he decided the first bold word must be *wanted*. All the notices had the same big word, and everybody called them Wanted posters. Made sense.

He looked at the words underneath, which must be her name. He looked at the letters. He knew some of them. After her name, he could read part of the word *run*. He didn't know the rest of the word: *a-w-a-y*. Under that word was the amount of money she was worth. He'd never had trouble reading numbers.

He understood *$2,000*. That was a lot of money. He could use it to pay against the note on his ranch. Maybe he should turn her in and forget his horses? No, he wouldn't do that. It would break Emma's heart. She loved Charlotte. He'd have to remind Emma that Charlotte wouldn't be staying with them when they got back to Cedar Grove.

If he could read the next word on that poster, he'd know what she'd done to become a wanted person. Should he confront her? Would she tell him the truth? He wouldn't know unless he could read it.

Who'd put up such a huge reward? *Reward*. That

must be the word before *$2,000. I can read another word*, he mused. Paul was so excited, he jumped up, banged his head on the wagon bed and covered his mouth, stifling a cry of pain.

At last he wound down the wick in the lantern until the flame went out. He rolled onto his back, holding his aching head, and prayed that sleep would drown the thoughts and pictures that swam in circles, round and round in his mind: Charlotte's first attempt to start a fire and wash clothes. Charlotte hanging clothes on a line. Charlotte stomping her foot and slamming the bedroom door when he told her they couldn't take the tablet. Charlotte making biscuits into letter shapes, Charlotte reading the Bible in the evenings in her lovely soft voice. Charlotte skipping through meadows with Emma. Charlotte picking wildflowers with Emma. Charlotte's tears as she waved goodbye to Hattie McClain. Charlotte's patience in teaching Emma to read. Charlotte's kindness when teaching him to read. No words of criticism, no words of scorn.

Charlotte driving the team through the river. Charlotte hiding Emma from the thieves. Charlotte learning to shoot. Charlotte's smile. Charlotte's laughter. Charlotte's fiery green eyes when he got her riled up or when he bossed her too much. How those same emerald eyes filled with compassion and tears when warranted. Charlotte's sun-kissed hair cascading down her back. Charlotte's fresh rose scent when she leaned in close to him. Charlotte in his arms, making his heart pound and his pulse race.

Charlotte monopolized his thoughts. How could this beautiful creature…his wife…be leaving him so soon?

Chapter Nineteen

"**P**aul, are you okay?" Charlotte looked at him. He rubbed his eyes. The lantern hanging on the pole glowed radiantly. He blinked and ambled toward the worktable. He didn't feel rested. He knew his hat was cockeyed but didn't bother to adjust it. Paul rolled his shirtsleeves without answering her question.

"Did you have a hard night?" she asked. Still he plodded on without a word.

He poured coffee from the pot over the campfire. Should he tell her it was her fault? Thoughts of her had stampeded through his mind all night long. He glanced up and his eyes met hers.

"Yeah. Wasn't good. Didn't get much sleep."

"I'm sorry," she said as she expertly added flour and a little canned milk to the sourdough starter. She patted the dough into a mound, rolled it and cut out the biscuits, adding them one at a time to the Dutch oven. Charlie had taught her well. It helped that she was an adept student, willing to practice until she mastered a skill.

"Will you search for the horses again today?" Charlotte plopped the lid on the cast-iron kettle.

"Yeah. I hope Bernie feels like going with me. Maybe we can circle out from the falls like he suggested." His eyes drifted to the bedroll occupied by Bernie.

"They're pretty scraped up. I wonder how they ever escaped." Charlotte carried the Dutch oven to the fire and snuggled it into the coals, heaping more on top. She used the rag to grab the handle of the coffeepot and poured another cup for Paul and one for herself.

The sun, a dark orange sphere, peeked over the mountaintop, illuminating the sky like a shimmering pumpkin.

Charlotte glanced up and took a deep breath. "I love mornings when the sun explodes in the sky." She smiled and hummed a tune on her way back to the worktable.

Paul's foggy brain imagined himself and Charlotte side by side with their morning coffee, reveling in God's glorious creation.

He stopped himself and turned away. *She isn't staying. She has another dream.* One that didn't include him and Emma or ranch life.

"Mornin' Boss. Mornin' Miz Charlotte." Bernie staggered to the campfire. Charlotte handed him a cup of the steaming brew.

"Do you feel better this morning, Bernie?" she asked, her eyes full of compassion as she peered at the gash on his head.

He took a sip and tried to smile, but his lips drooped. "Well, Miz Charlotte, I ain't never been runned over by a freight train, but I'm thinkin' it might kinda feel like this."

"Oh, Bernie, I'm so sorry." She patted his arm. "Breakfast will be ready real soon."

Charlie rolled up his bed, stashed it under the wagon, hobbled to the worktable and grabbed his cup. "Lookin' like a good breakfast, Missy."

"Thanks, Charlie. I hope it is. If it isn't, just remember, you're the one who taught me. Are you feeling any better this morning?" She stopped midcut, held the knife in the air and looked up at him.

"Fair to middlin'." He shuffled to the coffeepot. Paul unhooked it and poured a cup for him.

"Boss, you look like you been rode hard and put away wet," Charlie commented.

"Bad night?" Bernie asked.

Paul pushed his hat back. "Yeah." He couldn't admit Charlotte had dominated his attention, not his absent herd. What kind of a rancher was he? A woman took priority over his lost livestock? Would she be his first thought in the morning and his last thought at night if they weren't parting company soon?

"Breakfast! Come and get it!" Charlotte called. They ambled to the worktable and scooped up bacon, biscuits, gravy and fried sugared apples.

"Fried apples?" Charlie winked at Charlotte.

"To celebrate your safe return," Charlotte explained, looking at Bernie and Charlie with a big smile.

Paul said, "If you feel up to it, Bernie, could you ride with me to search for the herd?" Bernie nodded.

"Charlie, can Bernie borrow Fred? I'd like you to stay here and keep an eye on Charlotte and Emma. That'd be helpful."

Charlotte sighed loudly, whirled and stomped to the front of the wagon muttering, "Does he think I can't protect Emma? I've already proved I can."

"Be glad to stay. Miz Charlotte don't need no help safeguarding Emma," Charlie remarked, "but I do need to rest. This old man is kinda tore up." He reached up to touch his bandaged head. "I gotta have some time to heal. I ain't as young as I used to be." He chuckled. "You two go on, and me and Miz Charlotte will mind the camp. Bernie, you're welcome to Fred." Charlie managed a half smile.

Paul deposited his dish and cup in the wash pan, then saddled Buck and Fred. Bernie rolled up his bed and joined Paul.

"We'll be back by supper." Paul and Bernie trotted off in the direction of the falls. Emma waved goodbye to her daddy while Charlotte scrubbed at the dish she held without looking at Paul.

On the trail to the waterfall Bernie searched for clues. Nothing. No identifying tracks, no broken branches where a herd of horses might have traveled. At the falls they rode in loops, distancing themselves farther and farther from the waterfall. Abruptly Bernie halted Fred.

"That's the sound." Bernie shifted in the saddle and cocked his head. "One of them guarded us. We had to wait around here while they moved the herd ahead of us. I remember the sound of the waterfall from here."

"Okay, good. Let's look around." Paul hunted for signs of a trail that an entire herd of horses could use. Nothing. Massive pockets of underbrush dotted the outlying area. He urged Buck forward alongside the bushes and saw a hacked-off fresh tree limb jutting out of a thicket. Curious, Paul moved closer. He discovered that what looked like an ordinary scrub-brush pile was actually a heap of chaparral stacked at angles to camouflage something. He dismounted and started pulling bushes to the side. When he'd thrown aside several big limbs, a pathway emerged that led upward into the rock formation ahead.

"Bernie, I think I found the direction they went."

He stared at his friend and asked, "Do you want to go on back to camp and rest? Let them know I'm on the trail of the thieves? I can scout this out and come back later and get you and Charlie."

"No, sir, Boss. I'm stickin' with you. You might need me." Bernie gave him a lopsided grin. Bernie's devotion to Paul was a sure thing Paul had repeatedly counted on. There would always be a place for Bernie in Paul's life.

"If we both get caught, how are we going to let the others know what's happened to us?" Paul asked.

"We'll escape like me and Charlie did. C'mon, daylight's burnin'." Bernie clicked to Fred, who stepped forward through the brush. Paul followed on Buck.

The trail meandered uphill through thickets and tall trees until rock outcroppings dominated the landscape.

"They kept me and Charlie in a dark shed. Whenever they let us out, they blindfolded us. I remember the shed was up a hill."

Paul encouraged Bernie to think of anything that might help them locate the thieves' hiding place.

"Maybe they don't even know we're gone yet. We heard them all ride off yesterday, a hootin' and a hollerin' about how much money they was gonna get. That's when me an' Charlie decided to break out."

Paul pondered the odds. It troubled him, Bernie and

him versus the four of them. And Bernie was hurt. No
other good option, though.

At the top of the hillside they stopped. A steep grade
led downward into a lush meadow surrounded by rock
hills. Down there in the volcanic-crater meadow, grazing as if they hadn't a care in the world, was Paul's entire herd.

"Bernie, you did it. You found the horses, and it's
not even noon yet. Look, there's the shack you must
have been kept in." Paul pointed to a small outbuilding
above one of the steep rock outcroppings.

Paul's best friend smiled and his sad eyes sparkled.
"Boss, we found 'em."

Paul started downhill. "Yeah. Now let's get them
outta here before those reprobates come back."

Charlie slept most of the morning. Charlotte and
Emma worked on reading lessons and then washed Bernie and Charlie's shirts and jeans. The picket line made
a perfect clothesline. Usually, the fellows did their own
laundry, but Charlotte had insisted she'd do their wash
until their wounds healed.

If she knew how to sew, she'd mend their torn shirts
and patch up their jeans. Once they were back in Cedar
Grove, perhaps the local seamstress could teach her to
repair clothes. She smiled. How grateful she was that
this school district did not ask for a teacher competent in
domestic arts. Charlotte would never have received the
appointment. However, she was now qualified to teach
a basic course in cooking, washing clothes and hitching
and driving a team. It'd be as easy as burning beans.

Charlie woke and Charlotte offered him a cup of coffee.

"Can you teach me to make a pie today?"

Charlie reached for the cup with a smile. "Sure." He sipped and ran his fingers through his hair, blinking. "Do we have apples or canned peaches?"

"Still have a few fresh apples. Should we peel them now?"

He sipped again and nodded. "About five apples should be enough."

Charlotte hopped up and called Emma over to the worktable. They put on their aprons and Emma wiped the apples off with a damp cloth. Charlotte peeled and cut. Emma poured sugar over the chopped apples, stirred and checked each piece to make sure it had an ample coating of the sweet white crystals.

Charlie hobbled over to the table to give Charlotte instructions on making the crust and on how to assemble it in the Dutch oven.

"Paul and Bernie will be surprised and happy to have an apple pie tonight." Charlotte's face beamed as she carried the cast-iron oven to the fire, centered it in the coals and heaped more on the lid.

Charlie gazed at her and smiled again. "It will be a fine treat, Missy."

"Charlotte, Charlotte, look." Emma tugged on Charlotte's arm and pointed at the horses charging toward the camp with their manes and tails flying. Paul galloped next to Sassy, her bell clanging. Charlotte cheered when she spotted Jack and Belle with the herd.

She couldn't take her eyes off Paul. It was as if he and the horse were one. He held the reins in one hand, his lariat in the other and urged the horses to stay bunched. Bernie followed at a trot, encouraging the stragglers to keep up.

How she'd miss scenes like this when she became a schoolteacher. How she'd miss Paul. She took a deep breath. He was so strong. So in charge. So capable. She felt safe with him. Was that all she felt? She wasn't sure. He made her insides feel warm and content, but he unnerved her at the same time. She'd miss talking with him and her time with Emma. She'd miss Bernie and Charlie too.

Nevertheless, according to their agreement, they'd part company. They would annul their marriage and be free from one another. Becoming a schoolteacher was her dream, after all. Wasn't it?

Remaining friends would be her goal. She could still visit and have moments with Emma. Perhaps Paul would continue his reading lessons? Well, no matter right now. They had to get the herd to Lyonsville. Only two days left to meet the buyer. Would they make it?

Paul trotted to the wagon and dismounted. "Charlotte, pack up the chuck wagon. I'll hitch up the team. We need to cover some miles before those thieves find out the horses are gone.

"Charlie!" he called. "Can you hitch up Jack and Belle?"

Charlie stored his bedroll and limped over to assist with the team.

Charlotte heard the urgency of Paul's command. She rushed to gather the utensils and stow them in the chuck wagon. This was no time to comment on his bossy attitude. Emma grabbed the clothes and tried to take down the picket line.

"I'll help with the rope, honey. Bring those things here, please," Charlotte directed Emma.

When Charlie came around the back of the wagon, he watched Charlotte dab at tears with a corner of her apron.

"What's goin' on, Missy?"

"My pie, Charlie. It'll be ruined. We worked so hard on it."

"Here, now. We can fix that. Hand me the kettle." Charlie reached for the Dutch oven. He pulled out one big empty drawer and shoved dishcloths on the bottom and sides and placed the cast-iron oven in the middle.

"Look at that. Fits as good as if it belonged. It'll be fine. You wait and see. The boys will be surprised to have pie tonight when we finally get to eat." Charlie gave her shoulders a hug and they doused the fire.

Paul took Emma's hand and motioned for Charlotte and Charlie to follow him. "Let's get Emma and the puppies in the wagon and head out."

"How far we goin', boss?" Charlie asked as he climbed into the wagon.

"When the sun goes down, we'll stop. We've got two days to meet the buyer." Paul lifted up Emma and then the puppies.

Charlotte took the reins. Paul rode Buck close to the wagon. "I'll take the herd on ahead. Bernie will ride back and forth and keep an eye on you three."

Sassy was haltered and Paul led her. He kept the herd at a trot to gain as much ground as possible. Since the trail was steep and narrow in places, Charlotte coaxed

Jack and Belle to keep a slow pace, staying a good distance behind the herd. She pulled up the scarf from around her neck and covered her mouth to keep out the dust particles spewing from the hooves of the fast-moving herd.

"Please, Charlotte. I want to ride up front," Emma begged.

"You have to use a scarf to cover your mouth. Are you okay with that?" Charlotte asked.

Emma nodded and a grateful Charlie crawled into the back of the wagon to rest.

Emma thought it was great fun to have a scarf across her mouth. When she wasn't pretending to be a bandit, she entertained herself with the sound of her muffled voice.

"Let's sing Christmas songs," Emma suggested. They warbled one piece, and Emma giggled at the muted words. One tune led to another and lots of laughter.

Shadows widened on the road. Charlotte called back to Charlie. "I can't see where we're going in the dark!"

He scrambled into the wagon seat. "Don't worry. Jack and Belle can see. They'll look for the other horses."

Her hands trembled. Where was Paul? Why didn't he come back for them? Or send Bernie to help?

They rounded a bend in the road, and Charlotte let out a sigh of relief. "There's the herd." She pointed toward the blurred trees ahead.

Bernie appeared and led them to the spot Paul had chosen for the wagon. "Boss says for me to unhitch Jack and Belle and for you to make some coffee." He looked at Charlotte. "He says not to worry about dinner, we can have somethin' cold. He wants to get to bed and get an early start afore daylight."

As soon as she stopped the team, Charlotte hopped out, got Emma and the dogs, and offered to help Charlie.

"I ain't dead yet, Missy."

Charlie got out the biscuits left over from breakfast and she sliced the cheese.

When the coffee was done Charlie said, "Don't forget your apple pie." He winked as he handed her the kettle. She pulled off the lid and plunged a big wooden spoon into the sweet-smelling pie.

After Emma was settled in bed, Paul gathered them. "I'm not sure we can make it to Lyonsville in time. If Bernie and I push the herd hard tomorrow, we might make Lyonsville by nightfall. Charlotte, you and Charlie and Emma drive on until dark, find a spot and make camp. I'll settle the herd in town and come back to stay with you."

Charlie nodded. Charlotte's stomach flip-flopped. She wondered if she could keep Emma safe. Charlie was in bad shape and wouldn't be much help if there was trouble. Paul had married her to take care of Emma. Could she do that by herself? She had the rifle. Would it be enough if the bandits came back? Could she handle another kind of threat, like a mountain lion, a coyote or a rattlesnake?

Disaster scenarios plagued her as she walked away from the wagon.

Paul followed her. He patted her shoulder and said, "You'll be okay, Charlotte. Charlie will be with you." An overwhelming desire to melt into his embrace coursed through her. She longed for him to hold her close and nuzzle her hair. Yearned to let herself be enveloped in those strong arms and soak in the familiar leather and coffee scent. Then she knew all would be well in her life. Since they were just friends, she resisted. It no longer seemed appropriate, even though his gentle touch had reassured her many times before.

Her heart sank. He would no longer be by her side after they reached Cedar Grove.

He'd withdrawn from her. Perhaps he was troubled about getting the herd to Lyonsville on time. Or was their impending separation on his mind? She knew he'd have to find another caretaker for Emma.

"Paul, I'm nervous," she whispered. "Charlie's not well and I'm not a good shot. What if Zeke and those thieves find us?"

"I don't think Zeke would hurt you or Emma. Bernie said those men are after the herd. So if the herd isn't with you, they won't bother you."

Paul walked her back to the wagon. "We'll start before daylight." He snatched his bedroll and slid under the wagon. Bernie and Charlie grabbed theirs and found places to sleep. Charlotte climbed into the wagon and plopped onto the wagon seat. Her mind whirled. She felt like a skittish cat.

Gazing up at the stars she prayed, *Lord, give me courage. Protect all of us. Help Paul and Bernie get the herd to Lyonsville on time. We count on You, Lord.*

Chapter Twenty

Charlotte woke before dawn. In the cool morning mist, she started the fire and made coffee. Paul and Bernie drank one cup and saddled their horses. Bernie haltered Jack and Belle and Charlie's horse, Fred, and tied them to the wagon.

Paul led Buck over to Charlotte. "Charlie can hitch the team for you. Try to get an early start."

"He's teaching me to harness the pair." She smiled at him. "I'll attempt it on my own since his injuries still trouble him."

Charlotte packed biscuits and a hunk of the cheese in a cloth bag, which she handed to Paul.

"We'll get as far as we can today. I'll stop before dark to make camp. It'll be less dangerous that way. I'll pray for your safety and that you make it in time to Lyonsville with the horses." She wanted to hug him but resisted.

He took the food and stared into her eyes. She felt her cheeks warming as his piercing gaze tunneled straight into her heart.

"Charlotte, thank you for all you've done for Emma," he said in a husky voice. "Thank you for your efforts to save my ranch, and most of all, thanks for your prayers."

He stepped into the stirrup and tipped his hat.

Bernie rode up next to him. "Daylight's burnin', Boss."

"Let's ride." Paul clicked to Buck and off they trotted toward the herd.

Charlotte filled her coffee cup, leaned against the wagon and watched Paul and the horses gallop downhill out of sight. She prayed his ranch, the home he'd built for Emma, would be saved.

Trust in the Lord... She remembered that verse from the other day when she'd read her Bible. She'd need to trust the Lord for her own situation too once they returned to Cedar Grove.

The list she kept filed in her mind of things she needed included finding a place to live, locating the school, discovering what supplies and books they had and finding out how many pupils were enrolled. The school board president, Mr. Higgins, mentioned the school population was small but the kids ranged in ages from six to fourteen.

Melancholy feelings surrounded her when she thought of not being with Emma. Her little responsibility wasn't old enough to attend school. Perhaps Charlotte could visit the ranch and continue with Emma's reading lessons. Her spirits sank deeper when she thought of her life without Paul and Emma. She'd grown to love Emma and she genuinely cared for Paul. Was this affection love? She shook her head. She knew nothing about loving a man, let alone a husband.

She smiled. However, she had gained some understanding of friendship. Once she and Paul aired out their differences of opinion, they worked well together as partners and enjoyed one another's company.

Lonesome. She'd be alone again without these two. A regretful sigh escaped her lips.

Emma's soft voice called, "Charlotte. I'm awake." The little girl climbed out onto the bench seat rubbing her eyes. Charlotte smiled up at her. Her heart ached. Oh, she'd miss this adorable wee gingersnap. She relished her time with Emma. She'd never considered motherhood, but her time with Emma had her dreaming about loving and raising a child. What would it be like to be someone's mother?

"Good morning. Did you sleep well?" Charlotte asked. Emma nodded with a big smile.

"Hand me the doggies." Charlotte lifted her hands up for Prince and then for Spots and then for Emma, who tumbled into her arms without hesitation. Charlotte whispered, "Charlie's still asleep, so we'll get ready for the day, get breakfast and then wake him." She winked at Emma and grinned when Emma tried to wink back at her.

"Did Papa go with the horses?" Charlotte nodded. She helped Emma wash and change into her clean gray-striped dress. Emma brushed her own hair, but still needed help with a ribbon.

"Nice morning, ain't it?" Charlie tossed his bedroll into the back of the wagon and poured himself a cup of coffee.

"It sure is. How'd you sleep?" Charlotte grabbed a galvanized plate.

"Not bad, not bad," Charlie answered.

"Paul and Bernie left before daybreak. We're supposed to travel as far as we can today," Charlotte reported. She offered him hot gravy and a cold biscuit. "It's all we have until I can make a proper meal. Paul is in such a hurry to get to Lyonsville. I didn't take time to get fresh biscuits or meat cooked."

"No worries, Missy. Sometimes all I had in the past was dried-up old biscuits with my morning coffee. You're turnin' out to be a fine hand. God sure did give you a spirit of doggedness." He chuckled.

Charlotte wished Paul felt the same way. She knew he was thankful for her care of Emma, but he'd never mentioned how she'd successfully taken charge of the meals and driving the wagon after Charlie got hurt. Why did she want Paul's approval? She wasn't staying, so whether or not he noticed all that she accomplished shouldn't matter to her. But it did. She bowed her head.

Under Charlie's supervision Charlotte harnessed and hitched the team.

Charlie grinned at her. "Good job. Jack and Belle like you. They stand still for ya even if ya fumble a bit with that harness. You'll get it mastered in no time, Missy."

The rising sun greeted Charlotte as she started the team down the steep incline. One skinny lane of dirt meandered through the thick-forested area. She hoped they didn't meet another wagon traveling in the opposite direction. She could back the team a few steps, but if they had to back up very far, Charlie would have to do it. When they came to a pullout before another bend, she halted Jack and Belle to rest them.

"Charlie, this is a rough, narrow road. What do I do if another wagon is coming toward us?"

"Pull as far as ya can to the right side of the road. Then, if it's still too narrow, one of us is gonna have to back up until there's room enough to pass."

Jack snorted and pranced a bit. Belle whinnied. "Whoa, easy now!" Charlotte called to them. She kept the reins taut and pushed the brake handle down.

"What's the matter with them?" Charlotte asked.

"Listen," Charlie said.

Charlotte heard the faraway sound of jangling harnesses and hooves pounding the ground. But there was nothing in the road ahead.

"Is another wagon coming?" She glanced at Charlie, feeling bewildered.

"Yeah. Keep 'em still and right here. Don't let 'em move. We'll be okay." Charlie grimaced. "Sounds like they're comin' mighty fast. Hold 'em tight, Missy."

"Emma, get inside the wagon!" Charlotte shouted. She worried the oncoming carriage might bump theirs and spook the team again. Emma bolted from the seat bench to the top of the bedrolls, grabbed Prince and Spots and held them close and whispered, "Everything is going to be okay."

"Whoa, Jack. Steady now, Belle. Easy, easy," Charlotte crooned. They flicked back their ears to listen and responded to her strong but gentle grip on the lines. Fred whinnied and stomped his feet, tugging his lead rope at the back of the wagon. Charlie hollered at him, "Whoa, Fred! Simmer down!"

It was as if a team of thoroughbreds were hitched to the coach that raced past them, leaving swirls of dust hanging in the air. Its breakneck speed rendered their driver invisible.

Charlotte sputtered and sneezed. Charlie coughed and brushed the particles from his face. Jack and Belle pranced, snorted and shook their heads, but stayed in place as the coach zipped on up the road. Fred let out a high-pitched squeal and pulled back on the rope but didn't break loose.

"Whew." Charlotte took a deep breath. "That was a close one. Sure glad we were already stopped. I wonder what would have happened if we'd been on the trail?" She glanced over at Charlie, her eyes wide with shock.

"No use wonderin' about trouble that ain't happened. Let's get movin', Missy. Like Bernie's always saying, 'daylight's burnin'.'"

Paul trotted beside Sassy. He had her haltered and on a lead rope. He didn't want her wandering off in the piney woods and taking the herd with her. He had to make up for lost time—he had to get to Lyonsville by tonight, and it was twenty miles away.

"Easy, Buck." He slowed his horse to a walk. If he alternated between a trot and a walk, he could cover about fifteen miles without endangering his mount. Maybe he'd give Buck a rest and ride Sassy. No matter how he did it, he knew he'd have to push the horses harder than he liked so he could recover lost distance and time.

Bernie mentioned again that Zeke talked about a Frank somebody he worked for. Could it be the banker, Frank Kenny? Why would he want Paul to fail? Why would he want the herd? Didn't he want the money on the loan for the bank? As soon as he sold the horses, Paul vowed to do a thorough investigation.

The trail zigzagged downward, following alongside a lazy stream. For the end of August there was quite a bit of water in the creek. When he saw a clearing up ahead, he led Sassy off the trail, into the eddies. By the time Bernie caught up to him with the stragglers, he'd saddled Sassy and had Buck on the lead rope.

The horses alternated between standing knee-deep in the water and grazing alongside the stream.

"Hey Bernie, that bay over there is pretty well broke." Paul pointed to a horse with a dark mane and tail. "I'll rope him for you, if you wanna give Boots a rest."

Bernie dismounted and filled his canteen. Paul handed him a biscuit and some cheese. "Yeah, good idea," he mumbled as he bit into the hard bread and warm cheese. He unsaddled Boots but kept a rope around his neck. When Paul brought the bay to him, Bernie spent a bit of time using his saddle blanket to wipe him down. Bernie saddled the prancing horse and mounted up. The horse snorted and strutted but didn't buck.

Coming out from the trees at a full gallop, four riders charged into the herd, firing guns and scattering the horses. Paul drew his pistol and shot into the air. The marauders turned and rode back into the grove of trees at a hard pace. One bandit's horse reared, and he fell off, hitting the ground hard.

"Let's round up the herd!" Paul hollered as he chased after his horses.

About a mile down the trail the herd had slowed to

a trot and bunched up behind Sassy. Paul stopped to collect himself and to talk with Bernie.

"Boss, do you think we should go back and see about that varmint that fell off?"

Paul pushed his hat back on his head. He rubbed his neck and then his chin and took a deep breath. "I don't want to, Bernie. Means I'll probably miss the buyer, but it wouldn't be right to leave him. I don't think God would look with favor on such an unkind act."

Bernie nodded.

"Let's get the horses over to that meadow there." Paul pointed to a small green clearing in the midst of the tall pine trees. "I'll go back. You stay with the herd."

Bernie nodded again.

Paul trotted back. He scoured the meadow for the injured raider but found no sign. Perhaps the other outlaws had come back for him? Or perhaps he'd been able to catch his horse and ride off?

Paul hurried back to his herd and they continued the trek toward Lyonsville.

The sun began to slip away…almost below the mountain peaks. Paul's heart pounded. He still had miles to go, but his thoughts were on Charlotte, his Lottie. Why did he think of her as *his*? In a few more days she'd leave. When he first met her, he'd decided he could endure a month with her. At first, he'd counted the days until he could be shed of her. He hadn't figured she'd want to be friends. Nor had he calculated that his heart would betray his mind. The risk of another broken relationship for himself and his daughter frightened him. He knew Charlotte loved Emma. She showed it in so many ways. So much more than Emma's own mother had.

How was that possible? Love was a funny thing, he decided. It didn't understand designations like birth mother or birth father. It didn't understand barriers like education or religion. It didn't know about walls like color or money. Love. God was love…simple and pure.

Paul admitted he had no idea how to love a woman. He didn't know how to trust a woman either. He knew how to love his child. He'd been starting to learn about friendship between a man and a woman until he'd seen the Wanted poster. Now his brain and heart were confused.

Charlotte's actions were all about love, no matter what the poster said. All about responsibility. About keeping her word and following through on her agreements. She was all about honesty. Except for the poster—and that puzzled him.

Still, he pondered, what would a true friend do? Defend the wanted person? Shouldn't he help someone in trouble? A friend stood by a friend, like Bernie stood by him even when he made mistakes. Even big ones. Like marrying Rachel.

If he were really Charlotte's ally, wouldn't he stand by her side even if she was in a fix?

From the hilltop in the twilight, Paul stared at the lights down in the valley. That must be Lyonsville. If they pushed on, they'd be there before midnight. Once he settled the herd, he'd ride back and find Charlotte, Emma and Charlie. He couldn't leave them alone on the trail with those bandits still loose. He halted Sassy and waited for Bernie.

"Let's trade mounts. I'll go on ahead and find the corrals and come back for you and the horses. That way we'll know the best route to bring the horses into town. You'll have to move slower with the herd since it's getting dark."

Paul and Bernie swapped horses and Paul maneuvered through the crowded streets of Lyonsville. He couldn't believe the number of people still out at this time of night. In Cedar Grove all businesses closed by dusk. In a ranching community, everyone had early-morning chores.

At last he found the livestock pens not far from the railroad tracks. The overseer agreed to let him use the corral overnight.

Paul hastened back to Bernie and the herd.

After the horses were settled, Paul said, "Bernie, get us a room at the hotel. You go on ahead and get some rest. I'll be there a little later." Bernie hadn't had a good rest since he'd escaped from those scoundrels who'd taken him prisoner. Paul figured he'd be back with everyone else about the time Bernie woke up. Bernie would never miss him.

Paul found Buck in the herd, saddled him and started back the way he'd come. His wife and child and that old cook were targets for those good-for-nothings. He aimed to make sure his people were safe.

Chapter Twenty-One

Were Charlotte's eyes playing tricks on her in the shadowy moonlight? Was that a man leaning up against a stump by the side of the road? Jack snorted. Belle threw her head in the air and twitched, but the horses continued to march forward. She nudged Charlie, who'd dozed off.

"Is that a person up there?" she whispered.

Charlie leaned forward. "Looks like it." He reached for the rifle and placed it across his lap. "Stop and see if he needs help. I'm ready if it's a trick."

Charlotte halted the team and stared down at the slumped body. The man's head drooped and his hat covered his face.

"Hey, there!" Charlotte shouted. "Are you okay?"

The man raised his head with a groan. He looked at Charlotte with a twisted smile. "Miz Charlotte, Charlie, it's me, Zeke. I'm in a bad way." He started to rise.

Charlie gripped the rifle in his lap. "Zeke, you low-down reprobate, you stay right there. Don't you think about movin'."

"What's wrong, Zeke?" Charlotte asked.

Zeke leaned back against the stump. His breath came in labored spurts. "I'm 'shamed to say I helped scatter Mr. Paul's herd again. I got hurt."

Charlotte looked over at Charlie and whispered, "We should get him to a doctor. Can we put him in the wagon?"

Charlie shook his head no. "No way is he gettin' in this wagon. We'll send the doc back after him. We can't worry about him lyin' again. Don't forget what he did to Bernie and me. He's a snake."

He glared at Zeke. " You don't deserve no charity after what you done to the boss, this lady, the little one and me and Bernie."

"I know, Mr. Charlie," Zeke whimpered.

Charlotte didn't feel it was right to leave the man to die. But she wouldn't risk Emma's safety to get Zeke in the wagon.

"Charlie," she whispered, "what if we let him ride along on Fred? You could sit in the back of the wagon and keep an eye on him."

Charlie looked at her and fingered his mustache. "Miz Charlotte, you're not gonna leave Zeke on the side of the road, are ya? Even if he is a no-good skunk."

Charlotte bit her lip and said, "Charlie, you're right. I just couldn't."

"Okay. If he can hang on to the saddle horn, he can come with us."

"Zeke, can you get up in that saddle on the horse tied at the back of the wagon?" Charlotte asked.

"Maybe." Zeke awkwardly pushed himself to a standing position.

Charlie poked the rifle in the air at him. "Drop your gun belt and don't try nothin' stupid."

Zeke unbuckled the belt and let his holstered gun slip to the ground. He hobbled to the back of the wagon. Charlie climbed over the bedrolls. "I got my eye on you, Zeke. And I'm gonna keep my eye on you. You try anythin', I mean anythin', I don't like, and I'll plug you like you was a no-good coyote."

Once Zeke was in the saddle, Charlie hollered at Charlotte to go on. She clicked to the team and they surged forward.

Charlotte kept the pair at a slow pace. The gloomy darkness obscured the road. She scanned the woodland for a safe camp spot. Emma leaned against her on the wagon bench seat, clutching her Lucy doll in one hand.

Charlotte spotted a clearing. It wasn't far off the road, but at this time of night, she wasn't particular. She lifted Emma and the pups out of the wagon and called to Charlie. He handed her the rifle and she ordered Zeke to dismount. He fell to the ground but pulled himself up and hobbled to a felled log. Charlie insisted they bound Zeke's hands and feet. Then he tied him to the log while Charlotte kept the rifle pointed at him.

She and Emma got a fire started. Charlotte ground coffee and hung a pot of water over the fire.

"Charlie, while he's tied, I need to look at his injury."

With a warm cloth, Charlotte tenderly cleaned his shoulder wound. He moaned about his ribs being broken. She gently wrapped another piece of her ripped petticoat around his middle. He thanked her and said it felt a bit better.

It took her a while, but she convinced Charlie to

untie Zeke and allow him to eat and have a drink. Charlie kept an eye on him the whole time.

She handed a cup to Zeke and said, "We'll get you to the doctor tomorrow morning. That's the best I can do."

Zeke's eyes misted. He took the coffee. "Thank you, Miz Charlotte. It's more 'n I deserve." His head drooped.

"Them's true words," Charlie growled.

When they finished their cold supper, Charlie retied Zeke with the comment, "I ain't lettin' this varmint get away. He's gonna pay for what he done."

Charlotte took Emma's hand. "It's too late for lessons tonight. We have to get an early start in the morning, so let's get you ready for bed."

Emma nodded but looked up at Charlotte with her ocean blue eyes. "Can I have a story after Bible reading?" Charlotte hugged her shoulders and agreed to read one story.

When she climbed down from the wagon, Charlotte saw that Charlie had thrown his bedroll in a direct line from where Zeke sat. She wandered over and whispered, "Charlie, you can't stay awake all night watching him. Why don't we take turns? You go get some sleep. I'll take the first shift. Let me know when you're ready to take over."

"Miz Charlotte, I couldn't do that. Why, if that ruffian was to get loose, I wouldn't want him to harm you or the babe."

"Charlie, Paul taught me to shoot, remember? I can do this." She stuck out her chin.

"Miz Charlotte, I know you don't like to back down from a skirmish. And I know you'd fight anyone who tried to hurt Emma, but you gotta promise to call me if that rattler makes a wrong move." Charlie stared at her.

Charlotte nodded in agreement. She took the rifle and sat with it across her lap, keeping an eye on Zeke. Why had he made a decision to betray Paul? What caused a man to do such things? She'd not suspected Zeke was anything but a cowboy glad to have work. When he woke, she'd ask him.

Her eyelashes drooped. She needed coffee. She grabbed the rifle, walked to the fire and poured a cup of the hot brew. She wished Paul would come back. She knew her strong husband could take care of any situation, even when things went sideways. She'd never felt like she could trust anyone like she trusted Paul. He was so bossy sometimes he was hard to get along with, but she knew he was fierce about protecting the daughter he cherished. She suspected he'd be that way with whoever he loved. She wondered what it would be like to be loved by such a man. She just wanted to be his friend.

Charlotte listened. Hoofbeats came at a trot down the road. Should she douse the fire or wait? The sound came closer. She stood and aimed the rifle where she thought the noise came from. Someone on horseback rode toward camp... She stepped away from the fire and toward the rider.

With firmness, Charlotte commanded, "Halt. Don't come any farther. I have a rifle and I will shoot."

The horseman dismounted. "Charlotte, it's me, Paul. Don't fire." He chuckled and moved forward in slow motion, his hands raised in the air until she could see him.

When she spotted him, she dropped the rifle, rushed

to him, jumped up and threw her arms around his neck. Her feet dangled in midair.

"Oh, Paul, I've been so frightened. I'm so glad it's you. I'm so thankful you're back." She buried her head in his neck and sobbed.

Paul closed his arms around her and whispered, "Lottie, my Lottie. Are you okay?" He held her for several minutes.

She let go of him and felt her toes touch the ground. "I'm sorry, Paul. I was so relieved it was you I couldn't help it."

Charlotte stepped back and faced him. "We found Zeke injured alongside the road, and even though we've kept him tied up, Charlie insisted we keep a watchful eye on him with the gun. Charlie's exhausted. I convinced him I could handle Zeke and that I could shoot him if I needed to."

Paul's mouth fell open. His soft, compassionate eyes turned to steel blue. He gripped her shoulders and fastened his eyes on hers. "You brought that heartless villain into our camp? You endangered Emma? How could you do this, Charlotte?" he chastised her.

Charlotte threw his hands off her, and her fists flew to her waist. Her chin jutted out and her eyes flamed. "I did not put Emma in danger. The man is severely injured and can barely move. I think he broke his ribs. Charlie and I have the situation under control. How dare you think I would cause any harm to Emma? I love her." Charlotte started to stomp away, heading for the wagon and wishing there was a door to slam when suddenly they heard a commotion and turned to see Charlie aiming the rifle at Paul.

"Put that down, Charlie. That's the second time to-night someone's pointed that gun at me."

Charlie stared at him. "Boss, I didn't know it was you. I thought that snake Zeke had wrestled the gun away from Miz Charlotte."

"I doubt anyone could do that. That woman has a temper when she's riled. Reminds me of a momma bear. Woe to anyone who crosses her when she's provoked." He shook his head and walked up close to the fire. "I guess you or me need to take the next watch."

"It's my turn, Boss. You been pushin' it—you better get some sleep."

"Not sure that's gonna happen, but I'll try. Thanks Charlie." Paul patted his shoulder, found his bedroll and tossed it under the wagon. As he prepared his bedroll, Charlotte could hear him muttering under his breath.

Sunlight streaked all the way down the wide street that led through town. Buckboards, freighters, buggies, farm wagons and horseback riders crammed the road-way. Store doors stood wide open. Men and women pushed past and around one another on the congested boardwalk.

Charlotte smiled at the women in their fashionable dresses with colorful fringed parasols, plumed hats and gloved hands. Cowboys, bankers and lumbermen dressed in their red shirts tipped their hats when they passed a lady. In the distance, up on the hillsides, smoke spewed from the tall towers of the lumber mills.

Paul flagged down a businessman. "I need a doctor."

The well-dressed man pointed to a small house at the south end of town. "You can't miss it. Nice white picket fence with roses in the yard. Sign says Doctor Robinson. He's the one real doctor in town, but if you need a dentist, we have two of those. One at Stacks Barber Shop, over that way," he pointed, "and one at the Last Stop Café which is that way." He pointed in the opposite direction.

Tipping his hat in Charlotte's direction, the man continued down the sidewalk.

Paul had looked at Zeke in the morning light and agreed to let him lie down inside the wagon for the trip to town. He took Emma with him on Buck and said, "I'll help you get Zeke to the doctor's office, then I have to get Bernie and find the buyer. When that's settled, I'll go see the sheriff about Zeke."

Charlotte stopped Jack and Belle in front of the doctor's home. She and Emma knocked on the door while Paul and Bernie carried a feverish, mumbling Zeke between them. "Sorry, Boss. Frank, he wants your ranch somethin' fierce. You got the hot springs on your place. He don't want you to pay off the loan. Hired me to stop ya. I didn't want nobody hurt. I'm sorry, Boss." Zeke's head drooped. Paul felt his brow.

"He's burning up. Must be delusional."

A plump woman with a big smile opened the door and then stood beside the doctor while Paul explained the situation with the hurt man.

"Vera," the doctor said to the smiling woman with the starched white apron, "show them into the examination room and have them put that man on the table." Vera led them to a well-lit room where they deposited Zeke on a clean cloth-covered table.

Paul took off his hat and said to the doctor, "I'll be responsible for any expenses. I'm in town for a few days. I'll drop back by or send my wife to check on Zeke."

At first Paul had resisted the idea of paying for Zeke's care. Then he remembered the story of the Good Samaritan in the Bible and relented.

Paul handed Charlotte a wad of folded bills. "Charlie will let you off at The Grand Hotel. Get two more rooms. Bernie already has one." She took the money and nodded without looking at him.

He glanced up at Charlie and handed him money, as well. "After the ladies are dropped off, take the wagon to the livery and have them brush down and grain Jack and Belle and store the rig. This should cover the cost for at least two days. If not, tell them I'll pay the balance when we collect the horses and wagon."

Charlie smiled. "Yes, sir, Boss." Paul peeked at Charlotte and wondered how she was dealing with being ordered around again. Her cheeks were pink and her green eyes flamed like they could start a fire, but she bit her lip.

He grinned. "Well done, Missy. I know you don't like takin' orders," he whispered. She glared as she handed Emma up to him and placed her foot on the wheel to climb in.

Paul placed his hands on her waist to assist and murmured, "Please pray for this sale. I'll be back soon."

The Grand Hotel was a two-story, white-washed structure. After Charlie helped them to the steps, Charlotte spent some time getting Emma's bow tied beneath her chin. Emma giggled and fidgeted.

"Emma." Charlotte took her chin in her hand and made her look at her. "Stand quietly, please, while I tie this bow. Your frock is already wrinkled. I don't want us to look like ragamuffins."

"But Charlotte!" she exclaimed. "We're staying in a real hotel. I've never stayed in one." She would have jumped up and down if not for Charlotte's strong hand on her shoulder.

Charlotte clutched their suitcases in one hand, along with the two ropes looped around each puppy's neck. In her other she held Emma's gloved hand as they strolled through the hotel door.

At the counter she said to Emma, "Here, you hold Prince and Spots while I get the rooms. Stand right beside me and don't move," Charlotte commanded. *Oh my,* she thought, *I'm starting to sound like Paul, barking out orders.*

Emma nodded and took the roped puppies. She managed to stay in one place while perusing the hotel lobby.

Charlotte smiled at the clerk and said, "I need two rooms. Also, I'll pay for two baths. Please have the tub brought to our room posthaste—" she glanced at his nametag "—Robert."

The clerk stared at her. He pushed his glasses up his nose and pursed his lips. "Madame, we do not have such services here. You got to go to the bathhouse down the road."

Charlotte raised her eyebrows and scowled. "How absurd, Robert. I will not take my daughter to a common bathhouse. I want a tub and hot water brought to our room before noon. We have been on the trail for quite some time, and there is nothing I want more at this moment than a bathtub filled to the brim with warm water. Would you deprive this sweet child of an opportunity to remove all the grit and grime she's had to suffer? "

Robert stared at her. He peered over the counter at Emma, and his face contorted with confusion. His lips twitched.

"Thank you, Robert. I look forward to the tub and hot water before noon." Charlotte pressed an extra folded bill into his hand, picked up the room keys, took Emma's hand and strode to the stairs.

The flustered attendant called after her, "But Madame, that isn't possible!" His brows furrowed. His lips quivered downward into a frown.

Charlotte turned and smiled. "Of course it's possible, Robert. I'm counting on you." Charlotte nodded. "Thank you." She continued up the steps, hoping he didn't mention the dogs. She hadn't asked about the critters. In her travels she'd noted almost everyone brought their dogs as companions and no one made a scene over it. However, she was west of the Mississippi now, so how would she know what was acceptable in cowboy country?

Charlotte checked out both rooms and chose the larger one for herself and Emma. She plopped their bags on the bed and opened the window to air out the stale smell. A bath. A real bath in a real bathtub. She felt like dancing.

She smiled and hugged herself, marveling at what she had accomplished downstairs. She'd confronted the man about the tub without losing her temper. She hadn't shrunk away from his refusal. Had she changed so much in three-and-a-half weeks? How had it happened that she did not retreat from an argument or a refusal?

Paul. It was because of Paul. She practiced with him. He was safe territory for her. Safe to disagree with. Safe to say what she wanted and how she felt.

"Emma, we'll put your clothes in the bottom drawers so you can reach your things." She unpinned her hat, then asked Emma take off hers and laid them on top of the bureau. Charlotte helped Emma arrange her outfits. She put her own garments in the top two drawers and hung her coat and other dresses in the wardrobe.

Prince and Spots raced around the room and then settled on the circular rug at the foot of the bed, content to rest.

Charlotte hugged Emma. "Your papa will be here soon. We'll have our baths and get cleaned up. Perhaps we'll celebrate with supper in the hotel dining room."

Emma twirled. "Oh, I hope we can have apple pie for dessert. It's my favorite."

"You had that the first day we met." Charlotte smiled at her. "Do you remember?"

The little girl tilted her head. "Yes. You had the prettiest clothes I've ever seen. And when you were angry with Papa, your head looked like a quail." She giggled.

Charlotte looked at her. "What do you mean?"

"Your hat had a feather on top that bobbed back and forth when you shook your head at Papa. You looked fierce. But I knew you were nice because you brought me a tablet and pencils."

"Oh, Emma. I'm glad you didn't forget. We can treasure those happy memories forever." Charlotte hugged her again.

At that moment someone banged on the door and hollered, "Ma'am, we're here with your tub!"

Chapter Twenty-Two

Paul staggered to the bench at the railway station and plopped down, burying his head in hands. He would lose his ranch. Emma would have no home. No inheritance. His stomach somersaulted. His head pounded. His heart throbbed like he'd been stabbed with a knife.

He felt like he was drowning. Like he'd stepped into quicksand and was sinking farther and farther. Would the quagmire swallow him like a snake devours a mouse?

How could he face Emma? Charlotte? Had it all been for naught? Stunned, he caught his breath. Now there was absolutely no hope of anything but a friendship with Charlotte. He couldn't ask her to abandon their annulment agreement. He had nothing to offer her.

Only a few moments ago, Mr. Leeman, the horse buyer, had explained to Paul that someone delivered a letter yesterday signed by Paul Harrison, releasing Mr. Leeman from the agreement to purchase Paul's horses. The letter instructed Mr. Leeman to buy horses elsewhere. Last night, Mr. Leeman had paid a different seller for a herd of horses.

"Mr. Leeman, the letter you received is a forgery."

Mr. Leeman apologized.

"Do you have that letter?" Paul asked him. Perhaps Charlotte would read it to him. Just to make sure Mr. Leeman was telling him the truth.

"Why, yes, I do." The stout man sifted through a pile of papers and handed Paul the dated, handwritten letter.

"That is not my signature, Mr. Leeman."

The man apologized again. "I had no way to recognize your handwriting or signature Mr. Harrison, since we have only corresponded by telegram."

Mr. Leeman described the man who delivered the message. The courier sounded like the redheaded man who had stolen Paul's herd the first time.

Paul had no way to prove his accusation and it seemed pointless to go to the sheriff. He did need to report Zeke and his attempt to steal Paul's horses a second time, though.

When they'd delivered Zeke to the doctor's, he'd mumbled about a man named Frank. Paul's mind was focused on locating the horse buyer and sending the money to the bank back home. He hadn't paid much attention to Zeke's jumbled words this morning.

Paul stuffed the letter in his pocket as he walked to his horse. He needed to talk with Zeke before he relayed the bad news to Charlotte, Emma, Bernie and Charlie. And before he went to the sheriff.

Paul rode past the church, then pivoted Buck and trotted back. He tied the horse to the hitching rail, took off his hat and opened the door. His mind reeled in turmoil as he ambled down the aisle of the silent building. Rainbows shone through the stained-glass windows.

The beautiful mahogany lectern with a carved dove stood in the front of the pews. Behind the podium on the wall hung a massive weathered wooden cross.

Paul slipped into a bench at the back. He bowed his head and poured out his confused thoughts in a muddled prayer. "Thy will be done, dear Lord." He rose and quietly retreated the way he'd come in.

A plan formed in his mind as he continued toward the doctor's office.

Vera greeted him and ushered him inside. "Doc, Mr. Harrison is here to see you."

The doctor looked up from the paperwork on his desk and asked Paul to have a seat. Paul slid onto the chair across from the doctor.

"Mr. Harrison, Mr. Smith will pull through. I stitched up his wound. Someone cleaned it real well, and there was no infection. His broken ribs will take longer to heal, but his fever is down and he's resting."

"Thank you, Doctor Robinson. My wife tended him until we could bring him here." Paul ran his fingers through his hair. "Can I talk to him? I need to clear up a few things. He rambled on a lot when we brought him in here earlier."

The doctor came around to stand in front of Paul. "He confessed how he'd tried to steal your herd twice and how he and the men he worked with kidnapped your hired men and frightened your wife and child. He's quite remorseful. Will you press charges against him?"

Paul looked up. "I don't know yet." He glanced out the window. "I know for sure he didn't plan this on his own. He mentioned someone named Frank. I need to find out who this Frank is."

The doctor allowed Paul to talk with Zeke. The injured man confirmed it was Frank Kenny, the banker in Cedar Grove, who'd hired him and the others to prevent Paul from arriving in Lyonsville in time to sell the herd. The banker told Zeke he wanted Paul's ranch for the mineral hot springs in the meadows. Mr. Kenny had already contracted with an architect from Reno to build a resort on the property. Frank Kenny had promised Zeke a job at the lodge after he took over the property. Zeke apologized over and over and said he was sorry he'd ever agreed to such a wicked plan and he hoped Paul could forgive him.

Paul's insides tossed about. He almost threw up. His head spun. He slumped into the chair beside Zeke's bed and stared at the wall. Frank had told him the board of directors had decided to call in the loan on his property. Paul had considered Frank Kenny a friend.

Betrayed.

Again. But not by a beautiful woman this time.

Where had he missed the clues with Frank, with Zeke, with Rachel? And maybe with Charlotte? Had she fooled him also?

Paul looked the bandaged man in the eyes. "Zeke, if I agree not to press charges against you for attempted theft and endangering the lives of my wife and child, would you testify against Frank Kenny?"

Zeke's eyes filled with moisture. "I'm so sorry, Mr. Paul. I never done nothin' like this in my whole life. I don't know what come over me to agree to such a vile thing. Even if you see fit not to drop the charges, I'll tell ever'thing Frank Kenny said to me. 'Course, it'd only be my word against his."

"Thanks Zeke." Paul pushed his hat back on his head. "When you're well enough to move, there will be a room reserved for you at the hotel where you can recuperate. I'll let the sheriff know that you'll give him your testimony so he can take it down."

"Thank you, Mr. Paul. I wish you and the missus and the little one all the best. Tell Charlie and Bernie I'm awful sorry for what I done to them. I'm so ashamed."

Paul trotted Buck to the livery stable and paid the man to take care of his horse, then he hurried to the hotel. He couldn't wait to share everything with Charlotte. He asked the clerk for the room number of his wife and child.

The hotel assistant smirked. "Your wife sure don't like takin' no for an answer. It appears she's used to getting her own way. I bet you got your hands full with that woman." He snickered when he dumped the keys into Paul's outstretched hand.

Yes, Paul thought, *Charlotte's a handful. She's opinionated, strong-willed, smart, fun, resourceful, hardworking, kind, thoughtful and beautiful.* Paul smiled as he took the stairs two at a time. His new plan wasn't perfect, but it would allow him to pay off some of his debt. He still had one week to make the full payment. He wasn't licked yet. Perhaps he could appeal to the bank's board of directors. He couldn't wait to discuss his plan with Charlotte.

Paul turned the key and flung open the door.

A dripping wet Prince yipped, running circles round and round the room. Emma, bath towel in hand, dashed after him, calling, "Prince, Prince, come here! You're still wet!"

Charlotte, her glistening damp hair pinned in a lop-sided bun, struggled to keep Spots in the tub of water. A bar of soap popped out of her hands and settled on the floor. She glanced up at Paul.

"Oh, I'm so glad you're here. Could you help Emma get hold of that silly dog?"

Prince halted at Paul's feet. Wagging his tail, he shook violently. Water droplets ascended into the air like sparks from a campfire, and then descended—drenching Paul from head to foot.

Wiping his face, he stared at the chaos. Heat spread from his neck to his forehead.

"What…are you two doing?"

Emma scooped Prince up in the towel. "Hi, Papa. We're getting the trail dust off the doggies. We already scrubbed ourselves." She smiled up at him.

Paul grimaced. Charlotte managed to bundle Spots and gather him into her arms. She vigorously rubbed the towel all over the squirming puppy. Her zealous movements jiggled her hairpin loose, and like a water-fall, her long hair tumbled across her face. The puppy sprinted away.

With a single stride, Paul kneeled and corralled Spots. Holding the dog at arm's length, he watched his lovely wife sweep hair back from her face. Her eyes sparkled. She grinned at the pup wriggling in Paul's hands.

"You rascal." Charlotte marched toward the dog. Her foot met the bar of soap on the floor, and she staggered and lurched backward. Her head hit the floor with a thud.

Paul released Spots and hurried to his wife.

"Charlotte." He gathered her in his arms. "Are you okay?"

No smile, no fluttering lashes. Her eyes remained closed. "Charlotte?"

"Papa, what's wrong with Charlotte?" Emma rushed to him.

Paul carried Charlotte to the bed and adjusted her head on the pillow.

"She'll be fine." He patted Emma's shoulder. "We'll let her lie here for a little bit. If she doesn't open her eyes in a few minutes, we'll go get the doctor." Paul was familiar with unconsciousness. Sometimes cowboys got knocked out after getting bucked off a horse. Usually they recovered. He'd never worried before. But this was Charlotte, not a buckaroo.

He lifted a wisp of hair hugging her cheek and tucked it behind her ear. He stared at the woman he'd come to depend on. How astonished he'd been when she'd taken his hand and stepped out of the stagecoach.

At that moment, he'd felt like the wind had been knocked out of him. Reluctant to trust her at first, he'd quickly become enamored with how she cared for Emma. Impressed with her dedication to learning new skills, he felt a kinship with her desire to overcome. Now he was eager to share his thoughts and ideas with her. Especially his new plan to sell the herd and pay off the bank.

Paul's heart raced. She should have awakened by now. He pulled a chair close to the bed. Emma climbed into his lap. He picked up Charlotte's hand, and Emma laid hers over Charlotte's. Paul bowed his head. "Lord, please bring Charlotte back to us."

* * *

Charlotte slowly blinked open her eyes. The back of her head felt like she'd been struck with a hammer.

Paul's brows furrowed; his eyes filled with concern. Emma, on Paul's lap, gazed at her.

Charlotte tried to push herself up. "What happened?"

Paul settled his hands on her shoulders. "Just rest easy." He gently assisted her back onto the pillow.

"You and that slippery bar of soap locked horns." He pointed at the meddlesome bar. "And you took a whopper of a fall."

Emma jumped down from her Papa's lap and stood at the side of the bed. "God answered our prayers. You came back to us." She squeezed Charlotte's hand with a smile.

Paul grinned. His blue eyes teased her. "I never heard of anyone taking a bath in the middle of the day, let alone giving dogs a wash in a tub."

She frowned at him. "Emma and I needed to get the trail dust off. That silly clerk downstairs was reluctant to provide a tub and hot water. He wanted us to go down to some common bathhouse. Can you imagine taking Emma to such a place? I flat out refused. He finally saw the light and arranged for the tub and hot water to be brought to our room."

Paul shook his head with a smile. Charlotte continued. "And since the puppies are staying with us in this room, I thought it'd be nice to have them cleaned up too."

His eyebrows raised. "No wonder that clerk got all balled up. You're a corker, you are."

Was he proud of her or was he teasing her?

Paul wandered to the window and pulled the curtains aside, letting the sunshine into the room. "When your head feels better, I need to discuss some plans. I want to talk over a few things with you."

Charlotte squeezed her eyes shut and bowed her head. Paul had never volunteered to talk about plans with her before. For the last three weeks he'd made the decisions, and then told her what they were doing. If she had other ideas, she'd told him and sometimes, after a heated exchange, he'd consider what she'd said. But he'd never asked to consult with her ahead of time. What had come over him?

She looked up at him and nodded.

"Do you feel like having a cup of coffee? Maybe some apple pie? And a glass of milk for my gingersnap." Paul glanced at Emma sitting on the floor with both puppies in her lap. He winked at his daughter.

Emma smiled up at him. "Oh, Papa, I hope they have apple pie. You know it's my favorite."

"Before we have coffee and pie, we should have them get that out of here." Charlotte pointed to the copper tub still full of water.

Paul grinned at her. "Right. I'll ask them to take care of it and place our order in the dining room. I'll be right back." He kissed the top of Emma's head, pushed down his hat on his own head, smiled at Charlotte and walked out the door.

Charlotte thanked the women who arrived to empty the tub. The same men who'd carried it upstairs came to retrieve it. They tipped their hats and grinned at Charlotte.

"Ma'am, you must be purty special. We ain't never

heared of anybody gettin' a bath in their hotel room and in the middle of the day. Boy howdy, that's something that'll be talked about 'round here for long while."

She handed them each a coin. "Thanks so much for all your hard work."

They bowed their heads. "Thank you, ma'am. Thank you much. It's a pleasure, shore 'nough."

There was a knock and Paul called, "Emma, come open the door!" The little girl hopped up and went to answer.

Paul carried in a platter with the pie. Right behind him, a young girl in a white apron toted a tray with the cups and saucers, a glass of milk and the coffeepot. Paul pressed a few coins in her hand and thanked her.

Emma's curls bounced when she vaulted off the bed and took a seat at the table. "Papa, the apple pie smells delicious. Almost as good as Charlotte's."

Things are sure different this time, Charlotte thought. Three-and-a-half weeks ago, when they gathered for pie and coffee in another hotel, Emma hadn't spoken a word in over a year. Both she and Paul had been nervous and edgy and uncomfortable with one another. She'd been scared.

Charlotte stole a glance at Paul. Something about that rugged cowboy had inspired a confidence in her to speak her mind, and she'd asked for a signed document. She marveled at her bravery. She hadn't retreated or run away. Remarkable changes had unfolded in each one of them, uniting them. Now their journey was almost over. Her heart wrenched at the thought of leaving Emma and Paul. She took a deep breath.

Paul stood beside her. "Are you okay? Do you want to lay back down? We can wait to talk."

Overwhelmed with his nearness, she was edgy. Again. What was it about this man? He always made her insides jittery. Her knees threatened to falter when he moved too close to her. Sometimes her breathing changed. Why did he have this effect on her? She wasn't afraid of him. What was wrong with her?

She faced him. Tears welled in her eyes. How could she speak what was on her mind? She couldn't tell him how much she enjoyed being his wife, even though it was in name only. She couldn't tell him that because of him, she might change her mind about men and rethink her ideas about marriage and motherhood. She couldn't tell him about a longing in her heart that was fierce, strong and powerful, a yearning she had no name for because she couldn't identify the feeling. She couldn't tell him she didn't want to face the future without him by her side.

"Sit down, Charlotte." Paul pulled out a chair and motioned for her to take a seat. He reached for her hand and for Emma's. Paul bowed his head and asked a blessing on the food. He also prayed for his men and that Zeke would be well soon. He asked the Lord for wisdom in the coming days.

She and Paul picked at their pie and sipped their coffee. Emma devoured hers. After she swallowed the last drop of milk, she scampered back to the bed with her book and her puppies.

Paul leaned close to Charlotte. "I wasn't able to sell my horses." He told her about the letter the buyer received and about Zeke's confession.

Tears flowed down Charlotte's cheeks. Paul picked up the hotel napkin and gently blotted her face.

"Does this mean you lost your ranch?" Her heart pounded.

"I might lose it. I still have about seven days to get that payment to the bank. I'm going to telegraph the sheriff in Cedar Grove and have him contact the bank board members with my proposal, and I'll let him know the sheriff here will send a note with Zeke's confession."

From his shirt pocket he pulled the letter that Mr. Leeman had given him. He handed it to her. Raking his fingers through his hair he said, "Please read it out loud to me. I want to know if Mr. Leeman told me the truth about what it says."

In a gentle voice Charlotte read the letter. When she saw the signature, she gasped. "This isn't your signature, Paul."

"You can tell?"

"Of course. I have the document you and I signed the first day we met. This is not your handwriting, for sure."

"Charlotte, do you have the agreement we signed?"

"Yes."

"Please hang on to it. I might need it when we get back to Cedar Grove to prove I did not send this letter and that Frank Kenny committed fraud to steal my land. I may be able to renegotiate my bank loan when the bank directors find out what Frank did."

He paused and looked into her eyes. "Will you help me, Charlotte?"

How could she refuse this man? He'd bolted into

her life and left footprints on her heart. Tears filled her eyes. She spoke with determination.

"I'll do whatever it takes to assist you in resolving this matter."

Chapter Twenty-Three

Today was the first day of the Polk County Fair, and people from all over had come to town for the festivities. Paul arranged to have his herd corralled for one more day. They'd stay another night before heading back to Cedar Grove.

Paul and Bernie trotted alongside the wagon. Charlotte was content to let Charlie maneuver Jack and Belle through the crowded streets of Red Bridge this morning. It was far busier and more crowded than Lyonsville or any town they'd been through in the last several weeks. She'd mastered driving the team through narrow mountain passes, across streams and rivers and down steep inclines, but she wasn't confident handling the horses in the bustling city with so many other horses and people and strange noises.

This morning Charlotte had helped Paul compose a telegram he'd sent to the sheriff in Cedar Grove. He'd asked the deputy to advise the Cedar Grove bank directors that he'd be mailing a message later concerning his loan.

Paul dictated the letter Charlotte wrote, outlining the evidence against their bank president, Frank Kenny. Paul requested a postponement of the foreclosure proceedings on his ranch. He also asked for a chance to renegotiate his loan.

"I don't feel hopeful that I can keep the ranch, but I'll sell as many horses as I can on the way home. There were a lot of ranchers asking to buy just one or two horses on the trip here, but I needed to be sure I had the number I'd promised Mr. Leeman."

Charlotte wished for words of wisdom to console or encourage him, but nothing came to mind except that verse about trusting the Lord.

"We'll have to trust God, Paul. And wait." She smiled at him.

At the fairgrounds, Paul stopped the team under a shady oak tree, and they tied Buck and Boots to the side of the wagon. Charlie handed Paul the heavy tether hitch from under the wagon bench seat. Paul looped Jack's lead rope into the link welded to the iron block, dropping it on the ground next to Jack.

Paul caught Emma in his arms, kissed her cheeks and set her feet on the ground. He offered Charlotte support as she climbed down from the wagon. He gently squeezed her hands and pulled her closer. She flushed and stepped back.

Charlotte pointed to all the wagons and buggies whose drivers hadn't secured their horses.

"Why do they let those teams stand without tying them to something?"

Paul looked to where she pointed. "Not sure. Maybe

these horses are used to lots of activity. I don't want Jack and Belle to spook and wreck our wagon."

Charlotte smoothed her gray-striped skirt, adjusted her hat and pulled on her gloves, then looped her reticule over her arm. She kneeled to retie Emma's blue bow, tidied her dark blue dress and straightened the white collar.

"Here are your good gloves, Emma." She helped her get all her fingers in the right places.

Bernie pointed to the crowd and sighed. "Boss, look at all them people. I don't think I ever see'd so many people in one place."

Emma reached up for Charlotte's hand, her eyes wide with wonder as they strolled through the entrance gate. Long colorful banners decorated tents and buildings. Fancy lettering and curved signage invited everyone to come and enjoy.

When Emma spotted the sign with animal pictures, she begged to go there. They ambled down aisles where piglets squealed and chased one another. The stout sow ignored them, snoring like a train in a corner of her pen. Little lambs and goats frolicked in their enclosures, bleating as if they were competing with the piggy sounds. Gentle-faced dairy cows and short, husky beef cattle chewed their cuds side by side, their calves resting in the straw next to them.

"Charlotte, Emma, come see this horse!" Paul called. Charlotte tugged a reluctant Emma away from the colorful strutting chickens to catch up with Paul, Bernie and Charlie.

In the tall wooden pen stood the most gorgeous horse

Charlotte had ever seen. None of the fancy carriages back East had ever flaunted a horse quite like this one.

Emma gasped. She tilted her head, straining to gaze up at the horse. Then she pointed to a sign strapped to a wooden panel. "Charlotte, what does that say?"

Charlotte read out loud. "'This is Mike. He is a Clydesdale horse. He is the heaviest and tallest horse at the Polk County Fair. He weighs two thousand three hundred pounds and is eighteen hands high.'"

"He's so beautiful," Emma said. "Look how shiny black he is."

"What I'd like to know is how the owner gets his four white stockings to stay so bright, let alone all that feathered white hair down by his hooves?" Charlotte quipped.

Paul laughed. "Must have to bathe him often. Wonder if he has as much trouble getting a bath as some people I know." Paul grinned and winked at Charlotte. She felt heat in her cheeks and pushed at his arm.

"Anybody hungry?" Paul asked.

They strolled back to the main thoroughfare, filled with people going in all directions. "Look, Emma. There are so many choices." Charlotte pointed to the hand-drawn pictures and printed signs assuring patrons of the delicious, magnificent food available at each booth. "There's Aunt Mabel's Southern Fried Chicken. Over here is The Famous Coney Island Hot Dog." Charlotte pointed in a different direction. "Why, there's even someone selling The Best Apple Pie in All the World." Charlotte smiled at Charlie, "I'm not sure it could compete with your apple pie, Charlie." He raised his eyebrows and chuckled.

Charlotte continued. "There's a Sally's Mile-High Cake food stand. They're serving lemonade or root beer to drink also."

Bernie licked his lips and pointed to a huge sign depicting a donut sprinkled with white crystals. "I ain't never tried one of them sugared cakes with a hole in the middle. That's what I want."

"Anyone else for a Fresh Delicious Donut?" Charlotte asked, following Bernie toward the donut stand.

Paul looked at all of them. "Everybody get whatever food you want and then meet back at the animal area in about an hour. Sound okay?" They all nodded.

"I'm gonna get me some fried chicken I don't have to cook." Charlie chuckled and headed out.

Paul reached for Emma's hand with one of his. His fingers touched Charlotte's gloved palm and he gripped her hand with a gentle squeeze. A quivering sensation rushed from her head to her toes, but she didn't pull away. Bernie ambled alongside as they approached the donut stand. Charlotte glanced at Paul. Her heart pounded and her eyes misted thinking about leaving her two favorite people in the entire world. Well, she liked Bernie too.

She cocked her head a little and smiled. What a perfect day. She wished for more of this. She wished it would never end. The four of them—altogether. She and Paul side by side. Always and forever.

Paul turned in the saddle to make sure the herd was following Sassy. Doubts about saving his ranch plagued his heart as his boss mare trotted beside him.

After they'd started on the trail again, Charlie

nudged Fred up beside Paul. "Why don't I take over with Sassy and you spend time with the missus and the little one?"

"You feel okay to handle riding and trailing Sassy?"

"I'm fit as a fiddle." Charlie chuckled.

Paul loped back to the wagon and asked Charlotte to stop. He tied Buck to the back and climbed up. "What's Emma doin' back there?"

"Said her tummy hurt," Charlotte said.

"Probably ate too much fair food. She'll be better in a while." He smiled at Charlotte and took the reins. "Thought I'd give you a break. Charlie wanted to ride since he's all healed up now."

Charlotte gazed at him. "You seem kind of down in the dumps."

"Yeah. It's still a shock not being able to sell the herd. It was a long, hard trip. I'm not sure I'll be able to keep the ranch. Maybe Emma won't have a home." He stared ahead.

Paul's insides jumbled. When he thought about Charlotte leaving in less than a week, his heart hurt for Emma. She'd come to depend on this woman. So had he. He didn't want to admit it, but he didn't want her to leave. They worked well together. As a team. Like good friends. Like him and Bernie…except she made his heart pump faster. He wanted to hold her and kiss her and wake up with her and enjoy every sunrise and sunset with her. He wanted her by his side for the rest of his life.

But he knew it couldn't happen. They had an agreement and he was a man of his word.

The sun faded behind the mountaintops. "Time

to find a good camp spot for the night." Paul trotted Jack and Belle to a meadow with a stream meandering through it. He pulled the team to a stop under some trees.

"This is a good spot." He leaned back to look at Emma. "How you feelin' gingersnap?"

"Not good, Papa." Her voice sounded weak. Her face was pale.

"You rest, honey. Drink more water from your canteen. I'll get Charlie to fix some broth for you."

He lifted Charlotte down from the wagon. He didn't let go of her hands as he looked into her eyes. "Go ahead and start the coffee. I'll send Charlie around to help with the meal. Bernie and I'll be back in time for dinner. Looked like there was a ranch east of here. We'll go see if they want to buy a few horses."

After Paul rode off on Buck, Charlotte unhitched Jack and Belle and let them graze before gathering wood for the fire. Charlie showed up, and while they talked over what to fix for supper, Charlotte heard Emma moan from inside the wagon. She hurried to Emma and gathered the child into her arms. Emma's eyes were glazed. Charlotte touched her forehead.

"Charlie!" she screamed. "She's burning up. What should I do?" Charlotte handed Emma to him and threw down a bedroll. They laid her on it and Charlotte dampened a cloth, then placed it across her forehead. Emma's eyes rolled back in her head. Her breathing was labored.

"Missy, I think she needs a doctor. Do you think you could carry her on Fred and find a doctor in that last town we passed?" Charlie's brows furrowed.

"I can. Help me, please."

"I'll saddle Fred. You hold her and keep that cool rag on her."

When Charlotte was in the saddle, Charlie wrapped Emma in a blanket and handed her up. Charlotte held her with one hand and trotted Fred back toward the town they'd come through.

She located the doctor's home. He examined Emma and gave her medicine for the fever and told Charlotte to let her rest. He agreed she'd probably eaten something bad at the fair and suffered from exhaustion.

Charlotte paid the doctor and decided Emma would be most comfortable back at camp where her daddy was.

Paul was furious when he found out Charlotte had taken Emma to the doctor without his consent.

Charlie argued with him. "I'm the one told Miz Charlotte to take the babe to town. That little one was burnin' up. Her eyes was rollin' back in her head."

Paul stomped around the camp for an hour, waiting for them to return. When Charlotte didn't come back, he decided to go after her.

"How do I know she didn't kidnap my daughter?" Paul shouted at Charlie and Bernie.

Charlie stared at him. "Boss, that's uncalled for," he said in harsh tone. "You know Miz Charlotte loves your sweet Emma. She'd never do anything to hurt her or you. I just hope nothin's happened to either one of 'em." His brow furrowed.

"I know she loves my daughter. Anybody can tell that. She loves her enough to want her for her own.

She's kidnapped my Emma!" Paul yelled as he galloped away.

He was losing his ranch and now his little girl was missing. He'd done it again. Misjudged a beautiful woman. He'd trusted her with his child. He wouldn't lose Emma. He could live without his ranch, but he couldn't live without his precious daughter. He'd find her. He'd do whatever he had to do. Charlotte wouldn't get away with this. He couldn't stop the last beautiful woman who'd ruined his and Emma's lives, but he'd sure stop this one.

Paul crashed through the sheriff's door. A sleepy deputy swung his feet off the desk and rose. Before he could say a word, Paul shouted, "She's kidnapped my daughter!" He waved the poster in the deputy's face, claiming Charlotte was the woman on the flyer. Paul insisted they form a posse to hunt her down. He wanted her arrested. He wanted his daughter back.

He rattled on about trusting beautiful women. He bellowed like a crazy man. "Don't trust a beautiful woman! They'll always betray you! No matter how much you want to be their friend or have faith in them—they'll deceive you every time!"

The deputy took the poster from Paul and shook his head.

"Look here." He pointed at the words. "This woman is wanted 'cause she's a runaway. She ain't done nothin' wrong, 'cept scoot outta town."

Paul stared at him. He pushed his hat back on his head and rubbed the back of his red neck.

"What? You mean…she's not a criminal?"

"No sir." He frowned. "Now, why don't you calm down and let's figure out how I can help you."

They discovered Charlotte and Emma a few miles from town. Charlotte had lost her way in the dark and circled back to town. Emma was warm and snug next to her in the saddle, and her fever was gone.

The deputy seemed satisfied with the results. "Y'all have a safe journey back to Cedar Grove. Be careful about the assumptions you make, Mr. Harrison." He winked at Paul, mounted and rode off.

Charlotte sobbed. "How could you Paul? How could you want me arrested? You know I love Emma and would never hurt her. Or you. How could you accuse me of such a vile deed?" She wiped her eyes. "How could you not trust me?"

Paul dug the poster from his shirt pocket. "I'm sorry, Charlotte. I could only figure out that you were wanted. I couldn't read the rest of the words."

She stared at the notice, then swallowed, took a deep breath and looked into his eyes.

"Yes, Paul. I am wanted. For running away. I escaped from my aunt. I desired a different life. My aunt couldn't understand and didn't respect me. She arranged a marriage for me with some rich old captain. I had to leave." Charlotte buried her head in her hands.

"I guess she had posters made and sent to all the law offices," she said, a sob in her voice. "My aunt has influence in high places. I'm sure she hired a detective too. Maybe they couldn't find me because she wouldn't dream I'm married."

She stared at Paul. "Why didn't you just ask me? Why did you act before you talked to me? You don't trust me." Charlotte gulped. "There can't be friendship between us unless there is trust." She sniffled and looked at the floor.

Paul didn't move. He was astonished. She'd dodged an arranged marriage. In his misery about not selling his horses, and convinced he was losing his ranch, he'd given up trying to read the poster. His thoughts had been to get home to his ranch and make new plans for himself and Emma. Charlotte had tried only to help Emma. She'd gotten lost. She'd walked out on her aunt, but she wasn't a criminal.

He'd hurt her. Badly. He needed to apologize. How could he have suspected her? Why were his first thoughts the worst about her? Why didn't he trust her? Why hadn't he listened to Charlie? Why hadn't he trusted God?

He bowed his head. "Charlotte, I am sorry for being a fool." He took off his hat and locked eyes with her. "Can you forgive me?"

Chapter Twenty-Four

Charlotte's heart beat wildly. She gazed at this man she'd thought could become a good friend. A man she could trust. A man she could believe in. Maybe even a man she could love someday.

How wrong she was. Disappointment flooded her mind. Was she more disenchanted with him or with herself for thinking she could trust him? Her suffragette friends were right. Men were untrustworthy.

"I forgive you," she whispered. She looked him straight in the eye. "But I don't trust you."

She took a deep breath. "I will fulfill my agreement and take care of Emma until we reach Cedar Grove. However, I do not wish to speak to you for the rest of the trip. After our marriage is annulled, I never want to see you again. Ever."

Charlotte kept her word. She acknowledged Paul but said not one word to him. If he asked her a question, she pointed or otherwise indicated an answer. She wasn't hostile. She was brokenhearted.

Soon she'd start her teaching career. Thoughts of her new adventure turned dismal. She'd have no one to share it with. Lonesomeness consumed her when she thought of life without Paul and Emma.

Charlie resumed cooking. Charlotte helped him, but there was no joy in her work. Charlie tried to tease her or comfort her. She'd smile, turn away and do what was needed. Emma was still included in the cooking chores.

Charlotte kept up with Emma's reading lessons and worked with her on simple number problems. But her heart wasn't in it. Emma tried to cheer her up with drawings and funny stories about the puppies.

The first time Paul picked up Emma's tablet and walked toward Charlotte, silently asking for a reading lesson, Charlotte disappeared into the wagon without a word. After that, she finished her evening chores and retired early. No more Bible reading or sitting around the campfire having coffee and chatting about the day with everyone.

After breakfast one morning Paul and Bernie left the herd grazing and rode into town to ask if the livery stable or any ranchers wanted to purchase horses. Paul had sold about a dozen horses since they'd left Lyonsville. He'd been pleased with the prices, but it was a drop in the bucket of what he needed to pay off his ranch loan.

Charlotte spotted two riders headed toward their camp. "Charlie, riders coming!" she hollered. "Emma, get in the wagon." Emma ran to the front wheel and Charlotte boosted her up.

"I'll be quiet, Charlotte," she whispered.

"Good girl. I'll come get you. Don't get out of the back and don't peek your head out either until I say it's okay," Charlotte instructed her. She strolled back to stand beside Charlie, desperate to control her trembling body and hoping it wasn't thieves coming to steal again.

These riders wore uniforms. They stopped a good distance from the wagon, dismounted, left their horses standing in the field and walked into camp.

The tallest one said, "Good morning. I'm Sergeant Boone, and this is Private Long. We're from the Sacramento army post." They tipped their hats at Charlotte and she nodded.

"Mornin'," Charlie said. "How can we help you?" He had the rifle tucked under the dishcloths on the worktable, his hand poised on the towels.

"We're looking for Mr. Paul Harrison. The sheriff back in Verda said he was headed north with a herd of horses."

"He's in town. The town just up ahead. I'm not sure what the name of it is." Charlotte pointed north and smiled at them.

The sergeant looked at the horses in the meadow. "Is that his herd?"

Charlotte nodded.

"Any of those horses for sale?"

"Yes, sir," Charlie said. "Most all of them. Our wagon team and a few saddle horses are mixed in with the band, though."

"Can we take a look at them?" Sergeant Boone asked.

"Sure," Charlotte answered.

Sergeant Boone and Private Long strode out and wandered through the herd, pointing at one horse and then another.

"Sure wish the boss would get back from town,"

Charlie mumbled. He rolled his piecrust and patted it into the Dutch oven. "Charlotte, hand me those canned peaches." She found the jar and brought it to Charlie. Prince and Spots barked. Thinking something was amiss, Charlotte grabbed the rifle and pointed it in the direction the dogs were barking.

Paul and Bernie rode into the clearing. Paul stared at the gun Charlotte held, then dismounted and came to the table.

"Who are those fellows?" Paul asked, nodding at the men in the midst of his herd.

Charlotte put the gun down and moved away.

"They're from the Sacramento army post. Lookin' for horses, I think," Charlie said.

"Guess I better go talk to them." Paul and Bernie ambled toward the men.

Charlotte helped Emma down from the wagon. She ran after her daddy calling, "Papa, Papa, wait for me!" He turned, looked up at Charlotte with questioning eyes and caught his daughter as she leaped into his arms.

He hugged her, then set her down, and she ran back to Charlotte with a big smile. "Papa said to say thank-you for taking good care of me." She giggled. "Papa talks funny sometimes, doesn't he?" She sat down and gathered the puppies into her lap.

It wasn't long before the men strolled back into camp. Paul gathered cups and poured coffee for all of them.

"Charlotte, will you please make more coffee," he said as he poured the last drop. She nodded and took the pot from his hands. His fingers brushed across hers and she shuddered, taking a step back.

After she made coffee, she took a book and wandered to the front of the wagon with Emma. "Let's let them talk business. I'll read you a story." They sat on a fallen log, and Charlotte motioned for Emma to sit beside her. The dogs joined them.

By the time she'd finished the chapter, Charlotte noticed the sergeant had handed Paul a wad of bills. Paul called to Charlotte. She and Emma walked to him.

He leaned his head toward her and whispered, "Charlotte, the sergeant here just paid for the whole herd, except for my black mare, Sassy, our team and the saddle horses." He smiled at her. "He has a bill of sale that needs to be made out. Can you do that while I count the money?"

She nodded, her heart thumping. It must be hard being vulnerable. Not being able to read and only being able to write your name. For one moment an edge of her heart softened.

Paul signed the paper and then turned to Charlotte. "Since you're my wife, I think you should sign this too."

She coughed and choked. "What?" She stared at him. She was his wife for a couple more days. Why was he doing this? Had the sergeant asked him to have her sign it? She had no desire to argue or make a scene, so she signed her name below his. He stared at it for a moment.

"Charlotte, that doesn't say *Harrison*." She looked down. She'd signed *Carpenter*. She made a dash and added *Harrison*. He thanked her and took the paper.

When the sergeant looked at it, he smiled. "Got yourself one of them modern wives, huh?"

Paul grinned.

* * *

At the next town Paul wired the money to the Cedar Grove sheriff. He asked him to locate one of the bank directors to make sure the loan got paid off without Frank Kenny's knowledge. He'd deal with Frank when they got to Cedar Grove, but he wouldn't take any more chances on losing his ranch.

Paul was grateful to the Lord that his ranch was saved. Grateful the army quartermaster had chased him down. But he was devastated that he'd lost Charlotte. He realized too late he wanted more than a friendship with her. He wanted to share his life with her. Wake up every day beside her, have coffee and savor the mornings with her. He wanted to resume his reading lessons. He wanted to have a family with her.

He begged the Lord to help him show her how very, very sorry he was for his childish behavior. She'd distanced herself from him, and her heart was somewhere else. He knew she wouldn't stay now, even if he begged her. Not even for Emma's sake.

He didn't know how he was going to live without her. He'd have to trust God. *Trust in the Lord with all thine heart*...

Perhaps Charlotte would accept Sassy as a token of his appreciation and as an apology. He knew Charlotte had longed for her own horse. She fancied Sassy, the boss mare. Sassy was the most valuable horse Paul owned. He had planned to start a new herd, and Sassy would have been one of his prime brood mares. But... he considered the woman he loved...

"Charlotte!" he called.

She wandered to him.

"Let's take a walk. I need to talk with you." She followed him toward the back of the wagon where Sassy was tied.

He pointed to the horse. "Sassy's yours. You need your own horse to ride when you start teaching. She's a thank-you gift for all you've done for all of us."

Charlotte caught her breath. Tears edged down her cheeks.

"Paul, Sassy's your favorite and most valuable horse. I know you want to start a new herd with this mare. You can't just give her away."

Her eyes locked with his. She shook her head. "Thank you, but I cannot accept." She turned to walk away.

Paul hooked her arm. "Is it because you still can't forgive me?"

Charlotte paused. "No. I have forgiven you. But Sassy is part of your dream. I won't take that away from you."

"I want you to have her. You'll be safe when you're riding to and from school. Sassy is very smart and reliable. She will take care of you." His eyes pleaded with her. "Please, Charlotte. Take her."

He moved a step closer to the woman who'd been his wife for nearly a month. He wanted to embrace her, to hold her close. To tell her that he couldn't abide thinking about her leaving him—them. He felt heat rising up his neck. He knew his face was probably red.

"I care for you very much. I'll be grateful to know you are safe."

Charlotte's eyes sparkled when she looked up at him.

She took a deep breath. "Oh, Paul, thank you for Sassy." She reached for his hand. "I care for you too. She will be a delightful reminder of this wonderful month we spent together."

Paul pulled her into an embrace and stroked her hair. "Lottie, my Lottie. I don't think I can live without you. I love you."

She stammered "I… I love you too."

Paul stared at Charlotte, then pushed back from her. His heart pounded wildly. "What? What did you say?"

Tears streamed down Charlotte's face. She sniffled. "I'm so, so sorry Paul. I… I am in love with you. I don't know how this happened. I promise I tried to keep my feelings under control. I struggled not to love you. But…but you snuck into my heart."

She swiped at the tears. "I worked hard to get you out of my mind. I did. I really did. I prayed not to think of you all the time. I strived not to think of how wonderful it has been being married to you. I promise… I promise to honor our contract. I have it right here."

Charlotte sobbed. "We can have our marriage annulled just as soon as we get to Cedar Grove. I hope I can continue to teach Emma, though. And you too, if you want. I'm so very sorry. I didn't mean to love you. I hope you'll forgive me."

Paul smiled and touched his fingers to her lips. "Shh."

He took her tear-streaked face in his hands. "I love you, Lottie. I've loved you from the moment you stepped off that stage. I love your heart. I love how you love Emma. How you love so fiercely. I love your spirit. I love your joy. I love being with you in the crazy times and in the happy times. I love working with you. I love mornings with you. I love evenings with you. I love fighting with you. I love planning with you. I don't want to live one day without you. I want you by my side forever."

Charlotte stared at him, seemingly trying to comprehend his words. "But…but why didn't you tell me?"

He smiled. "I love you so much. I want you to have your dream. To teach school. I want you to have your heart's desire. I want you to do something you feel is important. I didn't want to take that away from you."

He looked down at her, his blue eyes full of hope and love.

Charlotte beamed. "Oh, my Paul. I am living my dream. Every day. I have two delightful pupils. I am doing something important, and this is my heart's desire—to love and to be loved."

He held her hands and gazed into her eyes. "Then will you be my wife, Lottie. My wife for real? Will you stay by my side and let me love you for the rest of your life?"

Charlotte nodded. "Yes, I will!"

Paul pulled Charlotte close, kissing her with all the yearning he'd held inside. She kissed him back with equal excitement and promise.

Chapter Twenty-Five

When the wagon rolled up to Paul's ranch house Charlotte gasped. A short, dark-haired woman stood next to a gray-haired gentleman in a navy uniform on the front porch. Aunt Arilla and the captain were looking toward the barn.

Charlotte scrambled down from the wagon and approached her aunt.

"Aunt Arilla. What are you doing here?"

Arilla whirled around and frowned. The captain turned to face Charlotte. Her aunt drew the spines of her parasol inward.

"Charlotte Carpenter, we have searched for you all over this horrible dusty wild west. Do you know how much trouble you have caused the captain and myself? I am positively exhausted. Do you know how much money it has cost me to find you? I had to hire the Pinkerton Detective Agency. I've spent hundreds of dollars on posters. I have spent thousands of dollars looking for you. I am appalled at your behavior. Why did you leave? And why would you come to this awful place? Northern California, an uncultured, backwater state if ever there was one. Why didn't you have the common decency to send word about where you were?"

Charlotte stood still, studying her aunt. Arilla had informed Charlotte of her own discomfort. She'd berated her niece for her lack of manners and her choices. But there was not one question about whether Charlotte was okay or how she was doing.

Perspiration dripped from Charlotte's forehead. Her throat felt dry, and her mind careened out of control. Charlotte knew what her aunt expected. She wanted Charlotte to apologize, to beg forgiveness and to comply with whatever was requested. Ever since she was a small child, Charlotte's pattern had been to acquiesce, to abdicate and to avoid confrontation.

"Aunt Arilla… I—I…"

Arilla grabbed Charlotte's hand. "You've had your modicum of an adventure. Now get your things and come along."

Charlotte pulled back. Her aunt held on.

"Aunt Arilla, I have something—"

Arilla tightened her grip. She scowled. "Did you hear me, Charlotte Carpenter? There is nothing you can say that will change my mind. We are going to that little church in this backwoods town." She pointed her parasol toward Cedar Grove. "You and the captain will be married before we leave this…this dump they call a town."

"Wait a minute, Aunt…"

Paul strode to Charlotte. He tugged her hand loose from Arilla's grasp and stepped between her and her aunt.

Arilla poked at him with her parasol. "Take your

filthy hands off my niece, you low-down, despicable cowpoke."

Paul swatted the parasol away. "You will kindly stop speaking to my wife in that ill-mannered tone." Paul stared hard at the woman and the captain.

Arilla glared at him. "Wife? Are you insane? Do you know who I am, you buffoon, you freeloading parasite? If indeed my niece is married to you, she will immediately annul it and marry the captain. He is a pillar of society and offers her an excellent situation."

The captain grinned at Arilla and nodded to Charlotte.

Charlotte's aunt glared at Paul. "You, sir, will butt out of our family business."

Arilla shifted in front of Charlotte and gripped her arm but did not pull her away from Paul. "Is any of what he said true?"

Charlotte nodded. Tears streamed down her cheeks.

Arilla took her shoulders. "Listen to me, Charlotte Carpenter. You are better than this. You will not remain married to this…to this reprobate. I demand you annul this marriage and immediately marry the captain. If you do not do as I wish, I will withhold your inheritance. You will live in squalor your entire life. You will have nothing."

"Stop it! Stop it!" Charlotte screamed. She straightened her shoulders and her hands flew to her hips. She leaned close to her aunt's face. "I would rather have one day with this cowboy, with my husband Paul and his darling daughter Emma, than all the money in the world. I experienced more love and joy in one month with these two than I ever received from you in all the years I lived with you. Keep my inheritance. I don't want it. I love Paul and I love Emma and I will never leave them!" Charlotte shouted at the short woman standing with her mouth gaping.

Arilla groaned, rolled her eyes and shook her head. The captain stiffened and frowned.

Paul grinned. "Madam, I suggest you and the captain take your leave. My family and I have some livin' to do!"

Emma jumped up and down and the puppies raced circles around everyone. Paul swept Charlotte up into his arms, pushed opened the door and carried her across the threshold where the lingering smell of burnt beans welcomed them.

Epilogue

September, 1896

Charlotte's hand rested on her growing abdomen. Emma sat beside her on the porch, reading a new book. Charlotte felt a jab in her belly.

"Emma, come quick." Charlotte reached for Emma's hand and placed it on her tummy.

"Oh, Momma, the baby's kicking." She smiled. "Can I help name her? We could call her Elizabeth May or Mary Rose or Anna Grace. I know lots of good names."

"What if it's a boy?" Charlotte teased.

Emma frowned. "I don't think I want a brother. Boys are stinky. Like that Bobby. He's always chasing me at the church picnics. He pulls my braids and thinks it's funny. I can't think of any good boy names anyway."

"We'll have to talk to your papa."

Charlotte's heart raced as she thought about her handsome cowboy husband. Oh, how she loved him. And Emma, her own little girl now. Emma insisted on calling her "momma." Charlotte hadn't known the emotions that would stir in her heart when that title designated her."

She still couldn't get used to the idea that she and Paul had married again. He'd insisted on a church wedding with all their friends present this time.

Now she and Paul would be adding another little one to their joyful family. How happy she felt knowing she'd set aside her doubts and embraced the love the Lord had given her.

Being married to Paul was exhilarating. He challenged her and laughed with her and brought out the very best in her. She'd learned more about life with him than any school could have ever taught her.

Paul's lessons had continued. He was a skilled pupil and proudly read the Bible every evening, surrounded by his family. The church often asked him to fill in when the preacher left to make rounds in the outlying areas.

Charlotte glanced at the man striding from the barn. Her heart flip-flopped. Emma dashed down the steps and rushed into his open arms. He swung her around and kissed her cheeks. "How's my Emmy?"

Charlotte no longer envied Paul's love for Emma. She knew now what it was like to be cherished by this dashing cowboy.

"Papa, I felt the baby kick. Can I help name her?"

Paul smiled up at Charlotte as he took the steps two at a time. "We'll have to ask your momma. She's got some pretty strong opinions on things, you know."

He pulled Charlotte from the chair, lifted her in his arms and spun her around. He buried his face in her hair and whispered in her ear, "My Lottie, my Lottie,

I'm crazy about you. I'll love you forever." He kissed her with great longing. Charlotte was grateful they had finally trusted the Lord, let go of their fears and embraced this love.

* * * * *

LOVE INSPIRED

Stories to uplift and inspire

Fall in love with Love Inspired—
inspirational and uplifting stories of faith
and hope. Find strength and comfort in
the bonds of friendship and community.
Revel in the warmth of possibility and the
promise of new beginnings.

Sign up for the Love Inspired newsletter
at **LoveInspired.com** to be the first
to find out about upcoming titles,
special promotions and exclusive content.

CONNECT WITH US AT:

Facebook.com/LoveInspiredBooks

Twitter.com/LoveInspiredBks

LISOCIAL2021

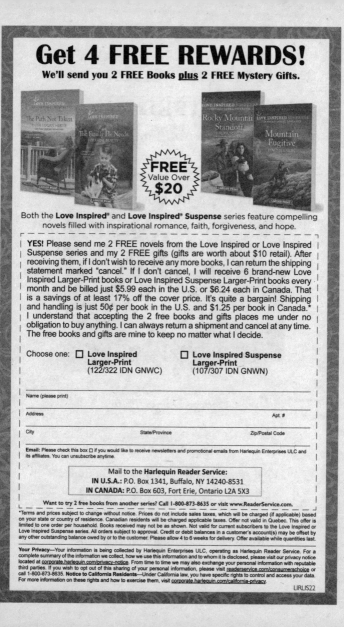

Get 4 FREE REWARDS!

We'll send you 2 FREE Books plus 2 FREE Mystery Gifts.

FREE
Value Over
$20

Both the **Love Inspired®** and **Love Inspired® Suspense** series feature compelling novels filled with inspirational romance, faith, forgiveness, and hope.

YES! Please send me 2 FREE novels from the Love Inspired or Love Inspired Suspense series and my 2 FREE gifts (gifts are worth about $10 retail). After receiving them, if I don't wish to receive any more books, I can return the shipping statement marked "cancel." If I don't cancel, I will receive 6 brand-new Love Inspired Larger-Print books or Love Inspired Suspense Larger-Print books every month and be billed just $5.99 each in the U.S. or $6.24 each in Canada. That is a savings of at least 17% off the cover price. It's quite a bargain! Shipping and handling is just 50¢ per book in the U.S. and $1.25 per book in Canada.* I understand that accepting the 2 free books and gifts places me under no obligation to buy anything. I can always return a shipment and cancel at any time. The free books and gifts are mine to keep no matter what I decide.

Choose one: ☐ **Love Inspired**
Larger-Print
(122/322 IDN GNWC)

☐ **Love Inspired Suspense**
Larger-Print
(107/307 IDN GNWN)

Name (please print)

Address   Apt. #

City   State/Province   Zip/Postal Code

Email: Please check this box ☐ if you would like to receive newsletters and promotional emails from Harlequin Enterprises ULC and its affiliates. You can unsubscribe anytime.

Mail to the Harlequin Reader Service:
IN U.S.A.: P.O. Box 1341, Buffalo, NY 14240-8531
IN CANADA: P.O. Box 603, Fort Erie, Ontario L2A 5X3

Want to try 2 free books from another series? Call 1-800-873-8635 or visit www.ReaderService.com.

*Terms and prices subject to change without notice. Prices do not include sales taxes, which will be charged (if applicable) based on your state or country of residence. Canadian residents will be charged applicable taxes. Offer not valid in Quebec. This offer is limited to one order per household. Books received may not be as shown. Not valid for current subscribers to the Love Inspired or Love Inspired Suspense series. All orders subject to approval. Credit or debit balances in a customer's account(s) may be offset by any other outstanding balance owed by or to the customer. Please allow 4 to 6 weeks for delivery. Offer available while quantities last.

Your Privacy—Your information is being collected by Harlequin Enterprises ULC, operating as Harlequin Reader Service. For a complete summary of the information we collect, how we use this information and to whom it is disclosed, please visit our privacy notice located at corporate.harlequin.com/privacy-notice. From time to time we may also exchange your personal information with reputable third parties. If you wish to opt out of this sharing of your personal information, please visit readerservice.com/consumerschoice or call 1-800-873-8635. **Notice to California Residents**—Under California law, you have specific rights to control and access your data. For more information on these rights and how to exercise them, visit corporate.harlequin.com/california-privacy.

LIRLIS22